Thirteen Shells

Also by Nadia Bozak

Fiction
Orphan Love
El Niño

Non-fiction
The Cinematic Footprint: Lights, Camera, Natural Resources

Thirteen Shells
Nadia Bozak

Copyright © 2016 Nadia Bozak

Published in Canada in 2016 by House of Anansi Press Inc.
www.houseofanansi.com

House of Anansi Press is committed to protecting our natural
environment. As part of our efforts, the interior of this book is printed
on paper that contains 100% post-consumer recycled fibres, is acid-free,
and is processed chlorine-free.

20 19 18 17 16   1 2 3 4 5

Library and Archives Canada Cataloguing in Publication

Bozak, Nadia, author
Thirteen shells / Nadia Bozak.

Short stories.
Issued in print and electronic formats.
ISBN 978-1-77089-987-2 (paperback).—ISBN 978-1-77089-988-9 (html)

I. Title.

PS8603.O998T45 2016   C813'.6   C2015-907619-6   C2015-907620-X

Cover and text design: Alysia Shewchuk

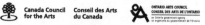

We acknowledge for their financial support of our publishing program
the Canada Council for the Arts, the Ontario Arts Council, and the
Government of Canada through the Canada Book Fund.

Printed and bound in Canada

MIX
Paper from
responsible sources
FSC® C004071

While parts of this book are adapted from childhood memories, it is fundamentally a work of fiction.

I dedicate this book:

To my dad:
a gifted artist and craftsman
who taught me to never give up.

To Michelle Lundy:
a true friend who truly sparkles.

CONTENTS

CONTENTS

The beauty of a shell is rarely evident
when taken from the water.
—Helen S. O'Brien, *Shell Album*

Thirteen Shells

Greener Grass

The one-floor rental where Shell was born is too close to the tracks—Shell's the only girl or boy around not allowed to lay pennies on the rails so the double-engine CNs can turn them into wafers—and even with the add-on studio at the back, Dad and Mum don't have enough room to do their pottery. Dad gets a pretty good council grant, finally, so they start looking for something else. Further east, near the fairgrounds and the factories, and maybe they can even buy.

Dad promises one day they'll get out of Somerset and go back to Toronto, where Mum and Dad got married, though there are no pictures in any albums or steamer trunks of Mum in a gauzy white dress and Dad with a tie and red rose and neither of them wear a ring. Mum says Somerset is the perfect size for a city. "You can borrow an egg from your neighbour, just like on the Prairies," and also there's a movie theatre with black-and-whites like *Mr. Hulot*, which Mum and Shell saw on a Saturday afternoon.

Dad, though, says Somerset is small-town in the way it thinks. "A million miles away from Toronto," even though the drive to the Toronto Zoo is only about two hours. The cars on the spaghetti of highways to get there are so much faster than their bouncy Dodge Dart. The kids staring back at Shell instead of at the gorillas wear T-shirts with spaceships and for sports teams Shell's never heard of; the toys they drag around are bought in boxes at department stores. When the sun's gone down and Dad finally clicks onto the exit ramp back to Somerset, something becomes less tight in the Dart and in Shell—like seeing Mum after a morning at Montessori two times a week. Shell waves at the smoky factories and rusty railroad tracks, the quiet streets with the lit-up bikes and big kids on front steps.

Shell has never been down Cashel Street.

"Cashew Street?" Shell asks. But Mum and Dad are busy pointing at Princess Anne Public School on the corner, the Bun King at the lights, also there's a library and plenty of droopy oaks and stiff maples planted on the boulevard. There are two churches in just one block. Mum's sure one will have a Brownie troop. Lawns are short and green and the houses small because they were built after wartime. People didn't have so many pairs of shoes or colouring books to put away.

Halfway down the second block, Dad slows the car, pointing out a two-storey red-brick house. The homemade sign pounded into a patch of dry garden plot declares the house for sale by owner.

"Of course, there's no phone number," says Mum. "I just hate that."

Dad parks the Dodge Dart right in front. Except for the car's speckled rust, its yellow is the same deep mustard as the boulevard grass. The blades break beneath Shell's sandals when she jumps down from the car and into the strong jiggle of Mum's open arms.

Hands on hips, sneakers planted wide, Dad surveys the length of the sloped tarmac drive, at the end of which, beyond a chain-link fence and a gnarled lawn, is a wide garage. The double doors are rolled open; the pair of bright school buses inside are parked face out. Shell starts kindergarten in September, but Mum promised it will be at a school close enough they can walk there and back together.

"Why?" Shell asked.

"Because buses like those don't have seat belts."

"So?"

"So they're not safe." But sometimes Mum doesn't buckle in either, and—

Dad goes up the front steps first, Mum and Shell behind. Rotten wood springs back under their feet and the handrail wiggles.

"Careful," says Dad. And then: "Don't say anything about the pottery, okay?"

Mum tells Shell, "Look with your eyes, Shell. This won't take long."

Shell nods. All of their living room furniture could fit

on the front porch — couch, chairs, stereo, Dad's sculpture of the giant clay horse head — and still have space left over. The thick honeysuckle climbing the trellis at the far end hums with yellow jackets, the worst kind of bees for hiding in rubber gloves and the toes of running shoes.

Dad's knuckles are sharp on the aluminum door. His hands make goggles around his glasses as he peers inside the screen. Stepping back, he smoothes his beard; Mum straightens both her spine and the billow of her blouse. From between the curtains of Mum's wide trousers, Shell eyes the bees.

"Don't you go near that vine, Shell," Mum says.

Dad raises his hand again but stops when a figure pops up behind the screen. The boy's face is meshed in shadow. But his bottle of Mountain Dew is visible, as is a pale blue T-shirt, the gaping arm holes of which reveal a red pepperoni of nipple each time he drinks. The boy's eyes shift from Dad to Mum. And then they find Shell peeking out from behind Mum's pant legs. Without looking away, he calls for Gary to come: "Gare, there's people want to see the house." Again and again: "Gare."

The door moans when the boy opens it then slams fast, caught in an inward gust. The boy, standing there, is about nine. He hooks his shoulder blades on the edge of the railing and leans back into the pain. A deep scar splits the boy's top lip in half, pulling it up into his right nostril and pinching it there as with a safety pin. He must have to really brush and floss, because no matter how hard he tries, he cannot hide his top row of blunt teeth. A snarling skull, he is, like there's just not enough skin to make a

4

full hood of lip. Somehow the boy swigs Mountain Dew without a dribble.

"Mmmmm," he breathes, too loud. "We drive all the way to the States for this," he says of the pop. The passage of his hand over his cloven lip leaves behind a trail of motor grease.

His eyes flick as the screen door wrenches outward. The thick caramel arm that holds it open belongs to a big man in overalls with a shark fin for a nose. Shark Nose has black nails. A hammer hangs from a loop at his hip. He wipes his free hand on his denim front and shakes with Dad, who asks for a look at the house. Mum's fingers curl into Shell's. And she is tugged inside. The boy's flat grey eyes hold tight to Shell, who squeezes her top lip hard between her fingers.

Shark Nose says there's hardwood under all the dirty carpet. "Place is solid."

The main floor is as jumbled as a desk drawer, and the only place to sit is on one of five folding chairs tucked into a card table in the dining room. The orange plastic tablecloth glows like a Creamsicle against the chimney-sweep surroundings.

"Everything works," Shark Nose says to Mum, waving her through to the kitchen. Mum's not looking at Shark Nose, like she doesn't look at Dad when his voice gets big.

"Nothing fancy," says Shark Nose.

Uncooked rice speckles the linoleum floor, which is way stickier than when Shell spilled the syrup. Up on the countertop there's a coffee urn the size of Mum's Filter Queen and the biggest box of Alpha-Bits.

The stairs to the basement are dark. The air tastes like the mushrooms Dad gathers along the train tracks and sautés for Friday night omelettes. At the bottom, Shark Nose pulls on a string dangling from the ceiling. A light comes on. Dad and Mum are not nearly as tall as Shark Nose, yet they too must stoop beneath the ceiling. The three grown-ups move like roosters along the crates of empty glass bottles — Sprite, Mountain Dew, Coke, Export stubbies — that partition off a bedroom. Four roll-away beds are lined up beneath a pair of muddy windows dimmed by uncut grass. Each mattress is wrapped in an unzipped sleeping bag, a crisp white sheet folded over like some dads have their shirt cuffs.

The ceiling lets out a long, creaky ripple. Mum's and Dad's eyebrows rise above their glasses as they follow the footsteps along the rafters. They look like brother and sister with the same full curls and heavy glasses, and maybe they are, because along with no matching gold rings they don't ever hug or kiss — or hold hands like mums and dads in the park or at the fair. Even in her Egypt sandals, Mum is taller than Dad. Her braids are long and thick. Everything about Mum is big and strong — except her voice. It is a bird outside the window, not quite there. Everyone goes, "Pardon me?" when Mum says something.

The ceiling stops creaking. Next comes growly laughter and snake-sounding words that make Dad frown. Shark Nose grins a bit and points at the beds. "Don't mind them up there. Just my boys."

The toilet under the stairs has for a doorknob a diamond that's baseball big. While Mum and Dad consider the washer and dryer that come with the sale, Shell traces the knob's jewelled facets.

"...but we just can't fight off the damp," Shark Nose is saying to Dad but not Mum. "And these foster kids tend to have asthma." He, Shark Nose, really thought he'd done up the basement okay for them, but still they get sick.

Dad follows Shark Nose through the backyard to the garage while Shell tugs Mum towards the red swing set in the neighbour's yard, on the other side of a high fence. Mum, though, is watching the boy. He crouches at the base of a dense black walnut, the empty pop bottle pressed hard between his knees like he's trying to burst it. The walnut's branches ensnare the power lines above and its fallen balls of hard green fruit stain a patch of concrete that might once have been a patio. Shell follows his eyes, which are on Dad and Shark Nose as they near the garage.

Of the two school buses inside, one has its engine torn out. Silver tools and blackened rags and drink cans litter the concrete floor, and a picture of an orange lady in a bathing suit hangs beside a dull stainless steel sink. Dad hitches up his jeans and disappears into the brush that grows thick between the garage and the neighbour's stretch of chain-link. A fit of barking erupts. Mum almost breaks Shell's fingers, she squeezes so hard. Ever since a needle-nosed mutt chased them all the way up their street and clamped its jaws on Mum's bell-bottoms, Mum carries a thick wooden chair leg in her bike basket. Shell had been strapped behind Mum in the carrier seat. Mum's long braids were, like Shell's, ribboned at the ends. The world was bobbing by—train tracks, Kit-Kat store, lace curtains, autumn leaves raked up like bowls and bowls of salad. Then the dog came tearing alongside, nails clipping the ground, orange eyes to match its coat. Mum shouted—screamed—and the bike had careened, nearly skidding out. Then the dog caught Mum's pants in its teeth. The fabric ripped to the knee. Shell was crying, her helmeted head weighing heavy on her neck. But Mum kept on going. She pedalled hard and got three streets over before she stopped and turned around. "Don't tell your dad," Mum said, her eyes wet and nostrils trembling.

Behind the garage, Dad whistles sharp enough to split ice. The dogs go quiet. When Dad comes back out, there are leaves in his beard and bright beads of garnet squeeze through a scratch along his forearm.

"Imagine the garden I could put in here," he whispers, holding in his smile.

Dad asks to see the roof. Shark Nose calls to the boy, who shoves the pop bottle into the back pocket of his loose jeans. They carry a ladder from the garage like it's a coffin. Shell counts the ribs—four—that show through the boy's gaping arm hole. Dad jams the ladder into the ground before he climbs it, ducking low sweeps of walnut branch. Mum and Shark Nose squint up into a bright ball of western sun. The boy is gone. Though Shell feels the pull of the swing set through the fence, she stays near Mum.

"Shingles're new," Shark Nose calls to Dad, hooking his thumbs into his pockets. "Me and the boys laid them not a year ago."

Dad lifts his glasses and peers down the tin chimney. He pencils something in his notebook then crouches down and scans the eavestrough. Behind Shell there is a soft belch. A shadow cools her back.

"There's all kinds of junk buried back here," the boy says. He was hiding under the low bush behind Mum, a cloud of red blossom. It must be his lip that wets his words with slur. "Here in the dirt, under where we're standing. You'll see." The touch of his finger on Shell's bare shoulder is warm and firm. Just as Shell and Mum turn around, he pulls back his arm and tosses away his pop bottle. It twirls, bottom over top, and lands with a thud in the tall grass, among the fallen walnuts. Shell waits for it to break, yearns for it, but the sound does not come.

Up on the peak of the roof, the sun blanks Dad's heavy glasses. "Hey fella," he hollers. "Pick up that bottle."

"Huh?" The boy squints up at Dad.

"Go on." Dad's voice is sharp. His beard juts out as he points to where the bottle landed. "Can't litter like that."

Shell mouths the word "litterbug" so only she can hear. In Montessori they sat in a circle and recited, "Pick it up!" and "Don't be a litterbug," while the teacher thumped notes on the wood piano.

The boy shrugs.

Up above them, Dad widens his stance. Then he makes for the ladder.

"You heard the man," Shark Nose shouts. "On with it."

Bowing his head, the boy walks the yard, scanning for the bottle. Red flush crawls up the back of his neck into the jagged edge of his hairline. His sneakers crunch the dry grass and then there is a too-long sigh as he bends over.

"Okay?" he says to Dad, holding up the bottle. But

Dad is already stepping down the ladder, his back turned.

Mum walks Shell out to the car. Several steps back, Dad and Shark Nose talk, arms crossed, looking down at each other's shoes. Canvas sneakers to leather boots. The boy and his bottle are so close behind Shell, she switches to Mum's other hand, finding it just as wet.

"*Hippie*," the boy whispers, tramping the back of Shell's heel. "*Stupidassholehippiedad.*"

Shell takes two steps inside of one, stumbling. Mum pulls her back to her feet, wrenching Shell's arm in its socket. "Don't look at him, Shell," Mum says, quiet but hard. "He's just waiting to get a rise out of you."

Mum and Shell stand in the shadow of the locked Dart. The boy sits on the front steps, his elbows propped behind him. His eyes are not really closed — the lids flicker, watching. His teeth must get so dry and dirty, exposed to all that air and bugs all the time. That's why his words are so ugly, so mean.

"That garage'll make a fantastic studio," Dad says, tucking his notebook into his shirt pocket and getting in the driver's seat. He leans over and opens Mum's door from the inside because the handle is broken. Mum's going on about getting away from those damn tracks. Imagine an entire night without being rattled and hooted awake. She clips Shell's seat belt; her dark, coarse hair has escaped its elastic, falling over her face. If Shell were to reach up and take off Mum's heavy glasses, Mum would be someone so much lighter she might just float away from Dad and Shell and the Dodge Dart and get lost in the clouds she sings about when she puts on Joni Mitchell.

Dad's glasses occupy the rear-view mirror. "We can get a couple of kilns in there. Hey? That chimney's good to ventilate." In Dad's side mirror, the boy moves across the front lawn. Hidden muscles swell in his arms. The Mountain Dew bottle dangles from a crooked middle finger. When he takes it up, full in his grip, Mum and Dad are busy talking about bank loans and reasonable offers. Dad pulls slowly away from the red-brick house. And slowly the boy in the mirror raises his arm, pop bottle wielded. Shell sinks low in her seat, covering her face so shattered glass won't poke her eyes or slice her nose when the bottle comes crashing through the rear windshield.

"Faster, Dad!" she bellows, kicking hard at the back of Dad's seat.

"What the hell?" Dad shouts. But the car's already turning the corner, south off Cashel Street.

THE DAY THEY move into the new house is bright white with summer. At five-thirty in the morning Dad rents a truck with a sliding door, picks up Kremski on the way. Kremski's already sweating. He gobbles the toasted cheese Mum gives him wrapped in a cloth napkin and puffs a rolled cigarette; paint freckles his shirt and shoes. Kremski works at jobs like building a fence or shovelling snow, but, like Dad, his real job is making paintings. Or sometimes sculptures, out of garbage scraps. Dad and Kremski laugh and grunt and get drenched loading the truck. Shell gets to ride between Dad and Kremski on the way to Cashel Street, so high she can see right down into passing cars.

Mum pulls up in the Dart, the back seat full of pottery boxes. The front door key is in an envelope in the bottom of her purse where she can never find it. Dad and Kremski already have the couch on the boulevard. Mum opens the door. Dust speckles the sunlight sliding in through the windows that Shark Nose took the blinds from even though he wasn't supposed to. For five whole days Mum and Shell have scrubbed away at the smells and stains of Shark Nose and those boys that weren't adopted but only fostered, which means Shark Nose'll be their dad until he decides he's had enough. Because who wants a son with a hairy lip? No, no: *harelip*. A birth defect that makes him look like a rabbit, except rabbits are soft and gentle.

"I hate that boy," Shell told Mum when it was time to bleach the basement. And she told her again and again until it turned into red-hot chanting.

It is too stuffy upstairs for sleeping, and though Dad really insists, Shell won't let anyone sleep in the cool basement. "Harelip is down there hiding." Behind the furnace. "I heard him laugh. I heard him open a bottle of pop."

Dad says Shell is being unreasonable. "It's our place now." Shell lies between Mum and Dad on their double mattress in what will be the living room, tossing and shifting among the sticky sheets and the silver-blue light falling through bare windows. A few times Shell wakes, blinking through a night so quiet and still they could be camping. Her eyes adjust to the dark—shadowed walls, lion-foot chair; the pine tree in the corner is just a teetering stack of milk crates. The silence and heat weigh equally heavy; waiting for one or both to break, she falls back asleep again.

Dad gets up first and takes his coffee outside. Mum can't find the porridge pot or the toaster, so she soaks sliced rye in beaten egg and fries each piece golden. There is jam and syrup on the harvest table that Dad and Kremski lugged in yesterday, a slab of cheddar for protein.

"Call your dad in." Mum bends into the oven with a plate of bread. The dishes are the cornflower ones Mum never uses because Dad doesn't like that fancy English stuff, but everything else is still packed.

And because Shell's sandals have likewise disappeared among the boxes and bags, rolls of curtains, piles of cushions, she runs outside barefoot.

"Shell!" Mum's cry fades with the slam of the screen door.

Down the rough steps, over the sandy patio stones, and onto coarse lawn, Shell jumps over fallen walnuts and the patches of turned soil where Dad has already started to garden. From up on the garage comes the *click-clock* of Dad's hammer. The yard, Mum says, is three or four times as big as the one they left behind. Shell can't have a swing set of her own, so she's going to make Mum ask if she can play on the one next door, and then Dad can cut a hole in the fence so she doesn't have to go around to the front every time. Are there kids living there? Mum doesn't think so. Then why have a swing? Maybe there were kids once but they're grown up and gone. Gone where? Where is that place grown-ups disappear?

Click-clock. Dad's hammer echoes. Shell twirls—one loop, two—towards the ladder propped against the garage that Dad already calls "the studio." Then, there: up ahead in the grass, a sudden sparkle. Mid-stride, the sparkle becomes a glint, then a jagged circle of emerald. It glows, dazzles. And it's too late: Shell's right foot lands hard. A sharp spike sinks deep into the meaty ball. She freezes, impaled by a pain beyond pain, like a thousand yellow-jacket stings all at once.

The back door seems to slam even before Shell cries out. Mum's clogs pound down the steps, across the lawn, and then Mum is drawing Shell into her body. She grips Shell's foot and pulls out the biting. Dad is there. Like a baby, Shell is draped in his arms. Below her, the ground shakes as Dad races across the yard and into the Dart, where Mum is already waiting with an armful of tea towels. She holds Shell on her lap and wraps Shell's foot. Down there, on the other side of the basement windows through which Shell can barely see, the harelip boy would have chugged a Mountain Dew and then broken the bottle — *smash* — on the concrete floor. His foster brothers, atop their roll-aways and wheezing for air, would have watched him, learning. Before wrapping the shard in a rag, he would have held it up to the bare bulb at the bottom of the stairs, like Dad when he examines slides. Then, maybe on the very day they packed up the school buses and moved out, he planted the broken end of the bottle in the grass, spikes upright. Maybe if she prays to God for him, the boy will get his rabbit face fixed and be regular enough a good mum and dad will want him. Then he'll really feel sorry for hurting Shell and one day come back to Cashel Street to say so.

DAD STRINGS THE Mexican hammock between two black walnuts and Mum cocoons Shell inside, propping her bandaged foot high upon a bedroom pillow. A cheese sandwich and a glass of milk teeter on a stool just in reach. Dad, above, rocks the hammock, slow as breeze.

"Eighteen is a lucky number," he says of the stitches closing up her foot. "One day you'll be eighteen."

When she's eighteen, Shell knows she'll remember Dad saying that, like she'll remember the way the sun above turns the walnut leaves into lace, and how good the bread and cheese tastes, sweet with mayonnaise. The painkiller tablets make it all fuzzy. Inside fuzz, outside fuzz.

When Shell opens her eyes again, Dad is digging up sod along the fence. Fresh washing stretches from porch to studio, above Shell's backyard bed. One, two, three, four tea towels brown with bloodstains.

"Look." From a wooden quart basket splotched with strawberry picking, Dad pulls a perfect circle of green glass. The circle is edged in spikes, curving up like mammoth tusks. Above the hammock, bed sheets and pillowcases float past, the rusty line squawking.

Dad says the glass is old. It had been buried in the backyard for a while. His gardening churned it up. Dad says that a long time ago there were no garbage trucks, so if something broke, people dug a hole and buried it. "That was it. Forgotten."

So they live on a dump?

"A midden," Dad says. Everyone had one. "Many in the world have them still." Dad lets Shell run her finger along the razor jaws of the glass.

"Mountain Dew," Shell says. "The same green."

Now Dad says Shell is being silly. "Green was the normal colour of glass back when this house was built." Along with the glass, Dad found a blackened spoon and some long, rusty nails, a few triangles of dinner plates, cornflower like Mum's. Unlike the clean green glass, each of these other bits is covered in hard dirt. "You just make sure you wear shoes, kiddo." Dad sets the basket on the wooden bench they brought from their old backyard and then picks up his shovel.

The hammock loses its sway. Behind Shell, someplace she can't see, Dad's shovel breaks deep into the dry grass, in search of fertile soil. Laundry lemon floats through the air. The back door squeaks open and Mum comes out with a basket at her hip. Through her eyelashes, Shell watches Mum lean over the porch rail. The undersides of Mum's arms do that jiggle as she pulls in bed sheets, Dad's crisp jeans, the tea towels with splotches of browned blood Mum will cut into rags. Shell wants Mum to watch Shell falling asleep. But Mum is looking somewhere far away from the Mexican hammock. Once, in Mum's bottom drawer, Shell found a smoke-and-cream photo of a little girl with a ringlet down her forehead. There was another of a teenager with Mum's thick dark hair piled high on her head, a cigarette between her fingers, beads around a lean neck, spotted with Mum's same moles.

"I lived twenty-eight years before you were born, Shell," Mum had said, tucking the picture back under a pile of peach-coloured underwear folded into the same squares as Dad's and Shell's are too. Mum is like the backyard garden, smooth on the surface but with surprises hidden deep.

AFTER SUPPER, WHEN the street lights come on, Dad piggybacks Shell up to the small room in the front that is hers now. Her bed and dresser are in place, curtains hung, and Mum has already unpacked some of Shell's clothes and toys. The horsehair button box that was once Mum's but became Shell's after she played with it without permission and broke the hinges on the lid is on the dresser. Cream silk lines the interior, empty apart from three brass buttons, a spool of pink thread, and a headless toy soldier Shell found by the tracks. Shell tucks the broken glass she took from Dad's basket inside the button box. Then the box goes under the bed, behind puzzles and board games, a tea set, and an Eaton's bag full of dolls she doesn't like anymore.

The heat has broken. The box fan in Mum and Dad's window circulates the air, like blood in a body. Cars pass, pushing and pulling shadows. And the house's silence speaks so loud Shell cannot hear Mum and Dad in the living room below.

By the wedge of hall light spilling across her bed, Shell unwinds the damp bandage from her foot. The stitches along the ball make a long, tight insect. And though there is a deep itch inside, the pain is gone. Because Mum had to cancel her swimming lessons, Dad's going to rig up the wading pool tomorrow. She can dangle her foot over the edge. Oh, and Kremski's coming to help Dad tear up more of the grass. They've got to get the basil in. While Kremski rolls one of his Drums, Shell will tell him about the hospital and show him the piece of glass Dad thinks is still in the berry basket. Will Kremski know what a hairy lip is? Somewhere a car horn blares—once, twice—lonesome and long. Though Mum hates them, Shell misses the burly CNs that used to rumble down the railroad tracks so far, now, from their new house.

Fiddleheads

Dad doesn't stop working on the house from the first summer they move into Cashel Street. Under the crumbly carpet, the floors are bright blond hardwood and then the bathroom gets stuccoed and tiled and fitted with a new tub that is an antique with claw feet that Mum complains is too deep and expensive to fill. Spring comes. Dad gets his pointy shovel out and the tomatoes go in. The scaffold he puts up along the driveway side of the house goes all the way to the roof. Dad works all by himself or with Kremski, who'll stay for dinner after. Shell helps too, passing Dad nails and stirring away the skin on the top of the paint. The studio is a studio now and not at all a bus garage. Shell even gets to write her name with a stick in the wet concrete Dad pours in front of the studio door. He says it will be there forever.

Each morning after breakfast, Mum and Dad put on

clogs and carry the last of the coffee across the yard into the studio, warm from the overnight firing. They are still in there, aprons on, radio going, when Shell comes home from grade one for beans and toast and lunchtime news. After school they are back turning pots on their wheel, and when dinner's done and Shell is supposed to be doing homework, she watches through their bedroom window as Mum and Dad move from wedging table to wheel to kiln, loading in a glaze fire.

The studio shelves fill with Mum and Dad's pots — stoneware ashtrays, onion soup bowls, goblets in celadon green — but Mum still takes in mending and once a week teaches adults at the community centre how to glaze and then Dad gets some gardening work in the north end of Somerset. Doctors and lawyers and professors live there. The woman who hires Dad is an engineer, though not the kind that drives a train. Someone who buys Mum and Dad's pottery gave the woman Dad's name. Dad says the woman's garden is twice as big as their own. Now, though, when she should be planting and keeping the earth moist, she's gone to Vancouver to visit her daughter.

Shell had answered when the woman called then listened from the kitchen while Dad laughed and joked with her and said her name as often as possible: Olivia. Dad doesn't call Mum anything but "you" and "her" and "your mother." If Mum's friends at the co-op store didn't call Mum by her first name, no one in the whole world would. And instead of looking at Dad or saying hi or giving him a kiss like in glossy ads for margarine, Mum's eyes are always down in her lap or her back is turned to him, scrubbing borscht beets in the kitchen sink.

Along with the wage for planting and watering, weeding and cutting the grass, Dad can bring home all the crops he wants, which, this being the start of spring, isn't much. But after he's been there once or twice, Dad says fiddleheads are coming up in droves in the ravine behind Olivia's. If he gets enough, he can sell them to the French restaurant downtown. Mum laughs at how something only poor folks once scavenged is now so gourmet. Fiddleheads are bitter, nasty things you can never get clean of grit, and she bets Shell dollars to doughnuts Shell won't like them either.

"Do they really look like fiddles?"

Dad says Shell will soon find out. And then he reads her a recipe for fiddleheads with wild rice and salmon. "Native people ate them in the spring, Shell, all along the east coast. Now we will too."

On Saturday, Mum's volunteering at the co-op. Shell can come help measure raw nuts into bags and twist on the ties and listen to Mum talk to all her friends who come in for the weekend kefir shipment, but instead she goes with Dad to Olivia's. If they wait any longer, the fiddleheads will be gone. Or, not gone; they will be ferns. Mum packs cheddar and rye sandwiches, a Thermos of coffee for Dad, and one of milk for Shell. Dad goes north, past the university and the big new shopping mall that Dad vows never to set foot in. A science show is on the radio. When an expert says it's true that robins can hear worms moving in the soil, Dad cranks the volume

way up. "That's why they lean in close to the ground...
Shell—are you listening?"

"Yeah."

"Look!" A robin, on Shell's side, is stamping its feet on
a lawn, mimicking the sound of rain just like the radio
scientist said. Then it cocks its head and lays an ear to the
earth. All the mealy worms it has tricked will be racing
to the surface in search of moisture. Dad steers with only
one hand so he can lean across Shell for a better look, his
beard brushing her cheek. The Dart veers into the outside
lane. A car horn blares.

"Dad!"

Dad turns down the radio, straightening the wheel.
"Wow." He shakes his head. "Imagine that, Shell. What's
it sound like to actually hear worms?"

When they turn onto Sumac Valley Road, the sidewalks end. And so do the streets: it's all lanes and trails
and avenues now.

Dad helps Shell read the names out loud—"Peri-
winkle Path, Trembling Aspen Terrace, Iroquois Lane."

"The names are for things we've destroyed in this
country, Shell," Dad says, shaking his head. "Native
people, plants, trees."

Dad makes the world make sense like that, and Shell
always feels smarter and sad after.

The houses are set way back from the curb and lawns
are bright green like the turfed shelves at Thrifty Mart
where they display fruit. Bushes have been cut into
cones or spirals, and there are Union Jacks and Canada flags flying, and the driveways, of which many are

crescent-shaped, are mostly inset with brick. Red cars, black cars, silver cars shine like armour. Any For Sale sign on a front lawn has a sticker that says POOL.

Olivia's street, Mohawk, is really a "court" and doesn't look nearly as nice as Sumac Valley. Her house is way at the far end, set deep in its own nook, and the style is called "ranch," which means there's only one floor, or maybe one and a half, and a big basement. Dad says ranch houses are American and not only ugly but wasteful when it comes to heating. Olivia has neighbours on one side only, a yellow-brick with red double doors. Each door has a brass lion head knocker; the rings in their mouths would make good bracelets.

Dad eases the Dart up the driveway's fresh black asphalt. There's an opening within the forsythia—brightest buttercup—at the end. After a grassy slope, they are in the back. The glass doors of a walkout basement are concealed with oatmeal drapery. A concrete patio is roofed with a main-floor balcony that spans the back of the house. Like their yard on Cashel Street, Olivia's is mostly vegetable patch. Squares and rectangles of soil that Dad has turned for Olivia—fresh and black, studded with white eyes of stone—are framed with tough orange mums and a ruffle of stiff green plastic. Seed packs stuck to Popsicle sticks show photographs of carrots, potatoes, peppers, peas, zucchini. Beyond the plateau of the garden, a stretch of grass ends like a cliff, at the bottom of which the ravine starts in. A net of high chain-link fencing contains thick treed shadows and cool sapphire dark. Dad says, "You'd think you were in Algonquin down in there."

A forest right in the city. Or a city right in the forest, but a forest that is a ghost now.

Olivia's tool shed is made of brick and could be a nice house for one girl and most of her stuff. Dad gets Shell a weeding fork and leather gloves and a rubber bushel basket. She can weed the lawn and anything in the vegetable beds that shouldn't be there. Along the wooden fence between Olivia's and the neighbour's there's a crop of knee-high nettle. She squats, gets her gloves around a prickled neck, and tugs. *One-two-three*. Dad is behind her. He grabs her tool, strikes it deep into the earth, right at the nettle's shaft, pulling back in a single sharp twist.

"Right down to the root, Shell." Dad shakes the dirt from the hairy roots and tosses the weed into the basket. "Okay?" Then, with a pitchfork and a sack of potting soil, he disappears through the forsythia and into the front.

But Shell's roots don't ever come out with the stem. The gardening gloves are too big and the earth is hard. Shell's knees get stiff, so she weeds sitting down, her legs stuck out. Then her back hurts. Sometimes her fork turns up bits of eggshell or a peach pit, but there's not a single piece of glass or porcelain or brass button like Dad's always finding in their yard. She follows the weeds along the fenceline. Through the slats, the perfect circle of swimming pool in the neighbour's yard is covered with a shiny sheet of silver foil: a casserole in the oven. The wicker lawn chairs have been painted white and there's a glass-topped table. Beside a forgotten pack of cigarettes, a glass of iced tea sweats—lemon slice belly-up and pink lipstick on the straw.

The sun creeps high and hot. Above, the sky is the colour of blueberry-flavoured slushies Mum lets Shell have sometimes walking home from swimming lessons as long as she doesn't tell Dad. Shell turns her jean jacket into a pillow. The grass beneath her is crunchy. Somewhere close, a fruit perfume. And were it not for the buzz of bee she could maybe hear mealy worms squishing through the earth. When she is just about asleep—high orange sun toasting her lids—a crow screams. There is the rustle of treetop and the hard beating of wings. Shell sits up. Just as the crow scoops up and away from the darkness of the ravine, Dad comes across the grass, swinging the cooler.

They wash their hands with the hose and hold it to their lips to drink. Dad's T-shirt is damp and dirty; so is his beard, and his sweaty hair wings out. Olivia's patio chairs have no cushions. Dad brushes the seats free of leaves and twigs but says to ignore the white traces of bird dropping. He takes big bites of his sandwich and swallows hard. The cheddar is sharp and the mustard is the grainy kind, and because the bread is crumbly, Mum put on extra lettuce and pickle. Instead of cookies there are Brazil nuts and dried apricots down at the bottom of a Mason jar, which Shell fishes out when Dad's pouring his coffee.

"Why does Olivia have a vegetable garden when she's got a job?"

Dad brushes crumbs from his beard and points next door, the silver pie dish of the swimming pool glinting above the wooden fencing. "You think they care that robins hear worms moving underground?"

Dad waits until Shell says no, they don't care.

"Well, Olivia does," says Dad. Then he says that Olivia grew up in the Prairies too. "She's got a farmer's soul," he says, making a fist.

Dad has a key for the sliding glass doors. They leave their shoes outside and walk right into the basement. The washroom down here is even bigger than the one Dad built on Cashel Street. There's a glass bowl of dried flowers on the toilet tank and a dish filled with tiny soaps shaped like fish and shells. Everything is navy and pearl— the soaps, the tile floor, the neatly folded hand towels looped through a silver ring attached to the wall. The real soap is in a ceramic pump bottle by the faucet. It smells so lilac, Shell washes her hands twice, and when they are dry, she plucks a scallop from among the soaps in the dish, wraps it in a pull of toilet paper, and tucks it in her pocket.

Dad says he'd better use the toilet too. The basement is dusky. Through Shell's socks, the slippery tiles are cool; the pine walls are warm beneath her palms. Olivia has stacked the drinks bar with canning jars and boxes marked *kids' stuff*. A big wooden TV faces a brown leather couch, and the pictures Olivia's got everywhere show a girl with a horse and a boy with a dirt bike and there's a bunch of ribbons and medals. The door next to the furnace room will be for going upstairs. Shell puts her hand on the knob and, heart beating, gives it a twist. But the knob stays fixed. She tries again, shouldering the door with all her weight. It will not give. Olivia has locked it from the inside, keeping her and Dad out.

THE LAWN MOWER grinds in the front. Shell picks up her gloves. Next door, the cigarettes and tea are gone. Then the patio door slides open. Between the slats, the lady is mostly visible: jeans, white T-shirt, dark hair in a tight ballerina bun. Cigarette smoke infuses the tartness of cut grass. The lawn mower stops. Dad comes trundling around the side of the house, blades of grass stuck to his beard and arms.

It only takes a minute: the lady is at the fence with her hand stuck out.

Dad says he's the gardener.

"Oh, yes. Olivia said she'd found someone." And what a coincidence both she and Dad have daughters about the same age; hers is called Fiona.

"Shell," Dad calls, "come say hello."

Shell waves her weeding fork. A wash of cloud suddenly conceals the sun. Chill bites the air. The lady must be standing on a box or she's really tall, because the fence comes just to her ribs. Through her shirt she gets what the big kids at school call "party hats." Mrs. Gibbons gets them too, and when she does, she crosses her arms or puts on her cardigan. But Olivia's neighbour just lights another cigarette.

Dad and Shell ought to know there was a coyote in Olivia's yard yesterday. "Normally there are dogs and grandkids outside all up and down the crescent. But," she says, smoke steaming out her nose, "folks are being extra cautious."

"There's a lot of life in the ravine down there," Dad says.

The woman shakes her head. She'd prefer not to think about that.

SHELL HOLDS OPEN the bag while Dad scoops in raked grass cuttings. The sun dips low. When the yard waste is bundled up on the curb, Dad gets some canvas grocery bags and his small curved knife from the glove compartment. Garlicky meat is roasting next door. To go with the fiddleheads, Dad left a big orange triangle of steelhead trout thawing in the sink, and Mum's making wild rice.

"What about the coyote, Dad?"

Dad's forehead gets those wavy ridges. "Don't be silly." Whatever animal hears them coming is going to run scared before they even see it. Shell should know that.

The fence at the back where the yard drops off is not as high as it looks from the garden but is still taller than Dad. When he crouches down, fingers interlaced, Shell grabs his damp shoulders and then steps into the cradle of his hands. *One, two, three* — Shell reaches high, grabbing the chain-link. She hoists herself up and over.

"Good girl, kiddo," says Dad when Shell hits the ground on the other side. Her skull shakes from the drop, as does the fence from her rough clamber. Then Dad makes his thick hands into starfish, grips the fencing, and scrambles over. His breath is heavy when he lands.

The ravine is musty and cool, all wet velvet. Crystals of sun spill down through the lacy canopy above. So he'd find his way back to the fiddleheads, Dad tied a strip of red ribbon to a thick white birch. Heads ducked, they plunge down into the depths of the ravine and as the earth slopes down, Olivia's garden, the tinfoil pool, and Mohawk Court seal up behind. Following in Dad's wake, willow switches whip Shell in the face. Low branches catch her clothes and hair, and thistles cling to her jeans. Their footsteps sink into layers of wet duff, unearthing crushed Styrofoam, drink cans, burned paper, all the way down into a gully of mud, its bottom lined with soccer balls and chip bags.

Dad stops. His hand clamps down on Shell's shoulder. "Smoke," he says, nostrils flaring.

A crisp earthen burn weighs in the air, but there is as yet no taste in the mouth, no sting in the eye. Shell says, "Someone's barbecue?"

Dad steps to the left. "Coming from over there."

In a clearing some ten feet ahead, a campfire smoulders. The dozen or so empty tin cans half buried in leaves — pork and beans, jalapeno sardines — throb with a glaze of red ants. Also there's a pile of wet clothes clumped in a ball near the mushy log that someone has shifted over so that he or she or they could sit near the fire. The embers are young. They glow the angry orange of roadwork pylons.

"Fools," Dad says. With his rubber gardening boots he stomps out the embers then douses them further with a toe kick of damp duff.

Shell tries to swallow but has no spit. When Dad and Mum and Shell are camping, they leave their site for the whole day to go canoeing. There's no way anyone would come ashore and look in their tent, steal their food. Because, Dad says, the rangers don't let bad people into Algonquin.

"Dad," Shell whispers. "They'll be coming back."

With hands on his hips, Dad steps around the clearing.

"This is city land, Shell. There's a reason why you can't just camp here."

"Why?"

Dad frowns and pushes his glasses up his nose. With right instep, he drags the cans into a pile. The scuffing sound is so loud.

"Because people are reckless, Shell. That's why. They don't know what they're doing."

Crows circle above, attracted by the silver glint of the cans.

"Let's go, Dad." Shell tries walking off, but Dad's poking around the brush now, peeling back the branches from a cluster of sapling oak.

"Shell," he calls. From beneath a tarp of army green, the yellow cord of a knapsack snakes across the leafy ground. Magazines and newspapers are wrapped in clear bags. Dad's brows arch way up over his glasses. "See that?" He releases the branches and the brush snaps back into place. "Come on, kiddo," he says. Dad's strong hand cups the back of Shell's neck, steering her away from the campsite.

The canopy tightens above. Some twenty yards along, the forest deepens to garnet. The shadows that fall from the trees are as thick as those in Shell's nighttime bedroom. Dad and Shell keep moving; air cooling, skin getting wet. Shell trips over a tree root, and when Dad glances back, she swallows down the water in her eyes.

Then up ahead: as cranberry, as cherry, as winter cardinal, as blood, Shell sees Dad's marker first. "Look, Dad!"

They move in on the red ribbon, which has been cut from the same spool Mum used on Shell's strawberry sundress. The morning of Shell's last birthday, when she turned six, the first thing she saw waking up was the dress. Mum had finished it the night before and placed it at the foot of Shell's bed. The best part is the shiny white buttons all up the front, as well as the pockets—big enough for a baseball—and the strip of red trimming the hem.

The ribbon is tied to a thick white trunk of birch, its bark peeling away in horizontal strips—the spiralling ringlets look like tails of pigs. This birch is one of a grove, throughout which fiddleheads blanket the earth, a miniature forest of furled-up ferns. Water trickles in what must be a nearby stream. Dad grins as he unsheathes his paring knife. There's a canvas grocery bag for each of them to fill. Shell crouches next to Dad, tiptoeing among the fiddleheads. He says that for so many hundreds of years the Malecite people would have been really happy to see these guys after a long winter of salt fish.

"Look how green that is, Shell," Dad says of an emerald disc pinched between his fingers. "In terms of vitamin content, that'd have been gold."

Dad shows Shell how to pick: gentle, right at the base. The smell, each time, is a burst of both rotten and fresh. Shell tells Dad the fiddleheads look like they're from prehistoric times. But they also look a bit like seafood and just-hatched birds.

They sweep across the boggy fiddlehead forest, rapidly shrinking its size. Shell hums as she picks. Dad just picks. In as little as twenty minutes their bags are jammed. They'll stop at the French restaurant on the way home.

Will the nice chef be there? "Remember he gave me a sherbet cone? Dad, remember?"

Dad carries both bags, trudging up what is now an incline. Amber lozenges of day shimmer through the trees ahead. As he walks, Dad's forearms flex, the handles of the bags pulling tight. After some minutes Shell calls out, "Dad! What about my ribbon?"

Dad's face, when he turns, is tired. His glasses have slipped way down his nose. "God, Shell." A spot of red ribbon is still visible through the brush. "We'll get it next week."

Dad turns. It only takes a minute before his footsteps disappear, leaving Shell alone. She runs after him, calling for him to come back.

"Look," Dad says, pointing. He's waiting for Shell by a crashed hickory. Spongy caps of white burst within the rotting pulp. Next time they'll forage for mushrooms too. They go on. A woodpecker knocks, high and hollow. Last week on the radio someone said the woodpecker's head is made of special membrane so they don't get brain damage from all that pecking. Shell thought they should make motorcycle helmets from that membrane too, and Mum told her to write that idea down and send it in to the show. "Hey Dad," Shell calls out. She's been meaning to remind Dad about the woodpecker helmets—

Behind her, brush crashes. Branches crack. Leaves ripple and surge.

Dad stops and twists around. Shell stands frozen, which is funny, because inside she gets very warm. Blood floods her ears, blending in with the sound of the brush snapping behind them. The white of Dad's grocery bags is too bright. Seeing Dad's face, now Shell knows what she looked like when he caught her rummaging for candy money in Mum's purse.

"Hey!" a man calls. Footsteps come crunching.

Shell's knees knock together. Bone on hollow bone.

"Hey asshole!"

At Dad's gesture, Shell walks quickly towards him, ducking behind his legs. His jeans are greasy and warm. Reaching up, she hooks a finger through a belt loop.

Like an actor entering through a curtain, a man emerges from the brush. In her chest, Shell's heart is about to burst. She presses into Dad's legs, whose tense muscles make them as hard as the tree trunks that surround them.

The man is Dad's size. His grey hair is yellow, sort of like his eyes. And, like Dad and Shell, he wears jeans and a denim jacket. The tight gloves stretched over his hands are full of runs.

"You the shithead that put out my fire?" His deep voice is as scratchy as the oldest of Dad's blues records.

Shell lets go of the belt loop and reaches for Dad's hand. But his hand is a fist; from it dangles the heavy fiddlehead bag.

"I hope you would have done the same," Dad says.

"No," the man says. "I would have minded my own goddamn business." He has no more matches, he says. "Shit!" Then he calls Dad and Shell a couple of goofs.

Blood, pooled in Shell's ears, rushes her eyes, her head. "Shut up!" Shell steps out from behind Dad.

Dad hisses at her to behave.

The man is missing his eye teeth, so when he laughs,

he looks like a horse. Then his face loses all expression. "Whatcha stealing in the bags?"

"Not stealing." The echo in Shell's head competes with her hard gym-class heartbeats.

"Fiddleheads," Dad says. He sets down the bags. Shell takes the handles of the bag that is less full while Dad opens the other. The man steps forward, bringing in the smell of damp wood and smoke.

Dad says, "They're baby ferns."

The man pokes a finger into Dad's shopping bag. The collar of his jacket is sprinkled with white flakes and he is wearing the same dirty-white tennis shoes with green stripes that Dad has in the downstairs closet.

Dad is going on about the vitamin content of fiddle-heads and how good they are with salt and butter. There's more back in the birch grove. The man should harvest them and sell them too. "Plenty for all," Dad says.

The man squints at the fiddlehead between his fingers. "How much you get?"

"Three bucks a pound. We've about ten pounds here."

"Could be okay."

Dad says to try the market downtown. "I know a few vendors there who'd be glad to have them."

The man looks at Shell. "You mean coming from you and her they'd be glad."

Dad shrugs and gathers up the bags.

"You live around here?" the man asks. He scratches his yellow hair. More flakes fall, settling on his shoulders now.

"Working for someone who does."

"Good gig?"

"Makes ends meet."

"Yeah. I need something like that." Shell gets a nod. "Got a boy about her age."

Dad picks up both bags and says, well, if he wants to pick, there's still some left. He's to look for a red ribbon tied to a birch some fifty yards on. Then Dad turns away. "Come on, Shell."

They leave the man behind them and walk, then jog, away.

MUM AND DAD don't say hi so Shell does, extra loud for everyone. The opera is on the radio and the kettle's going. Mum's biting into a whole wheat fig roll and also there's bags of raw cashews and sticks of black licorice with brown inside.

"The rice is already cooked," Mum says, without looking up from a book Shell's never seen before. There is no picture on the cover. Mum takes the cooler from Shell and Shell tries sounding out the book title.

Laugh of the Medusa, Mum says.

"Medusa with snakes for hair?" There's a story about Medusa in Shell's kids' mythology.

Mum says, "Not really." The book is a loan from Barb Nutt, the co-op manager whose son Soren is a bit older than Shell and lives with his dad and not Barb anymore. Barb speaks French to Shell, though Mum has told Barb a million times that Shell's not learning French yet.

There are only enough fiddleheads for three, but

Dad's got a pair of twenty-dollar bills tucked in his wallet and there's a carton of lemon sherbet for dessert.

Shell does as Mum says, changing into a clean shirt and washing up to her elbows. The scallop of decorative soap is stuck with bits of toilet paper. She dries it off, wraps it up again, then tucks it into the button box under her bed.

Dad, beer in hand, gets the charcoal going for the fish. Mum is rinsing fiddleheads in the tin colander. Then Shell double-checks for bugs. The baby ferns are rubbery between Shell's fingers and they smell of tar, peppermint, moss. Mum switches on the double boiler.

By the time they sit down, the hockey game has already started. It's the playoffs and Montreal is on home ice, so Dad keeps the kitchen radio on low. He opens another beer, of which Shell gets a juice glass, half full. Mum spoons Dad a big pile of steamed fiddleheads, taking for herself only a few—Shell counts ten, the same number as Shell receives when she holds out her plate. Butter is passed, pepper and salt. Dad declares the fiddleheads excellent. "Come on, Shell," he says of Shell's untouched pile. "Folks're paying big bucks for these downtown."

"Poor-people food," Shell says quietly. Shell picks up a fiddlehead with her fork and holds it to her lips. Across the table, Mum's put one in her mouth, then a quick forkful of the wild rice. Dad watches Shell chew. The bitterness makes her throat close, so she shifts the clump to her front teeth, where it mixes with trout residue.

"They're okay, Dad," Shell says, swallowing.

Dad grinds pepper on his fish. "If the weather's cool, there might be some left next week."

Dad turns up the radio as Montreal scores.

"I want my red ribbon back," Shell says over the announcer, who must be bouncing in his seat, yelling like Shell's not allowed to.

"What ribbon?" Mum says.

Dad and Shell keep eating.

"What were you up to?" Mum asks again, looking over at Shell, who can't remember the last time Mum looked at Dad or Dad at Mum.

Shell gobbles the rest of the fiddleheads and smiles big at Dad, and when he smiles back, rice in his teeth, Shell's sure he won't go away and leave her like the man in the ravine did his son.

Dad takes his sherbet out to the studio. Mum and Shell have theirs in cones. The sherbet is smooth and pure white, though the flavour is the biggest brightest yellow, like swallowing the smell of Mum's laundry soap.

"Mum," Shell says, "I don't want to go back to Olivia's again."

Mum frowns. "What happened?"

Shell thinks of the locked basement door and the piece of soap that she treasures but Olivia will never know is gone in a million years. "They name the streets for the cut-down trees and dead Indian people and there's no sidewalks, so how can it be safe for a kid to learn bike riding?"

If Shell doesn't want to go back, she can bag nuts with Mum next week. Mum touches Shell's head. "We really need to get you into some kind of activity." The dishes are draining in the rack, but Mum won't let out the dishwater until she goes to bed. "It's such a waste to keep running the tap," she always says. This is also why she takes a bath in Shell's used water. Mum, like Dad, grew up hauling water and milking cows and saving pennies to get the bus to some other place.

"I'm glad there's no ravine and we've got sidewalks," Shell says, getting into her pyjamas.

"Yes," Mum says. She tucks Shell into bed and leaves the door open a crack and then halfway when Shell asks.

Downstairs, Dad comes in from the studio.

"Did something happen at that woman's?" Mum says.

Dad says no. "Why?"

Next are those hard whispers. Shell doesn't need to understand the words. She feels in her bones the vibration of Mum's clenched jaw and Dad's shoulders pinching at the back. Shell stands at her door. She's going to run downstairs and shout how they, like her, are so lucky to not have to eat sardines in a ravine. But then the back door closes again. Mum lets the water out of the sink and Shell climbs back into bed.

Please Don't Pass Me By

A Thrifty van trundles up Cashel Street and parks on the lawn of the angel-brick bungalow five doors down. Two men with sunglasses on their heads carry loads of belongings through the shadowy front door. Shell goes in from the porch and says this time there's a little girl's stuff among the furniture and boxes. Mum frowns, pouring hot milk into a row of little glass jars. In twelve hours there will be tart, runny yogurt. "Starting at a new school is hard at the best of times, never mind so far into the year." If she's in Shell's grade two class, Shell can help her catch up. Mum says they will have to wait and see how old the new girl is.

It seems like overnight, purple crocuses with egg-yolk centres rise up all over the front lawn. Then water starts running in the gutters, and dirty snowbanks recede down to grass, revealing last year's chocolate bar wrappers, cigarette butts, and so much dog poo. Then the special seeds Dad ordered in January arrive in the mail and the baby tomato plants that have been growing under lights in the basement are almost ready to go in.

Down the block, the garden under the front windows of the angel-brick bungalow stays muddy and the driveway, since the Thrifty van left, has only ever been empty. If the new girl and her fat mum didn't walk down to Princess Anne Elementary in the morning, Shell would think no one lived there at all. The girl's hair is what Mum calls "strawberry blond," and she wears those runners with Velcro closures Mum won't buy because they lack arch support. The girl's mum wears Velcro runners too, and her chubby feet hang out over the edge like when your skates aren't tied up tight enough and you end up sliding around on your ankles. And though they only live three blocks from Princess Anne, the mum walks so slow that sometimes she sends the girl in an On-the-Town taxi.

"Oh, Shell, you should offer to walk with her!" Mum cries when Shell says she would like to go to school in a taxi too.

Shell says the girl is too young for her. "Only in grade one."

"That's why you should walk her, then."

But she probably can't even read yet. What would they talk about?

Mum sighs and sends Shell down to Bun King to get onion buns for a hamburger supper. She gives Shell a one-dollar bill, enough for four buns, and makes her promise to walk up an extra block when she crosses because there's no other corner with a light.

Then, on the way back, the new girl pops out from

40

the screen door of her bungalow. Shell keeps going, head down, stepping over a dirty puddle.

The girl goes: "Hey, you my age?" She scrambles onto a collapsing lawn chair, kicking out her legs. "Hey girl!"

Shell's so close to home. Dad's pruning the mountain ash on the front lawn. When he's done with that, he'll light the charcoal. They're always the first ones on the street to have a barbecue, and that's not even counting the sausages and bacon Dad and Kremski smoked this winter in the tin smokehouse they built out back.

The girl stands up. "I'm six."

The sun is right above the bungalow, so when Shell turns around, she has to squint. "I'm seven," Shell says.

"My mum already said you can come over." The girl is down the steps and halfway across the muddy lawn. "You shy? I used to be too."

"Well, really, I'm almost eight," Shell says, clutching the onion buns. There's an Aero bar wrapper under the girl's sneaker.

The girl's name is Vicki.

"Shell."

Vicki says, "What's that short for?"

"Nothing. It's just Shell. Not Sheila or Shelley or Michelle or she-sells-sea-shells-by-the-sea-shore, so don't even try."

Vicki says she's just Vicki too. Not Victoria, even though that's pretty, like the actress on *Dallas*. She says Shell can come inside and see her room.

"Gotta ask my dad." Shell points down the block. Dad—cap, glasses, beard, and overalls—is on the kitchen

41

stepladder. Shiny mountain ash leaves fall away from his clippers.

Vicki says her dad lives in Michigan and Shell should see how much cereal you can get down there but not here. "Peanut Butter Balls, Tropical O's...How about just sit on the porch?"

"Don't know."

Vicki kicks around in the muck, spattering her Velcro shoes. "I got a Cadbury's Easter Creme. We can share it."

Vicki's cement porch is covered with green plastic carpeting like in minigolf. It's damp, so Shell sits on her hands while Vicki goes inside to get the chocolate. Not even Mum, who sometimes hides a Kit Kat at the bottom of her purse, will ever let Shell taste a Cadbury's Easter Creme Egg. "There's far too much sugar for a child in one of those things." The older kids at Princess Anne say there's a commercial where a boy asks the man in the store for six thousand Creme Eggs. They say too that Creme Eggs are available only at Easter.

Shell knocks a snail off the step with the toe of her sneaker, then opens the Bun King bag and one by one picks the onion bits off the top of one of the buns. The bits are dark and chewy and sweet. They could come as a snack like chips or sunflower seeds and Shell would buy them like that and eat them. Dad thinks they're the best part of the bun too. If they're out of onion buns at Bun King, Shell is to get the poppy seed ones, though poppy seeds have no taste at all.

The egg is wrapped in red and purple foil. Cross-legged, Vicki pushes back her hair and peels it.

Shell tells Vicki how last week her grade two class went real roller skating. There was a class trip to Bootin' roller rink, and their teacher fell and broke her wrist.

"Oh, sure." Vicki goes to Bootin' with her mum and Clarke, her mum's boyfriend, all the time. So often that she's getting her own roller skates for Easter. Not the adjustable kind with the key like Shell has, but the boot ones, with laces and everything. "What're you asking the Easter Bunny for?" Vicki balances the unwrapped chocolate egg on her knee, covers her face with her hands, and sneezes.

Shell didn't know you could ask for stuff for Easter.

"Oh, sure you can." Vicki sinks her small teeth into the top of the egg. She flutters her eyelashes. Then she pulls the bottom half away from her lips, passing it to Shell; white goop oozes out. The yolk centre is the same colour as the inside of crocuses.

Shell puts the whole of her half in her mouth. Sweetness creeps up her jaw into her eyes and gets wedged at the front of her scalp. She chews slowly, squishing slime between her teeth.

Vicki says, "If the Easter Bunny brings you roller skates, we can go around the block."

But the Easter Bunny doesn't bring toys, that's Santa's job.

Well, the Easter Bunny brings *her*, Vicki, whatever she wants. It's simple: instead of hanging up stockings, Vicki and her mum put baskets on top of the TV, and on the morning of Easter there are wrapped presents inside.

Doesn't Vicki hunt for chocolate eggs the Easter Bunny hides around the house? Shell says that's what happens in her house, and sometimes they're in such hard places only Dad can find them.

Vicki says, oh, yeah, she does an egg hunt too. But after she opens her presents. "Maybe you need to pray to the Easter Bunny if you want presents."

Vicki crumples up the chocolate foil and throws it onto the muddy lawn. She says that once at Bootin' a kid tried to wear those old-fashioned strap-on skates and he had to leave.

"Really?" And because Vicki says maybe Shell can come to Bootin' with her mum and Clarke someday, Shell lets her eat the bits off the last onion bun. Now the buns are evenly plain and she can tell Mum Bun King was out of the poppy seed kind too. A rich charcoal tinge floats in the air. Shell gets up and—"Well, goodbye!"—goes home.

IN THE FURNACE room, among ice skates, ski boots, and wooden snowshoes, Shell finds her roller skates. Since she put them away last summer, the rust has deepened in both colour and texture, and the wide plastic toe guards have turned the shade of the Yellow Pages. Though stretched and cracked, the leather ankle straps have not rotted through. The length of kitchen twine attaching the wide metal key to the left skate is easily cut away with the utility knife on the top of Dad's tool box. Having worked the key into the socket of the left skate, Shell wrenches at the hinges so it comes apart, front from back. Then she does the same to the right. She wipes her rusty orange hands on her pants and buries the key under the cardinal bush out back.

"Well, then, you'd better remember where you put it," Dad says of the missing key. Without it, he can't put Shell's skates together. That or they'll look for another pair when the garage sales start up. Then he goes back to his cookbooks. Easter is only a few days away and Kremski is coming to celebrate.

Shell asks what they're supposed to be celebrating when there's no God in their house or Jesus to rise again.

"Look," Dad says, putting down *Old-Fashioned Ukrainian Cookery*. "Kremski's from a place where you can go to jail for believing in the wrong things."

Shell nods and repeats after Dad that what they're celebrating is the coming of spring and how lucky they are to have enough to eat when people in the Soviet Union wait six hours in line just to get a sausage.

GOOD FRIDAY MORNING, *Scooby-Doo* is blaring through Vicki's screen door. Shell's never seen that cartoon before. She watches through the mesh before she knocks.

"Hi!" Vicki's eating Froot Loops from a Tupperware jelly mould; the milk she slurps has gone violet. Her pyjamas are just a long T-shirt and her hair is in what Mum would call a rat's nest.

Though Shell is still full of Dad's wheat-germ pancakes, she asks Vicki for a bowl of cereal. It tastes of Life Savers candy, like Shell dreamed it would. While Vicki's couch is shiny black velveteen, the rest of the living room furniture is lacquered wicker with forest-green upholstery. Giant Chinese fans and framed Rolling Stones posters decorate the lavender walls, freshly painted. On top of the TV—wood panelled like the station wagon across the street—Vicki and her mum have their Easter baskets all ready to go.

Vicki's mum is named Bonita. She wants to watch *The Twilight Zone* now that Vicki's show is over. She already has eyeshadow and blush on, and though she is so fat she can't sit in the wicker furniture, she's still so pretty.

"Let's go," Vicki says.

Vicki's bedroom is a clammy add-on in the back. The plywood door bangs into the desk when she opens it, and because there is no closet, Vicki's clothes are in garbage bags piled on the floor. Her mum doesn't work right now, but Vicki has all the latest toys. And she doesn't have a car either, so they get to bring their colourful groceries home in a cab. Shell watched them unload last week— Viva Puffs cookies, cheese Bugles, cases of Heinz soups and Chef Boyardee ravioli. Posters of Blondie and Bruce Springsteen are taped up over Vicki's bed, which is itself a mountain of blank-eyed Barbies in stretchy jeans, Big Birds, Holly Hobbies, and a Snoopy Punch Me toy.

Vicki's Easter roller skates are on page ninety-four of the Canadian Tire catalogue she keeps under her pillow. The sturdy boots are sleek white, while the thick wheels and stopper on the front are clown-nose red. Her mum's skates will be the exact same, only she's getting black ones.

"See?" Vicki flips to page ninety-three.

"They're nice," says Shell. Maybe it's easier for her mum to skate than to walk.

"You been praying for yours? Easter's only tomorrow, you know."

"Pray?" Shell doesn't know how.

Vicki scratches her knotted head and leans against her bed, knocking a pile of toys onto the floor. She picks up a stuffed rabbit with matted pink fur. An ex-boyfriend of her mum's won it at the county fair. While the rabbit's torso is squat, its arms and legs are spidery; iron-on facial features are coming unstuck; and the paws and belly and ears look like the dirty patch of snow on Vicki's front lawn.

"Here." Vicki tucks the rabbit into Shell's arms. It smells of sticky perfume. "Take Kevin home and just think really hard about roller skates. I bet you'll get some skates in your Easter basket too."

Vicki lets Shell out the back door. The stoop is piled with wet cardboard boxes marked *Living Room* and *Fragile, Kitchen*. One big one marked *Toys* is full of *TV Guide*s and what look to be dozens of balled-up Cadbury's Easter Creme foils.

Kevin goes next to the creaky antique teddy bear lounging on Shell's bed. In the gardening shed there is a wooden strawberry basket not too stained with which Shell makes her own Easter basket. She fills it with the Styrofoam peanuts Mum saves, and decorates it with pictures of chicks and rabbits and hot cross buns cut from grocery store flyers. Because they do not have a television, the basket goes on top of the turntable.

Shell sits on the floor in front of the stereo thinking hard about new roller skates. She truly believes in God, but only in secret. But it's always been okay to believe in the Easter Bunny. Sort of like how Shell gets to hang up a stocking and open presents on Christmas morning. Dad's always bugging her about how Santa can't get in because the doors are locked and they have no chimney. But on Christmas Eve he'll sit for hours, with whiskey and a bowl of nuts, watching the fairy lights glow on the spruce tree they themselves cut down in a farmer's field every year.

Dad reminds Shell not to touch the stereo. He sets the berry basket on the floor. "This filthy thing belongs outside."

"But the Easter Bunny won't find it outside, so how will he leave my new roller skates?"

Shell already has skates. Sorensen Sports called to say they're fixed.

"They're not the right kind. When me and Vicki go to Bootin', they'll kick me out."

Boot skates are ridiculous for a growing child. "In six months you'll need another pair."

With his hands on his knees, Dad leans in to read the spines of his records. "Besides, who says you're going anywhere with Vicki?"

"The Easter Bunny says," Shell answers. Then: "I'm praying to him so he'll bring me boot skates along with my chocolates."

"*Your* chocolates?" Dad pulls out the Leonard Cohen record with the live recording of the "oh please don't pass me by" song. Mum hates this record worse than the other Leonard Cohen records, and Mum hates those a lot. Once, Dad turned that song up so loud Mum got up in the middle of supper and went for a walk in the cold winter dark without a hat. Dad did the dishes and tucked

Shell into bed. Shell rubbed Dad's beard and asked what she had done wrong.

"Mums and dads aren't always good to each other," Dad said. But it never means it's Shell's fault. He promised he'd stay in the house until Mum got home.

Shell counted the beeps of a snowplow and the cars going slow until one stopped in the driveway. It was Barb Nutt who drove Mum back. Mum hugged Shell at the top of the stairs. Her glasses fell off. Without the thick lenses and round frames, Mum was not Mum, but the faraway girl from the pictures in Mum's underwear drawer. "It's not your fault," Mum told Shell just like Dad did.

Dad pushes up his glasses and opens the lid on the turntable. He shows Shell how to remove a record from the sleeve, touching only the edges. Just as the needle connects with the sound of clapping and whistling, Dad says, "The Easter Bunny is a load of rubbish, kiddo." Then Leonard Cohen's deep God voice cuts in. She's to listen carefully to the lyrics.

SHELL AND MUM make a million little Ukrainian piroshky for Kremski when he comes for Easter dinner the next day. The smell of fried onions and mushrooms that began after breakfast deepens, spilling out the open windows along with Mum's radio opera, this being Saturday.

Dad bought a leg of lamb to go with baby-size potatoes. But first there will be borscht and a full course of appetizers: herring in sour cream, semi-ripened dills, fish roe, and black bread. The way Dad cooks for him, you'd think Kremski is missing the Soviet Union. But Mum says that, really, Kremski is happy as a clam eating his chicken dinners before he starts his Swiss Chalet shifts.

"That's why he came to Canada," she says.

"For the tangy sauce?"

Mum nods. "That's exactly it."

When Mum goes down to change the laundry, Shell sits on the back porch with one of the books Mum got at the library: *Freckle Juice*. The clothesline, from the porch all the way to Mum and Dad's pottery studio, is crammed with pyjamas and bedding, but not underpants; those get hung in the basement. And in the middle—too high for Shell to reach—is Kevin, pinched to the line by the tips of his long skinny ears. His fur is no longer bubblegum colour but peachy, and the grey parts—paws, belly, ears—are as white as the sheets fluttering adjacent. Along with dirt and grime, most of Kevin's stick-on face is gone too; only the plastic whiskers, lower lip, and inward-looking left eye remain.

Shell sets an overturned bushel basket under the line. She has to really stretch to connect with Kevin's damp paws. Her tug is closed-eyed and hard. Clothespins go flying. Teetering, clean sheets rippling around her, she holds Kevin close, smelling sun and Mum and lemon soap. The bottom of the dried-out basket gives way. Shell and Kevin tumble into a patch of fresh-turned soil already seeded with beans. Dad gets mad.

"That basket was perfect for weeding."

"But the pins were hurting Kevin," Shell says, brushing dirt from the rabbit's mashed face.

Dad narrows his eyes and clicks his dentures. "Who's he, the Easter Bunny?"

Above, the clothesline begins to creak. Mum is on the porch, pegs between her lips.

A bed sheet cuts between them.

"Maybe," Shell says.

SHELL WAKES TO birds; her curtains smoulder in half-light. Across the hall, Mum is snoring—that low-pitched gargling before she wakes—and the air is hung with the mushroom and onion of yesterday's cooking.

It's Easter.

The hallway is silent. Shell switches off the light that stays on all night and then—without brushing her teeth or peeing—goes down the stairs. Somewhere, behind the couch or high on a windowsill, a Laura Secord egg will be hiding, or else a hollow rabbit with candied eyes and a tiny brass bell around its neck. Then there'll be the assortment of foil-wrapped eggs tucked around the house.

Down the stairs—one, two, three steps—Shell stops. Frozen as a Popsicle. There on the landing, where the stairs twist before descending into the front hall, is Kevin. Shell had snuggled him in her arms as she went to sleep, thinking about those boot-style roller skates and also no nuclear bombs or famine in Africa. But now he's face down on the landing, his head wrenched to one side. The long rusted pipe under which he lies is bent into an exaggerated U, for the strike that killed him had been just that forceful. Positioned near his right paw is a brown paper bag, from which jelly beans spill, a rainbow of them, all the way down the stairs.

The older grades at school eat jelly beans; so do kids with good allowances or paper routes. Edibles downtown at the market sells really fresh jelly beans from England, along with chocolate-covered potato chips and tiny chocolate bottles with real booze inside.

Shell goes back upstairs to pee, brushes her teeth. Dad's joke is still there. She tiptoes down, stepping over Kevin, the pipe, the jelly beans, and hunts through the silent house for a few eggs wrapped in bright foil or a hollow rabbit. She even checks in the fridge, garlicky with marinating lamb, inside the stove, and in the shed. There is nothing but a new pair of gardening gloves in the berry basket she'd left on the porch.

Shell sits on the bottom stair. She doesn't want to cry but does a bit when she picks up a yellow jelly bean and all it tastes like is the Freshie always in Vicki's fridge. A green one also tastes of Freshie.

"Happy Easter!" Mum says. She is standing on the landing. Her hair is flat on one side and her bathrobe skims the ground. "What happened to your rabbit?" Mum's frowning.

Shell swallows the candy in her mouth and looks away. She will not eat any more of Dad's jelly beans.

"Oh, Shell." Mum releases Kevin from beneath the pipe, fluffs him up. Then, stair by stair, she gathers up the jelly beans, along with dust and stray hairs, then gives Shell back her rabbit.

"We'll go to Laura Secord and get a chocolate bunny." On Monday the leftovers will be on sale.

Shell shakes her head. Instead of chocolate she wants the boot kind of roller skates. "I prayed for the Easter Bunny to bring them."

Mum whisks eggs and milk in a metal bowl. Peameal bacon goes in the big iron frying pan and also there are hot cross buns, like they're supposed to have at Easter. "Maybe next year for the skates, Shell," Mum says, nibbling a hot cross raisin.

Upstairs, the water is running. Dad is brushing his teeth.

"It's okay to not think it's funny, Shell," Mum says.

Shell nods. Her mouth still tastes like jelly bean. "Can we get a Cadbury Creme Egg instead of Laura Secord?"

Before Mum can answer, Dad comes down and switches on his Handel's *Messiah* record, extra loud.

Shell butters everyone a toasted hot cross bun. The choir voices brighten her skin with tingle. Mum and Dad laugh when she says the music makes her love Jesus.

"I HEAR YOU had an intruder last night," Kremski says. Kremski's beard is full of bald spots from the small pink scars that Mum says will never grow hair. His baggy jeans are always falling down though he lives on French fries and cherry pies that come in boxes. When, at a dinner party, Shell offered him one of her best barrettes to keep his oily bangs from getting in his eyes, the grown-ups all laughed. Kremski smiles at Shell, his brown teeth are purple with borscht, and there is sour cream daubed along his moustache, like snow on pine needles.

Kremski toasts Dad as a vigilante hero and they both laugh. "A real John Wayne."

After everyone's had seconds of lamb and potatoes and the piroshky are gone, Mum puts the coffee on and slices the poppy seed cake Kremski brought. Even with a smear of honey Shell doesn't like the cake's bitter taste and Kremski doesn't eat his slice either.

"*Ehk*," he says. "I never really went in for that seedy stuff."

"Shell," Mum says, "maybe you can share your jelly beans?"

"Beans!" Kremski cries, showing his metal molars. "The magic fruit!"

Mum puts the candies into a glass bowl, picks out a long dark hair. She gives Shell directions to pass it around the table. Everyone nibbles the orange and lime first.

"All are Freshie flavoured," Shell says.

Mum and Dad and Kremski don't know what Freshie tastes like. And neither should Shell, Dad reminds her. "What else do you have at Vicki's?"

With a rolled Drum smoking between his fingers, Kremski sucks on the black ones left over.

"Licorice!" That's his favourite.

After the bowl goes around a few times, Kremski pats his lean belly and asks Shell if now he's going to have jelly toots.

"Maybe." Shell frowns. "But no chocolate toots. 'Cause I didn't get any chocolate."

Dad says Shell always thinks she's so hard done by. She should ask Kremski about that. So she does and finds out that Soviet chocolates are always" old and crumbly. But the wrappers are beautiful, illustrated like art pieces—Kremski especially remembers the wrapper with Misha the bear from childhood stories.

Dad and Kremski take their Scotch and cigars out back, along with one of Dad's pottery ashtrays. Shell sits on the back steps, reading, drinking in the rich brew of cigar smoke along with her warm milk. Dad and Kremski shake their heads and talk a lot about the USA. The words they use are long and sticky: *fundamentalist, hegemony, ideology*. "Imagine if Ronald Reagan actually gets in?"

Kremski keeps forgetting you're not supposed to inhale. When he stops coughing long enough to take a drink, the sound of something scraping comes from out on the front sidewalk. Then a trundling, like wheels. It starts quietly and builds. Could be a skateboard—that big kid down the street had his out yesterday. But this noise isn't steady. Rather, the scrapes alternate with the jagged rolling: side to side, side to side, like cross-country skiing.

Shell wonders what took Vicki so long to come and show off her new roller skates. Dad and Kremski compete to blow the biggest smoke ring and Shell stares hard at her book, waiting for Vicki to go by. And she does. But then in a few minutes the scraping passes by again, and again, until it sounds like Vicki is skating rough, clompy circles right out front on Cashel Street.

"Vicki's outside," Mum says from the couch as Shell passes through the house on her way upstairs. A lone green jelly bean hides in the carpet of the landing. Shell scoops it up and, as she shoves it deep in her jeans' pocket, crawls into her room and up to the window.

The street lights are coming on now, but Vicki's mum doesn't shout for her to come back home. Vicki's new helmet, elbow pads, and knee pads are so white they glow in the dusk. And she needs them, for each time she attempts to skate backwards, she falls—hard—onto either the sidewalk or Shell's boulevard. When she lands, she waggles her feet in the air and laughs, giving Shell a good look at her new Easter skates—the adjustable key kind. They have the same wide plastic toe guards and ankle straps as Shell's; the only difference is that Vicki's straps are Velcro. Hanging from a shoelace around her neck is the big metal key for opening and closing the hinges to accommodate a kid's growing feet.

Shell keeps her light switched off. Through the open window, the chill breeze pimples her arms. But still Vicki does not go home. The white sweep of street light on the sidewalk is for Vicki the flashing disco lights of Bootin' roller rink, across which Vicki tries skating backwards, again and again. And then she makes it, and off she goes, swishing her hips for propulsion, twisting around to see what's coming behind, brand new skate key swinging from the string around her neck.

Mum has stretched Kevin out on Shell's bed. Shell crawls in beside him and wakes in the morning still in her clothes. Mum or Dad has pulled up her blankets and their room is dark, so Shell is quiet on the stairs. She eats the top off a hot cross bun and unlocks the back door with a tea towel because the handle is so stiff. The skate key is still buried beneath the cardinal bush.

Shell skates over to Vicki's, tripping on a sidewalk

56

crack just once, and sits on the steps. The angel-brick bungalow is sleeping. When the cartoons come on, Shell knocks on the living room window.

"Hi, Shell," Vicki says through the window screen. "I like your skates." Then the door opens. Vicki is in her new skates. "My mum let me sleep in them." She is chewing a pink Pop-Tart. She gives Shell a bite and sits down. The pastry is cold and hard, the goop inside is sweet.

"Don't you toast it?"

Vicki shrugs. Her toenails are polished lilac. "What did the Easter Bunny get you?"

Shell says, "Kevin got hit on the head with an iron pipe and almost died."

Vicki's eyes get wide. Red Pop-Tart filling makes whiskers at the corners of her lips.

Shell's voice gets proud. "But then we had a jelly bean feast. My dad knows where to get really fresh English ones."

"Like the big kids?" Vicki wants to know. She's never had a jelly bean.

Shell digs the green one out of her pocket and gives it to Vicki.

"Yummy," Vicki says. "It's just like Freshie." She sighs. She wishes her dad was there for Easter too. "It would be better than new skates or anything."

"Why does your dad not live here?" Shell says.

"Because he doesn't love my mum and my mum doesn't love him, but they both love me all the same. I didn't do anything wrong," Vicki says.

"Oh," says Shell.

Before Vicki can ask Shell if Dad loves Mum and Mum

loves Dad and Shell has to say she doesn't really know, Shell grabs the railing and pulls herself up.

"Let's skate."

Tooth Fairy

The pottery studio in the backyard is too dusty for painting, so Dad and Kremski go in on it together and rent a painting studio above Sorensen Sports on Clayton Street. Saturdays, Dad and Shell drop Mum to volunteer at the co-op, and then Shell climbs in the front seat and she and Dad drive to the studio. Dad stretches canvas or talks to Kremski if he's around, and Shell sits on the wide window ledge watching Clayton Street below. No one, not Mum or Vicki or anyone in Shell's grade three class, knows how small downtown is from up here. Even on a Saturday it all sounds pretty quiet. Sometimes people stand on the corner or in front of the bank long enough Shell can draw their picture. Shell wants to know how she would look if she could see herself from the third floor but doesn't know how to do that. She wonders because from up in Dad's studio she sees things only God maybe could.

Like people looking a bit sad even if they're smiling or at Christmas when the parade goes by and Santa's sleigh is full of Bud cans. Or the time when this boy on a bike got hit by a car and a box of Smarties went flying right out of his back pocket. All those chocolates — tiny polka dots of pink and yellow and red — had scattered across the grey asphalt and also there was a small puddle of blood where the boy had stopped skidding. Dad went down and joined the gathering crowd, and Kremski called later that night to say Dad had flashed by on the local news.

Dad used to go paint just on Saturday, but now it's evenings too. After supper, a Thermos of coffee and a slice of loaf cake in his shoulder bag, he walks down the drive and turns left. But he can't leave without making Mum mad by rinsing his denture plate in the kitchen sink. One winter on a prairie ice pond when Dad was not much older than Shell, a slapshot took out five of his upper teeth. Dad's a caveman without those dentures, especially when he pulls out his ears and rolls back his eyes.

"Bring something back tonight, Dad?" Shell calls down from her front window. Dad waves, says he'll see, but really Shell can already guess what it'll be. Tuesday's garbage night, so Wednesday there's something from the trash in front of the stationery store: accounting ledgers or typewriter ribbon or outdated calendars. That or maybe some loose tennis balls or sticks of ski wax from Sorensen's. Wednesdays, Kremski washes dishes at Swiss Chalet, so Dad brings home round plastic boxes with barbecued chicken and soft fries inside, a white bun that's just toasted, and there's never enough of that red gravy sauce that goes best with the bun. Mum warms up these chicken dinners for lunch the next day, Thursday. Today is Thursday. On his way home, Dad stops at Enriched Bakery on Derby Street where some friend who works there saves day-old pastry. Dad says every shift this friend finds bums scrounging in the garbage bins.

"Behind any of those restaurants, Shell, the Dumpsters are brimming with perfectly good food." Dad shakes his head. "And yet men go hungry."

But the bums don't get everything, because Friday mornings there's almost always a paper sack getting greasy on the kitchen counter. There's ham and cheddar biscuits inside, sugared apple strudel, sausages wrapped in soda pastry, and sometimes almond croissants or the chocolate bread that Mum ate for breakfast in Paris when she lived there at age eighteen. But Mum won't eat the chocolate bread from Enriched or anything else from there. Dad clicks his denture plate with his tongue as Mum scoops herself porridge.

"All the more for us, Shell," he says.

Nights, after the dishes, Mum plays the records Dad doesn't like. And now that Dad sleeps more and more on the couch, the pile of them by the record player gets bigger. The street lights will be on and Mum will sit in the Quebec rocker, her toes hooked over the broken rungs, mending clothes with a needle so fine it's near invisible. At the harvest table, Shell draws in the margins of her school booklets because she doesn't like the homework. They hum along with Joni Mitchell or the McGarrigles, but mostly it's Bob Dylan, who Dad says is a hypocrite.

Shell doesn't know what hyprocrite means, but she uses it on kids in her class anyway. Well, whatever it is can't be that bad if Mum plays Bob Dylan over and over while she's patching Dad's shirts. There's that one song she likes about the lady with the Egyptian ring who is an artist and don't look back. Mum has a scarab ring in her jewellery box upstairs and making pottery counts as being an artist and because she's a grown-up she has no place to fall either, right? It's a love song for Mum, or once was. And maybe it still is, though Mum's black hair is greying and her feet are covered in corn pads and there's a drip of tomato sauce down the front of her blouse from supper.

FRIDAY MORNING, SHELL wakes up first. Maybe it's the paper boy's squeaky wheel or the way her curtains billow open with dawn breeze. The hall light's been on all night. She reaches up and pops the switch. All Shell can hear is the wind from the furnace and—there—the curdled notes of a blue jay. Mum and Dad's door is always a bit open because the latch has been painted over so many times. Shell nudges it further inward, lowering her face against the sour warmth thickening within. Heavy wool covers the window, the panels of which are safety-pinned together so Mum can out-sleep the sun. And yet, as pastry flour through a fine sieve, morning penetrates the wool, falling across the sturdy pioneer bed where Mum snores and Dad lies on his back, arms crossed over his chest like when he's talking to another adult. The rug burns Shell's knees as she slides towards the three-legged stool next to Dad, her hand outstretched. Cookbooks wobble high, pages marked with bits of newspaper. Dad's eyeglasses are folded up next to a spill of sticky lozenges and the notebook he keeps in his top shirt pocket, curved as the shape of his chest. Dad's dentures smell a bit like cheese and there's some wet stuff on the underside of the smooth metal roof. When Mum lets out a snort, Shell palms the teeth and slides backwards out the door.

The bathroom is cold and smells like last night's bubbles. Dad's teeth rest in a puddle beside the sink, the basin strung with hair and chalked in dry soap. The dentures might be something out of *National Geographic*. Except that Dad's plate is roofed in silver rather than flaked bone and its teeth are grey pearl, not the black and brown of ancient man. Shell squeezes not too much Aim onto Dad's toothbrush, runs it under the tap.

You wake up in the morning, it's quarter to one
And you want to have a little fun
You brush your teeth ch ch ch ch ch ch ch ch
You brush your teeth ch ch ch ch ch ch ch ch

She always starts with the three front teeth, brushing in circles like the dental nurse showed with her giant toothbrush and set of fake teeth called Stan. The pointy tooth at the side goes next, followed by the lone molar. Shell dries the teeth on a towel before putting them back on Dad's stool. Today, like yesterday and the day before, when Shell gets up early to brush Dad's teeth, he'll be less unhappy. And that means Mum will be too.

Mum says they're having porridge for breakfast.

"I want a croissant."

"Shell, stop. The table needs bowls."

Shell's eating when Dad comes down in his overalls and cap, sleeves pushed to the elbow. "Wow, Dad, your teeth look nice this morning." Shell makes her voice extra happy the way she learned to do in choir.

Dad smooths Shell's hair and calls her kiddo.

"Where's the pastry bag?" He turns to Mum and frowns.

"In the compost." The cheese was rancid, Mum says, never mind that meat.

Dad says low and hard that he wants a croissant. Mum says go get them yourself if he doesn't believe her. Shell is so glad for the radio sometimes, the smooth voices and regular bouts of news. Her runners and school bag are by the back door. Mum sits spooning porridge, one hand holding her velveteen robe together, and Dad's slicing bread for the toaster. When Shell opens the back door, Mum looks over, a droplet of milk wobbling on her chin. Shell's to be home for lunch.

"Don't dawdle."

There's a concrete block by the compost pile so that when the slimy pail under the kitchen sink is full, Shell can lift off the sheet metal cover and empty the pail inside. The Enriched bag is right on top, soaking into coffee grinds and vegetable peels from last night's lentil soup. Behind her, Dad moves across the back-door window, coffee in his hand and his mouth opening and closing. Shell holds her breath and purses her lips against the flies as she sticks her hand into the paper bag. There's got to be an almond croissant inside. Oh, and she'll take that chocolate bread too, chunks of which she pokes in her mouth walking down the driveway. The pastry is dry and tastes like onion. Shell ducks beneath the open kitchen window. Above the sound of water and radio, Mum's voice is as big as it's ever been. She's saying over and over, "What the hell is happening with us?"

WITH A SOFT HB PENCIL, Shell sketches the man begging for change in front of the Canada Trust down on Clayton Street. With purple and orange pencil crayons and in her best cursive, Shell writes out the man's deepest wishes — for scrambled eggs and hot coffee — so they swirl above his head. Even from way up in Dad's studio, the man's eyes are puffy and red; "Hemoglobin" is the name of the pencil Shell chooses for them. "Chestnut" darkens the man's hair, and because his skin is closest to "Buttercup," Shell thinks he must be sick.

When Dad and Kremski left for the auto wreckers, the coffee warming in the pot by the sink smelled like chocolate and wood. Now, though, it's more like when Mum burned the popcorn because she didn't use enough oil. Shell leaves it on because, along with linseed and the tang of Kremski's acrylics, it smells as Dad's studio should. The pottery studio at home smells like wet bones and toasted paper, and that's completely different.

The people brushing past the beggar man end up in a pencil-crayoned tornado of rainbow hair, X'd out eyes, and mouths like zippers. When Dad and Kremski walked by him on the way to the car, Dad said something to make the man laugh and tip his corduroy ball cap. Most people don't even look when the man sticks out his hand and speaks right to them. He sort of bobs up and down as he tries to find the eyes of all those passing. Dad says you have to acknowledge a human being when he speaks to you because no one is invisible.

"Everyone once had a mum and dad, Shell," Dad says. "Everyone was once a baby."

Once I was a baby, Shell writes under the man's blue boots. She gets limp in the sunny window, melts like butter in a hot skillet. Leaning against the glass, Shell closes her eyes. Her half sleep is prodded by car beeps, the click of the coffee pot, the crook in her neck.

Secret footsteps — where? There! Outside Dad's door.

Shell pops awake. The beggar man with the hemoglobin eyes is gone from his spot in front of the bank. Dad's door — pinned with Cuban flags and *Buy Canadian* stickers and brightened with Kremski's acrylic swirls — is chained from the inside like Kremski and Dad said to do. The beggar man shuffles in the hallway. What's Shell doing spying on him when all he wants in the world is a plate of scrambled eggs? How would she like it?

The knock is shy — one, pause, two. Air rushes through vents. In the wall, pipes clang, low and slow.

"Dad?"

The yellow Dart should be passing by any minute now; the jut of Dad's and Kremski's beards will be in the front seat along with the peak of their ball caps. And there'll be some car parts tied down to the roof rack—bumper, spare tire, undercarriage. Kremski and Dad have some new sculpture idea going.

The next knock makes Shell more mad than scared. Then a lady's voice calls out. It says Dad's name and then, "It's Paulina." Paulina asks Dad to open up. She says she can smell the coffee all the way out in the hall and she has some apple strudel to go with it—Dad's favourite. Though she is light as a tadpole, as fluff in breeze, the floor creaks as Shell moves towards the door.

Again, Dad's name. Then Kremski's. "I can hear you in there."

Shell steps onto the fruit crate Kremski painted in stripes to look like a tiger, with beer caps for the eyes. Through the keyhole, denim blurs. Red hair all knit up into swirls.

"You okay in there?"

Even Paulina was a baby.

At Shell's knee, the doorknob slowly turns.

"I won't stay long."

Shell steps down and opens the door even less than the chain allows. Paulina's red hair is done up in those French braids that Mum doesn't know how to make, and she's wearing a long blue-jean dress with a shawl that looks like a fishing net, or the Mexican hammock before Dad hangs it up. The Enriched bag she cradles is going to make her front all greasy, and the strudel inside smells buttery sweet and fresh compared with pastry Shell finds on the counter Friday mornings.

"My dad's not here."

Paulina squints through the crack, leaning in as far as she can. "Oh?" Her voice is a squeak. "Your dad?"

"Yeah."

The sigh that comes through Paulina's nose is wet and whistly. "Well, tell him Paulina came." She reaches into her purse, squishing the pastry. "And give him this." Shell takes the postcard from Paulina's freckled fingers. Her light footsteps disappear down the stairs.

The homeless man is back in front of the Canada Trust. He's sipping takeout coffee and there's a cigarette tucked behind his ear. When Paulina steps out onto the sidewalk, the sun bronzes her hair. Her braids are coiled up on top the way Mum showed Shell how to make a clay pot. She pulls her shawl around her shoulders and crosses Clayton. When she passes the beggar man, Paulina does not seem to see his outstretched hand. She goes as far as the movie theatre, and with a sweep of her shawl she rounds the corner. But then she stops and turns back. Maybe she needs some money, because she's heading right for Canada Trust. But instead of going inside, she speaks to the beggar man, pointing up to Dad's window. The beggar man looks up, squinting. His hemoglobin eyes meet Shell's. But just for a second. Shell hops down from the ledge. Now everyone on Clayton is going to know Shell's been spying. Well, Dad does it and Kremski too. When she peeks out the window again—head low, her eyes like rising suns above the chipped pane—Paulina is gone. The beggar man is leaning up against the Canada Trust, one foot propped on the wall behind him, toe pointing down. Between sips of coffee he reaches into the Enriched pastry bag and takes big squishy bites of apple strudel. And it's true—Dad always says how well apple strudel goes with coffee. But that doesn't make it his favourite.

Shell looks down at the postcard Paulina handed to her. The picture shows rolling green hills and a purple sky and a stone cross with a circle in the middle. *Celtic Wonder, Celtic Light: Watercolours by Paulina.* She rips it up into tiny pieces and sprinkles it into Dad's garbage bin.

THERE IS AN Enriched bag the next Friday, but no meat or cheese pastries this time. Plus there's an art show announcement stuck to the fridge just like the one Shell ripped up at Dad and Kremski's studio. The opening is tonight.

Dad toasts croissants for himself and Shell while Mum eats porridge. Shell says she wants porridge too.

"No croissant?" Dad hands Shell a plate. A warm buttery pastry smiles up at her.

"No."

"Don't be silly." Dad sets the plate in front of Shell's crossed arms.

Shell doesn't want to eat that second-hand food. "We won't go hungry," she says. "Why does that lady think we want it?"

"What lady?" Mum looks confused.

Dad clicks his denture plate and spreads peanut butter on his pastry. "No wasting food in this house, Shell."

Shell flicks the croissant like she does marbles, sending the pastry clean off the plate. Though his dentures are extra scrubbed this morning, Dad's voice rises: "Why are you so ungrateful?"

Shell's body ripples and her eyes get watery. The croissant, smiling in the middle of the table, begins to collapse.

"You're a hypocrite," Shell whispers. "Worse than Bob Dylan, that's you."

Dad freezes, his teeth about to sink into the nub of his second croissant. He always saves the end parts for last because they stand up best to peanut butter. Mum's hands cup Shell's shoulders from behind, pulling her away from the table. While Shell finds her bag, Mum puts her coat on over her pyjamas, tucking the cuffs into gardening rubbers.

At the school gate, Mum takes a napkin from her pocket and stands there while Shell eats the croissant she had wrapped inside.

"Don't make things any worse than they are," Mum says.

Shell is hot inside. Their house on Cashel Street is so full of things she's not supposed to notice. "You mean so Dad stops sleeping on the couch?"

Mum looks across the schoolyard. Her eyes stay there. Kids are all running and laughing. Their mums and dads must hold hands and celebrate wedding anniversaries and don't get mad over croissants like the one sticking in Shell's teeth.

The bell rings. Kids let out a final scream. Shell swallows the last of the dough and watches Mum disappear home. Her shoulders fall so forward now. After school, Shell will make Mum a back brace like the one in *Deenie*. There are always extra coat hangers and Dad must have some wood under the back porch.

DAD'S GOOD COWBOY shirt is ironed and laid out on Mum and Dad's bed. The black cowboy boots from the back of the closet are polished and the shower's been running overtime since Dad was in the garden all day. Shell leans up against the bed. The shirt's embroidery is silky beneath her fingers: wildflowers, blue birds, free-falling feathers of silver and gold. On his stool, Dad propped one of Paulina's announcements next to his teeth. This announcement is different from the one on the fridge, for it has been folded in half and is still warm from Dad's pocket. On the back, Paulina says she hopes Dad will come celebrate her big night.

"Shell, come help please," Mum calls, the smell of supper drifting up from below.

Shell puts the postcard back but upside down. In the bathroom adjacent, the shower stops running. There is the squeak of a foot along the bottom of the tub. With Dad's false teeth in her pocket, Shell— "Okay! Coming!" —goes down to help Mum.

Mum is frying onions for the T-bone steaks that have been thawing on the counter. They're eating early because Dad's going out.

"Where?"

"Oh, just to that opening." Mum's hair keeps getting grey threads in it, and while she used to braid it with ribbons or sweep it up with combs, it falls now into a tent shape, from which her nose and lips just peek. Mum's leg is a strong tree trunk in Shell's arms. The side of Shell's head feels poured into the curve between Mum's knee and thigh like clay into a mould. Shell squeezes. Since it's Friday, can she still stay up and listen to the hockey game, like with Dad? Mum points her paring knife at the cupboard beneath the sink.

"Take out the compost and we'll see."

Grey oatmeal jiggles at the top of the rubber pail and onion peel burns with stink. Dad's coffee grounds are heavy, so Shell needs to hold the handle with both hands. The compost's sheet metal cover is warm with sun and fermentation, and when Shell lifts it, heat and fat green flies burst out. Breathing through her mouth, Shell flips the pail and gives it a shake, thin orange liquid dripping down her wrist. She swats at the flies that have found the wet parts of her face. Before sliding the sheet metal back, Shell takes Dad's denture plate from her pocket and tosses it in too. The white teeth sparkle next to the coffee grounds and blackened carrot peels while the plate's roof looks extra silver. With the long-handed claw, Shell mixes the teeth into the compost. Now Dad will stay home with Mum tonight. Popcorn and beer — apple cider for Shell — hockey on the radio, or a play from England for Mum. Fridays were like that when they lived by the railroad tracks.

DAD'S A CAVEMAN cowboy when he comes down for supper, hair wet and glasses steamed.

Or else he's a cowboy caveman.

He can't eat his steak until he finds his dentures. Mum offers to cut up his meat, but Dad ignores her. Mum puts pot lids over their plates while Dad goes back up to the bedroom. Likely the teeth just fell off the stool and got kicked under the bed.

When Dad comes back, he takes Shell's plate away.

"It's not funny, Shell. Kremski's going to be here in twenty minutes."

Shell's heels bounce as they hit the legs of her chair. When she's told, she goes up to her room. Loud voices rumble below and then her door opens without a knock. Mum stands over Shell, who is flopped on her stomach on top of her bed. Why in the world would she take Dad's teeth?

"Come on, Shell." Then Mum says it again: "Don't make things worse."

Shell's face gets hot and moist jammed into her pillow. A steam inside her rises up as Mum slides open every one of Shell's drawers then shuffles through the pencils and drawing paper on the desk. After that, she pokes through the garbage in her can and then gets on her knees and looks under the bed.

"Don't you touch it!" Shell screams when Mum fishes out the horsehair button box. But Mum opens the lid anyway. She sighs and pokes around until Shell, standing above her, snatches it away. Mum says Shell is a mystery sometimes.

"Why not just co-operate?"

Kremski dings his bell when he rides up. While Mum and Dad open and close all the kitchen drawers and even pull the pots from the cupboards, Kremski talks to them from the dining room, his mouth full of Shell's steak. Kremski didn't know Dad had dentures and can't get over that it was from a slapshot.

"Really? You had to walk all the way into town to get

to a dentist?" Kremski says as Dad gets into the Dart. Kremski waves at Shell, peeping down from her window. They both laugh, Kremski with his cigarette teeth and Dad as toothless as the hockey player Shell jokes is Booby Hull.

SHELL CAN'T GO outside until she gives back Dad's teeth. On Saturday afternoon, sixty-seven cars pass down Cashel Street—twenty-six pedestrians, seven dogs, and eleven bikes. Mum makes easy-to-eat soup for Dad. The back door clicks behind Mum each time she takes the compost out to the pile, further burying Shell's treasure.

As Shell eats squash soup from a tray at her desk, Mum sits on her bed and tells Shell how much a new denture plate will cost. "What, exactly, are you trying to prove?"

Shell's voice is husky from not speaking all day. She asks Mum to define a hypocrite.

Mum says check the dictionary for yourself. "And look up stubborn obstinate uncooperative ungrateful daughter too."

Dad spends Wednesday in the garden. When Shell comes in from school, she goes through the front door so she doesn't have to see him. She crawls between her bed sheets, pulling *Otherwise Known as Sheila the Great* from under her pillow.

When Dad appears at the door, his face is shiny and filmed with dirt, and he's got his shirt sleeves rolled up. The sweet scent of rotting apple follows him in. He holds Shell's eyes in his for a long time, then sits down on the end of the bed.

Dad holds out his closed right fist. Fingers squeezed tight, knuckles dirty.

"Come on. See what it is."

The air is cold as Shell sits up, and her hand, next to Dad's, is small but not much cleaner. One by one Dad lets her unfold his thick fingers. The false teeth are cupped in his palm — a lily pad of silver with five yellow pearls attached; tea leaves stick to the enamel.

Shell lies back on her pillow.

Dad asks if it was Shell who ripped up Paulina's postcard.

Shell nods. "I don't like her giving you strudel."

Dad rubs his dentures on his knee. His shoulders go down. He says he has friends who are men and friends who are women. "The world is not so black and white, Shell. One day you'll see that."

Shell blinks.

"Paulina is married to Ted, also my friend. They have a boy, a bit older than you." The three of them were at the opening on Friday. "Next time you'll come too."

Shell touches Dad's elbow. She wants him to make the caveman face. He does. But it is a sad caveman, a tired caveman. Shell wishes Mum would love Dad so much too. Maybe if she brushes Mum's hair like she does Dad's teeth, they will hug and kiss like Vicki's mum and Clarke do right in front of Shell and Vicki, who just goes on talking or whatever and Shell looks away.

Dad leaves, pocketing the teeth. Water runs in the bathroom across the hall. Shell turns the pages in her book, the sound of Dad's shower sweeping over her.

Children of the Corn

Shell will be in grade four after the summer. It's time to stop reading so much Judy Blume. After breakfast now, Dad gives her the World section of the newspaper and talks about things like what makes a war "cold" and what it means that the USA elected a cowboy president. Then there's a photo in the Saturday paper Dad wants Shell to see. It is really simple: a close-up of a man's hand—a white hand—and in the palm is a teeny-tiny black hand, the limp wrist of which disappears into the frame. Because the black hand is so small and brittle, the man's hand looks giant. The picture was taken under a hot sun, for the light is stark, blinding.

FAMINE WORSENS IN WAR-RAVAGED KARAMOJA DIS-TRICT OF UGANDA

"Dad, is it a little girl's hand or a little boy's?"
"Does that matter?"

76

Shell stands looking at the photo for so long, her legs get tired. The white man must feel like he is God—he could crush that tiny black hand like a snail shell. But does he want to feel like God? The photo makes Shell feel like God, and Dad putting the coffee on in the sunny kitchen—he will have felt like God when he saw the picture even if he doesn't believe in God. Shell doesn't know if she's sadder for the starving child or for the man who held its hand.

Shell and Vicki make "Feed Uganda" T-shirts by turning their own inside out and drawing on them with Vicki's sparkly pens. But then Vicki can't wear hers. Clarke, her mum's boyfriend, lives with them now and he makes Vicki throw hers away, saying starving Africans should eat their cows instead of worshipping them. So even though there's only ever bran muffins or dehydrated apples for snacks, Shell's house becomes the Feed Uganda headquarters. They make posters at Shell's desk, and with Mum's help plan for a lemonade stand where they will also ask people to donate canned goods to send over to the war-torn region. Wouldn't it be great if they could just hire a plane and bring the Ugandans to live here in Somerset? There are lots of parks around for their tents. And by the time winter comes, they could have apartments like the Cambodian people who live so quietly in the pink house beside Shell's school. You know? Theirs is the yard where the soccer balls always land. Whenever there is a photo of Ugandans in Dad's paper, Shell clips it for Vicki. But no picture makes them feel as sad as the one of the hand holding that of the world's most breakable baby. They drink milk and stare quietly at the picture, and though neither knows how, they pray.

It doesn't have to be that way. Right here in Somerset, there are enough food factories to feed the world. Even Dad agrees with that. All over the east end you've got the Kellogg's factory, plus McTavish's cookies, and Hot House — that's for spices. Cling-On Chicken is out that way too. And what about the Washko candy factory where Sparkle Dips and bubblegum trading cards come from? A kid whose dad works at Washko brings broken pieces of trading card gum to school in sandwich bags. He says the sweet white powder coating keeps the gum from sticking to the cards. The flavour lasts about three chews before becoming wax, but when the kid pulls out one of those Baggies, the whole schoolyard gathers around him like they're chickens and he's a farmer throwing seeds.

When Dad drives to East Somerset Lumber, Shell always goes with him — first, because the guard dog has no vocal chords and can't bark at her, and second, for the factory smells. Even in winter Shell keeps the window down, drinking in the waves of sweet cookie giving way to rich chili powder, then to toasty cereal, and then something sharp but smell-less hits the back of her throat: that's the ammonia Cling-On uses to clean the dead chickens. Finally they get to sugary pink bubblegum. Oh — and Phipp's Brewery is in Somerset too, but right on the edge of downtown, so the wind blows the sick tang of yeast as far as Cashel Street, where it smells up the yard. The smell is not unlike the one that comes from Kellogg's. Dad says that's because both beer and Corn Flakes come from cereals. But that doesn't mean you can have beer for breakfast, he laughs.

Mum and Dad and Shell don't eat food from factories but instead from the backyard garden, the co-op store, and from Schwartz the organic farmer, who delivers barrels of apple cider and whole sides of meat, which Dad and Kremski and other artists grind up into sausage right on the harvest table or smoke in the tin smokehouse out back. Once, when Kremski was feeding pork into the sausage grinder, he found the bullet used to kill the pig. Now Shell has the bullet in her horsehair button box, proof—Dad and Kremski said—that they are in touch with their food sources. Kremski grew up on Soviet sausages, which are even worse for you than Swiss Chalet.

Mum says Swiss Chalet isn't really junk food though. She even drinks her sauce right out of the cup. And also she cheats by getting cream for Dad's coffee or tonic water for his gin at Thrifty Mart and not the co-op. Shell can't come to Thrifty Mart with her anymore, though. The rows upon rows of bright boxes and sleek squeeze tubes, jars filled with orange goop, bags of marshmallow cookies make Shell greedy. She begs Mum for just one box of Shreddies or else an Aero bar by the cashier. And if she doesn't get a treat, which she doesn't, Shell steals: Fruittella, Trident, a Christmas orange wrapped in green tissue. Once, Mum tried to drive to Thrifty Mart in secret, but Shell hid in the back seat and popped up when the car came to a stop in the parking lot. Mum screamed *oh-my-god* so loud everyone packing bags into their trunks turned to look and a boy pushing a row of carts ran over to help.

Mum doesn't cry very much or at all, but she couldn't stop once Shell scared her. She kept her sunglasses on in the store and all through the aisles she was wiping her eyes. When Dad found out, he grounded Shell for a whole week.

SHELL GETS OUT the Uganda clippings and cardboard, but Vicki doesn't come over. She's in her backyard uncoiling a pile of dirty hose. "I'm sick of Uganda," she says. Together, Shell and Vicki fill Vicki's wading pool with freezing water then Shell rocks herself on the tire swing while Vicki pretends to swim, but she's just splashing. Vicki's mum comes out with a broken-in-half Popsicle: blueberry, bearded with frost. Does Shell want to stay for cartoons and a grilled Velveeta? Dad says Shell eats too often at Vicki's, so Shell shakes her head no then drips Popsicle all the way up the block.

Shell stops when she sees the blunt rearend of their yellow Dodge Dart parked in the drive. Dad was supposed to have driven the car up to the painting studio to meet Kremski today. Shell hopes he's walked there and is not home because then she can have lunch alone on the front steps, dumping the lentil soup she hates into the thick Rose of Sharon bush. Mum always does something to the soup that makes it taste like coffee. Maybe it's the bitter leafy bits floating on the top.

Laundry turns the backyard into a sea of sailing ships, and in the kitchen sunspots dance across the walls. Shell smiles and kicks off her sandals: Dad's painting shoes are gone from the mat by the door. Shell makes for the milk bottle in the fridge. Then she stops, looks around: something is different.

"Dad?" Shell's voice is soft.

Someone is hiding—in a cupboard or behind a door—watching her, waiting for the right time to jump out and scare her, like Dad has done too many times, once making her pee.

The washer bangs in the basement.

"Mum?"

From the brown stove to putty-coloured cupboards to the ceiling of peeling yellow Dad needs to redo—the kitchen is all the same. But, also, it's not the same at all. There are two new bottles of tonic water standing between Dad's splattered coffee pot and the antique toaster that cooks only one side of the bread. And—up, up, up—there it is, on the top of the pea-green fridge, a big white box of store-bought cereal. The bird on the front is done up in bright primary colours: green breast, white eye; the comb crowning its head is the same red as the teardrop wattle hanging beneath a sharp yellow beak. Shell knows that bird, would recognize it from a million miles away. But Corn Flakes are what other kids eat—Vicki sometimes, kids at school, or kids in magazine ads whose mums use crumbled Corn Flakes to coat chicken and bake it up crisp or they stir Corn Flakes, peanuts, and hot marshmallows together and, once congealed, cut the stuff into squares which are wrapped in that cling film which leaks toxins into the very food it is supposed to protect. Some kids eat the sugar-coated kind, which are not Corn Flakes at all; they're called Frosted Flakes and they're also made by Kellogg's right here in Somerset.

Shell's breakfast is never cold or from a box. Usually Mum slow-cooks oatmeal porridge; eggs and bacon are for the weekend, or Mum pours buckwheat batter into the heavy antique waffle iron to make thick cakey waffles, which they drizzle with syrup Dad and Shell tapped at a sugar bush.

With the Corn Flakes rooster's empty eye fixed in the corner of her own, Shell waits for Mum at the bottom of the stairs. Mum's faded red T-shirt says in peeling lettering: *Life's a Picnic.* She's carrying a basket of laundry.

"Hand over that filthy shirt," she says to Shell, who crosses her arms over the blueberry drips and sparkled letters and shakes her head.

Mum frowns. "Come on, Shell. People will think we don't own a bar of soap."

Beneath Mum and Shell, the washer stops banging, concluding its spin cycle with a groan of relief. As Mum steps towards the basement door, Shell grabs her elbow. Squeezes.

"What?"

Shell points at the rooster crowing on top of the fridge. Like Kookaburra in the old gum tree. *Merry, merry king of Corn Flakes he.*

"Those," she whispers. "What are we doing with Corn Flakes in this house?"

"Oh," Mum says before disappearing into the basement. "They're for Jégou. He's coming to visit."

ONE TIME WHEN Dad and Jégou were sharing a place in Vancouver during art school, Dad found him fast asleep

82

in the shower: standing up, the spray of water gone cold. In Dad's stories, Jégou is always falling asleep — while holding hot soldering irons, during Christmas meals, driving. Either that or he is getting hurt. Like when he was changing a tire and the jack collapsed so the pickup rolled backwards right over his foot. He screamed at his neighbour to come help, but the old guy was deaf. And all that was *before* Jégou moved to Newfoundland, which is the really funny part, Dad says. Or not funny, "iron" something. Now, after ten whole years of unanswered Christmas cards, Jégou calls. He's at the Saskatchewan farm where his dad still lives, driving back to Newfoundland. Though Somerset is about three days out of his way, he'll be dropping in to visit. And because back in art school the only things Jégou ate were Corn Flakes and homo milk, Dad added them to Mum's shopping list.

Will one box of Corn Flakes be enough?

Will I get to have some too?

Will Dad?

If there's leftovers, will you get some marshmallows to make squares?

Can we open them now?

Now?

MUM GETS THE vacuum cleaner out right after the next morning's oatmeal. She washes the kitchen floor and wipes fingerprints from the bottom cupboards. Along with tonic and gin, there are two six-packs of Radeberger in the cold room. Mum says Jégou will need more than six beers if he's going to fall asleep in the shower again or back his car over his own foot. Dad, sampling a garlicky Greek olive that goes perfect with beer, says, "Hey, that's not fair." For supper Dad will make homemade fettucini with fresh pesto from the backyard basil. One of his good stoneware ashtrays is out on the coffee table in the living room and a selection of records leans up against the turntable: George Jones, Hank Williams, and the Miles Davis record that has a cartoon-like Fat Albert on the cover, even though it's not for kids.

After Shell cleans her room and helps Mum fold laundry, she can raise funds for Uganda. She puts on her clean Feed Uganda T-shirt, but the sparkles have smudged and the U has melted into an O. Mum says it looks fine and she's not to ruin another T-shirt no matter how worthy the cause.

With a Tupperware jug of lemonade and a stack of plastic cups, Shell goes out to the sidewalk where Dad has set up a card table and chair.

"You're also raising awareness, Shell," he says. "Remember that. It's just as important."

Last night at the harvest table in the dining room, while Mum sewed new cloth napkins and listened to Kate and Anna McGarrigle on the radio, Shell made a campaign sign. Because the newspaper photo was worn out from being in her pocket, she'd made photocopies down at the library, one of which is glued in the middle of a piece of cardboard. Above it, Shell wrote, "Won't you please lend a hand?" Then she copied some facts about the famine from a magazine at the library: how children are the real casualties and most are killed by anemia and also the country is in a state of anarchy. When elections are held there in September, Shell will already be in grade four.

Shell sits alone in the driveway with the lemonade. She wishes she could be sick of Uganda too and go to the pool like Vicki did about an hour ago—Clarke at the wheel. Likely they will stop at Putterman's after for a soft ice cream. Mum comes out and coats Shell in Coppertone and makes her put on a hat. A few adults on bikes stop. They read Shell's T-shirt, gulping down lemonade which they say needs more sweetening.

"Oganda?" They've never heard of the place. One guy with a ponytail and damp cowboy shirt says it's just imaginary. "The kid's making it up." But then they see the picture and read the facts. "Oh, right, *Uganda*."

Even though the lemonade costs only a quarter per cup, each of them puts a two-dollar bill in the jar Mum usually ferments the kefir in. Then a bunch of kids come by, bathing suits still wet from the pool. The kids go to the Catholic school about five blocks from Princess Anne. Shell thinks it's because of being Catholic that they spend such a long time looking at the photo of the hands. One boy who is tanned very dark with long eyelashes reads the information to his friends. Then, blowing his nose into his towel, he says he has no money. A few of his friends say they will come back with canned goods. What do Ugandans like to eat? Shell remembers that the magazine she read talked about aid workers giving out cereals and grains, like rice and maize, which she knows is corn because in Social Studies they learned how the Native

Indians right around Somerset used to grow it. She tells the Catholic kids to bring rice, corn, cereals, and also baked beans because Mum says they are nutritious.

Shell's about to drink the last cup of lemonade herself when Kremski rides up on his bike, a paper Swiss Chalet hat in his back pocket. He squints against the smoke blowing up from the cigarette clamped between his teeth and says he's looking for Dad. Dad owes him money. Kremski's right pant leg is rolled up. His calf is so thin compared with the size of his sneaker.

"Uganda, huh?" Kremski digs two quarters from his jeans' pocket. But before he drops them into the kefir jar, he wants to know what Shell's going to do with the money. Shell can't answer. Kremski shakes his head and says that's the most important question about foreign aid and one people fail to ask. Why don't the goddamn Americans intervene in a real crisis instead of creating them in Nicaragua, Guatemala, El Salvador?

"Shell, you ask your dad what *corruption* means," he says, wiping spit from his lips. He deposits his money but says Shell can keep her refreshments, he doesn't like lemonade.

Shell, her cheeks burning, watches Kremski ride away, chicken leg flexing its sinew, and she feels hate for him, and if he wasn't Kremski she'd run after him and throw his quarters at his bald spot. Instead, she plucks them from the kefir jar and drops them, along with Kremski's pocket lint, down the sewer grate. Then she packs up her stand. The Catholic kids never come back with their cans.

DAD IS KNEADING pasta dough. He's good at it because of all his work with clay. Though Mum has her doubts, Dad bets Shell an ice cream cone that Jégou will show up for dinner tonight. Outside on the porch, Shell watches the cars, trying to guess which one will be Jégou's.

Dad comes out with a Radeberger. Shell says she's not sure what to do with the seven dollars and twenty-five cents she raised for Uganda. And what does *corruption* mean, because Kremski came by and called her that. Dad says, being from the Soviet Union, Kremski's nature is to be skeptical. For example, if Shell kept the seven dollars and twenty-five cents for herself, that would be corrupt.

"Or if I went and threw it all down the sewer drain? Is that corrupt?"

Dad furrows his brow. "That doesn't make sense, Shell. Why would you do that?"

Shell asks Dad what he owes Kremski money for.

"The mortgage," Dad tells her.

Before she can ask what a mortgage is, Vicki comes by on her training wheels. "Having a barbecue?" she calls out.

"Waiting for Jégou."

"Jay who?"

"Jay-goo."

Vicki says she'll go look up the street. She rides back and asks if Goo-Goo is coming in a taxi. Shell looks at Dad, but he shakes his head.

"Oh, 'cause I saw a lady in a taxi up on Maurice Street." Then she turns her bike around in the driveway and pedals off. "Time for *M*A*S*H*."

Dad has another beer and Shell a lemonade. Mum

brings out a bowl of crackers and a plate of cheddar. "Well, I'm not surprised with that character." Mum shakes her head.

Dad says nothing.

"He's gonna come," Shell says. She doesn't tell Dad she's praying to God for it.

Cashel Street gets busy with traffic cutting through to avoid some construction. Though there are lots of cars that seem to be slowing down in a meaningful way, none pulls up in front of the house. After a while the air fills with the smell of hot charcoal and then the smoky-sweet of grilling meat.

Dad says Shell raised people's consciousness today, even Kremski's. That means people will act more reasonably about what they eat and be thankful for it. If she waits for Halloween, she can put the money in her UNICEF box.

"But maybe by that time the famine will be over?"

Dad doesn't think so.

"Or we could put it towards the mortgage."

Dad sips his beer instead of answering.

When the street lights come on, Mum says they've waited long enough, it's time for supper. The pesto goes on whole wheat spaghetti; the homemade pasta will keep in the fridge until tomorrow. Dad and Shell keep watching out the window, and every time a car goes past a little slowly or a car door slams, they jump up.

"Is that Jégou?"

THE CORN FLAKES box gets so dusty Mum wipes it down with a damp dish towel.

"Are Corn Flakes expensive? Is that why we can't eat them?"

"No, it's because they're cheap," Dad says. "And that they're American."

When Shell says no, they are made right here in Somerset, Dad tells her Kellogg's is part of a larger network of American global imperialism — same as McDonald's, Burger King, Ford, and Bruce Springsteen.

"And Miles Davis?" says Shell, because she hates the shrill sound of his trumpet. "Why's he better than the Boss?"

Dad sends Shell to her room for talking back and when she's allowed to come down for supper, the rooster is gone from its perch on the fridge.

Mum's face is wet from standing over the spaghetti pot. The pesto is warming on the counter next to that carrot salad with raisins and nuts that Shell picks out.

"What about the Corn Flakes? Does that mean Jégou's not coming?"

Dad sips his gin and tonic. He smiles and says the Corn Flakes are on their way to Uganda. Shell owes him the seven dollars and twenty-five cents in the kefir jar for postage.

"Like you owe Kremski?" Shell says. "Is that what a mortgage is? Spending money that's not yours?"

Dad sets down his drink and looks hard at Shell.

When Shell says, "Or that's corruption?" Dad pushes his glasses up his nose. He's thinking of a punishment. Shell steps back just as Mum hands Shell forks and knives for the table, three cloth napkins, crispy from the line.

Now it's Mum's eyes that are hard. "Enough about politics, Shell," she says. "You have your whole adult life to worry about that."

REALLY, THE CORN Flakes are on the high shelf in the broom closet, behind the Javex, Ajax, and packets of bright-coloured sponges. For weeks Shell sits on the floor and looks up at the box, the green and red just visible behind the cleaners, and she prays for Jégou to still please come.

She manages to leave the Corn Flakes until late in September. By the time Mrs. Ball introduces Shell's grade four class to the "Countries in Need" unit of Social Studies, Jégou is nine weeks late. For the main project, everyone in the class has to pick a country and make a report. Instead of reading encyclopedias when they go downstairs to the library, Shell finds a corner and reads *Are You There God? It's Me, Margaret* for the tenth time. The very next week, she hands in the stuff she has on Uganda and the whole class says she cheated.

How'd she do it so fast?

Look how perfect it is.

She couldn't have done it herself.

That picture's a fake. Who ever saw a hand that small? I bet it's the hand of a little monkey.

No, her dad did it—they make all that weird stuff behind their house.

Shell says she had her own fundraising campaign in the summertime. She has her T-shirt and the seven dollars and twenty-five cents still in the kefir jar to prove it. That shuts them up. But then Mrs. Ball says handing in work you've already done is a kind of cheating.

"Like corruption?"

Mrs. Ball tilts her head and thinks. To be fair to everyone in the class, Shell will have to do her "Countries in Need" assignment over again.

But Uganda's the only country in need Shell knows.

"How about another place in Africa, Shell, if that's what interests you? They're all in need, really. Like, whatever happened to that place, you know, Biafra, for example? Or, what's it called, Ethiopia, there's famines there sometimes." Oh, and don't forget that the work is due tomorrow.

SHELL WAS SUPPOSED to have gone to bed an hour ago. Through walnut branches and phone wires, Shell can see from Mum and Dad's room right into the studio. Mum is mixing clay while Dad's painting uptown. Yesterday, Mum and Dad didn't talk for the whole day and for the first time ever Mum didn't eat supper.

"I'm going for a walk," Mum had said. Shell watched Mum going down the street without even her purse. Dad and Shell ate minestrone soup thawed from the freezer, and because Shell finished her entire bowl, she got vanilla ice cream for dessert and an extra tablespoon of maple syrup. She was doing her homework when Barb Nutt drove Mum back home. If Barb is Mum's best friend, she should come in the house and stay for dinner sometimes, like Kremski and Vicki. Instead, they just sat out front in Barb's Volvo, talking and talking while the engine idled like Dad says is a waste. Then the house filled with Mum's quiet footsteps and the smell of her buttered cinnamon toast.

Above the studio, the three-quarter moon is marshmallow. A red kerchief ties back Mum's curly hair, her plaid shirt rolled to the elbow, and heavy glasses slip down her nose. Crisp autumn air cools the house, though Dad put the storm windows on a few weeks back. By the low light coming in from the hall, Shell scans the books on Mum's shelf. None are about a country in need. There's lots of books on ancient civilizations, though, as well as a whole row on painters. At eye level is a shiny spine with bright yellow letters: *Gauguin's Tahiti*.

The house is silent and dark. Shell's nose drips from the cold. She finds her paper scissors and spreads the book on her desk. The ladies in the paintings don't look very hungry, but at least they are brown and their dresses kind of look like towels and no one seems to have shoes. The lettering in the book is too small and the words are too long, so Shell just makes up her own data. Like how there's no men in any pictures of Tahiti because they all died in a war and the island is so far away hardly any tourists go there. The people eat nuts and berries, just like birds, and then they eat the birds too. Mrs. Ball asked for pictures of natives of the country. Shell tries to be careful as she snips out a painting of three naked girls on a beach, which she then glues onto a piece of cardboard. She also snips a map from near the beginning of the book, which fits alongside. The thick, glossy paper makes the pictures look better than they are. But it is all kind of messy, so no one will say Shell's corrupt.

Shell puts the book back on the shelf. Out in the studio, Mum hunches over her potter's wheel, tongue between her teeth, rolling her shoulders as her fingers coax the wet clay into a wide, squat bowl. The kitchen still smells of the sausages and apples Mum made for supper. Apart from the brightness of the moon, the only light comes from the dim bulb glowing in the hood over the stove, and there is nothing to hear but the fridge. With the collapsible stool Mum keeps beside the stove, Shell climbs up and reaches into the broom closet. Behind the Javex and Ajax and sponges is the box of Corn Flakes.

Shell tugs on the box, knocking the sponges to the floor. Shell thought the box would be kind of heavy, but instead it's pretty hollow. She sits down on the floor, toast crumbs and dried peas littering the linoleum. The top flap opens easily; not only is it already unsealed, it has been opened many, many times before. Inside the crumpled bag there are only two handfuls of cereal left in the bottom, most of it just dust. Now it's Mum who has done something corrupt.

The remaining Kellogg's Corn Flakes almost fill a breakfast bowl, which Shell tops with milk and brown sugar. Replacing the box just as it was, including putting back the packet of sponges, Shell carries her Corn Flakes up to her room. Usually Shell only ever eats at her desk if she is grounded. She keeps her lamp on low and tucks a pencil behind her ear — a flower, just like plump brown girls-in-need in the painting she clipped from Mum's book. Shell slurps cereal from her spoon. The fine golden silt really does taste like corn, sweet and earthy, and the smell is just like driving though east end Somerset with Dad.

Fair Trade

Because Shell's house is built on what used to be the neighbourhood dump — really it's called a midden — every time Dad digs up more of the backyard's grass, he finds some kind of treasure: a cat's eye marble, a diamond of topaz glass, a hollow splint of chicken bone, a brass coin embossed with a ship Dad calls a schooner. Morning, before it gets too hot, Dad attacks a stretch of weedy grass beneath the high, wide windows of the backyard pottery studio. Mum's inside the studio glazing mugs — it's cool in there — shaking her head to the politics show on the radio.

"Goddamn it." Dad bounds over to the tomato cages. The squirrels tunnelled right underneath and — *shit* — they even dug up a couple of iris bulbs too. Buggers take just one bite and leave the rest to rot. That's what Dad really hates, the waste of it. He rolls a ball of half-eaten fruit between his thick fingers and — "goddamn" — chucks it into the compost.

"Maybe you should try the chili powder like Kremski said."

Dad doesn't hear. Hands on his hips, he takes in the panorama of the garden. Soon the whole yard will be just berry bush and vegetable rows, plenty of herbs, nasturtium vines, and a patch of specialty irises. Thick beds of poppies and cosmos conceal the rusted fencing enclosing the yard, and even in winter they never need to buy root vegetables or pickles or pesto or tomato sauce or compote — Dad harvests so much for Mum to can, jar, and freeze, she's started complaining.

Dad scratches his beard and murmurs about the basil patch that's coming up: he'd better lay chicken wire. He plunges his shovel into the sod. Stepping down on the blade, he pulls back, ripping out the grass by its roots.

Shell uses a short red spade to tear away at the backyard too. As they go deeper into the dark soil, bright bits of treasure bubble to the surface. Each time Dad turns up something new, he whistles Shell over. Shell pokes around the shovelful of dirt he holds out. This time it is one of those decorative combs that ladies once stuck in their coiled-up piles of hair. Shell sucks in her breath and picks it out. The rhinestones lining the comb's curved edge are almost all intact, but of its teeth, only three remain. The comb smiles at Shell: a toothless old woman, once beautiful.

"Real tortoise," Dad says, rubbing the comb on his jeans.

He lifts it to the sun, which turns it amber yellow, just like the stains under the armpits of his T-shirt. Dad gives the comb back to Shell then picks up his shovel and heaves it deeper into the earth, glasses sliding down his nose.

When it gets too hot in the garden, Shell follows Dad into the studio. She'd better go find someone to play with.

"What about Mamoon?" Mum says.

Mamoon goes to a special French school even in summer and lives in the apartments beside Cashel Street United Church. He's older than Shell but is never allowed to do anything except on Saturdays or after five, and that's only if his mum knows about it well beforehand.

"She's very protective," Mum says, dipping her hands into a bucket of wet clay.

"Why? Because he's Muslim?" Mamoon's mum has long yellow hair, blue eyes, skin as white as Elmer's glue. It must be Mamoon's dad who is the Muslim parent. Shell imagines him as Gandhi sitting cross-legged on a mat like in the book Mum borrowed from Barb Nutt, who said of Gandhi he was too busy making peace to be a good dad.

"Or," Mum says, "there's always Vicki."

SHELL WASHES THE tortoise comb in the bird bath and, without taking off her sneakers, gets her purse from her room. Barb Nutt brought Shell the purse — her first such accessory — all the way from the east coast. The outside is red quilted fabric, but the inside is mustard yellow with flowers; a button in the shape of a scallop shell holds it shut. Barb gave it to Shell at the co-op store. Shell and Mum were in the freezing walk-in fridge arranging bulk bags of Parmesan cheese. Barb's long curls looked even more white against her tan face. Barb was doing a summer course in Nova Scotia. "In a few years more, I'll have a PhD in folklore," she told Mum and Shell. She saw the purse and thought of Shell.

Shell said thank you, shivering.

Mum said, "You are just so brave to be pursuing what you love, Barb. Good for you."

Barb said, "Any woman can do it." She looked at Mum and then Shell.

Shell tucks the hair comb into the Nova Scotia purse and walks up the block. Vicki's on her front porch, a colouring book open on her lap. A Cool Whip tub of crayons softens in a pool of sun. In the driveway, the chrome trimmings of Clarke's emerald two-door gleam bright. He'll be inside the angel-brick bungalow, watching TV in his La-Z-Boy, bamboo shades closed.

"Look what I inherited from my great-great-grand-mother," Shell says, climbing the concrete stoop and holding out the comb. "She brought it all the way from the old country."

Vicki's eyes get big. Her smudged fingers touch each of the comb's sharp teeth.

"What's *tortoise* mean?"

"Turtle." Shell says they can make a trade. "Maybe for another nail polish. The last one's all dried shut."

Vicki's got a whole Barbie suitcase full of her mum's old makeup, but slowly, piece by piece, it's migrating to a shoebox hidden under Shell's bed. Along with nail polishes she can't unscrew, Shell's got a chalky coral lipstick, a compact of orange rouge, a dry mascara, and a dull eye pencil that cuts into the lid if you press too hard.

Vicki shakes her head. "Can't trade you no more."

"Why?" Shell's face gets hot and she wants to hit Vicki.

Then Vicki's eyes crinkle. "You gotta bring all my stuff back. Okay, Shell?"

She rummages in the Cool Whip tub for a purple and starts scribbling. Vicki still likes colouring because she's nine, a whole year and a bit younger than Shell. Vicki gets all the toys and stuff she wants, but she also gets swatted in the face for doing things like starting to eat before Clarke does. Clarke's a foreman at Silverhorn Dairy. His right pointer finger got caught in the machine that puts the caps on milk jugs, so all that's left of it is a shiny red hook from which he dangles his car keys. He's skinny and pale from sleeping all day, and because Vicki's mum is fat, Dad calls him Jack Sprat.

"What stuff?" says Shell.

"Our trades." Vicki presses the crayon very hard into the butterfly outlined in her book.

Because the only makeup Mum wears is some Vaseline on her lips, Shell doesn't know what to do with the tubes and bottles in the shoebox. But she likes reading the Archie comics she got in exchange for the china teacup Dad dug up when he was putting in a trellis for the runner beans. Even better is how soft the Head & Shoulders shampoo gets her hair, well worth the tiny brass ring Mum found weeding.

"But what about that ancient teacup I gave you?" Shell says, bending a warm red crayon into a U. "The princess ring? Or the pirate coins?"

Vicki slams down her crayon. "Clarke says it's just old garbage."

"It's not, dummy," Shell says. "You just don't know antiques. My dad does, though. You've seen our house. All that old stuff's worth a lot."

Vicki's stayed for supper at Shell's just once. Clutching the Strawberry Shortcake doll her dad sent up from Michigan, she had looked around at the dark, mismatched farmhouse antiques and the paintings and woven rugs hanging up on the walls, and after a while asked how come there was no TV. She was okay to drink her milk without chocolate syrup, but she wouldn't put the stew in her mouth after Dad said it was moose. She did try the wild rice, though, but spit the first bite into her cloth napkin. Dad shook his head and talked about how many hungry children there are in the world while Mum made some toast and heated a can of baked beans. Then she took away Vicki's stew and rice but not Shell's, even though she wanted beans too.

After that, Clarke started calling Shell a hillbilly.

"If your folks eat moose, you must eat squirrels and raccoons too." The first time he said it, he was watering the lawn in his bare feet and drinking a can of Pepsi. Shell went home before Vicki came to the door.

Shell crouches beside Vicki, eyeing the colouring book. "Stay in the lines," she says. Shadows move behind the screen door and somewhere Pat Benatar's on the radio. She knows the words to "Hit Me with Your Best Shot" just from playing all the time at Vicki's.

Vicki whispers hard, "Shell, I gotta have the stuff or else."

Shell shrugs and puts the comb back in her purse. When she says, "No, a trade's a trade," Vicki's face crumples up like newspaper on fire. She turns away to cry, but Shell catches her by the shoulder.

"I'll bring it back," Shell says. "Promise."

The tire swing at the back of Vicki's is suspended from the lower limb of a thick black walnut. Timmy, Clarke's soft brown dog, watches Shell and Vicki from where she hides in the shade beneath the back stoop. Timmy is gentle and smart and doesn't need a leash. Smiling and tail swishing, she trots behind Clarke when he walks down to the corner store for chips and cigarettes and then sits and waits for him to come out again.

The back lawn is littered with logs of Timmy's poo, which turn white in the sun. When Clarke cuts the grass, the old-fashioned push mower grinds the poo into powder. Sometimes he'll put down the mower and push Vicki and Shell really high on the swing. Shell was telling Vicki all about Mamoon coming over to her house for supper, and Clarke laughed and said they should call him Baboon. Shell felt sick at that and now hates Clarke even more. But she loves the tire swing and Timmy's soft fur and the Tupperware pitcher of bright Freshie that is always in Vicki's fridge. Plus, when Clarke's on night shifts, he sleeps during the day and Shell doesn't have to see him.

Shell and Vicki—legs interlaced and holding tight to the swing's rope—give themselves over to the spiralling pull of gravity and the swish of dusty breeze. Shell gets Timmy to jump in with them, but the dog—slick as an otter—squirms out of her tight embrace, lands with a yelp, and runs back beneath the stoop.

Shell says, "Let's have some Freshie and after that I'll go home."

They weave through the yard, stepping around Timmy's poo.

"Can I come meet Mamoon?" Vicki asks.

"No," Shell says. Timmy pops out from under the stoop and runs a wide circle around them.

"Why not?"

"Because Clarke calls him Baboon."

"But I don't say it. It's not me that calls him that." The straps of Vicki's halter top have slipped down, exposing strips of pale, unfreckled skin.

"Doesn't matter," says Shell. "It rubs off on you."

The kitchen is long, narrow, and without light. A black Thermos and matching lunch box are on the table, ready for Clarke's night shift. Vicki's mum's hips are wedged between counter and fridge. The way she twists around reaching for things, it's like she's trapped in a kayak. The door to the darkened bedroom off the kitchen is open an inch. Clarke's white-socked feet are splayed on the waterbed.

Vicki's mum takes a pizza and a bag of fries from the freezer and says it's Vicki's suppertime. Vicki goes to wash her hands. Vicki's mum reaches down for a cookie sheet, chubby hands on her knees; the breast cleavage that squishes out of her V-neck is as big as a regular person's whole bum. A clock radio goes off in the bedroom—"Still Rock and Roll to Me" blasts against the throbbing buzz of alarm. The waterbed sloshes. Clarke's up. Shell leaves before Vicki comes back from the bathroom.

AFTER SUPPER, DAD rummages through the camping gear in the basement. It smells like wood fire, baked potatoes, and wet leaves. In August, Dad will drive them up to Algonquin for a canoe trip. Kremski will come again this year, even though last time the suitcase he brought fell into Rain Lake and the flimsy straps on his fisherman sandals broke after the first portage. He stood there eating trail mix and smoking while Mum mended the sandals with twine, and when he threw his cigarette butt into the bushes, Dad yelled so loud Kremski's eyes watered. Shell found the butt smouldering in a pile of moose droppings. When she came back with it, Kremski patted her on the head then snuffed out the still-burning end right between his bare fingers and Shell heard the singe.

Shell sits behind Dad on the stairs. He's going through the fishing tackle. She gets a knot of lures to untangle. The fly ones with the pink feathers would make pretty earrings.

"Bingo," he says of a dish of ball bearings. These go with the slingshot hidden in a box with the Coleman stove.

Shell follows Dad out to the back porch. There's a load of washing still hanging on the line. Dad clears away the baskets and pegs. Shell holds on to the ball bearings while Dad fits his left hand through the slingshot's wrist brace. Then he wraps his thick fingers around the sturdy Y grip. The tubular band of yellow rubber extends off each end;

the pocket of leather joining the ends is where the ball bearing—when Dad asks for it—goes.

When Dad pulls back on the band, his forearm hardens and the veins running along his bicep puff out. Behind his glasses, the left eye squeezes shut. He freezes. Waiting. When a squirrel dashes through the yard, Dad releases the shot.

Snap! Ping!

They are fast, the squirrels, but after a couple of tries Dad takes out a grey one nosing in the nasturtium vines. Dad doesn't need to smile. He puts down the slingshot. Shell trots down the steps after him.

"Tell your mum to give us a garbage bag," Dad says, poking among the thick green nasturtium leaves. Shell comes back with an apple bag. The squirrel is belly up. Its eyes are pure black glass and its lips are pulled back to show off all four sharp yellow teeth.

"Rats with fluffy tails," Dad says.

But the tail is not fluffy at all; rather, its hair is coarse and there's a bony spine so it looks like a bottle brush. Dad grabs the apple bag, covers his hand with it like a mitt. He swoops down and gathers up the body, tail first. Then Dad ties the bag and puts it in the green rubber garbage can already out front on the boulevard, waiting for the garbage trucks that will come at seven the next morning.

"One down, Shell," Dad says. As the street lights start to glimmer, he sends her in.

MAMOON IS A boy but not really because his mum drives him everywhere or walks him if it is close enough. He could never have a paper route like the other boys, Shell knows. He is slender and taller than Shell by a whole head, and his face is shaped absolutely like an upside-down teardrop. Mamoon's skin is the colour of the way Mum drinks tea — strong but with plenty of milk — and the dark curls on his head are softer than Head & Shoulders. The first time Mamoon came over to Shell's, he brought her a necklace made of dried pasta in the shape of shells. Mum said it was beautiful and it is still hanging on Shell's bedroom door. The day after, Shell took the second-best green glass medicine bottle from Mum's collection on the kitchen sill and walked down to Mamoon's. After she gave it to him, Mamoon touched his cheek to hers.

Mum calls Mamoon special. And Dad is extra gentle to him. The time he was allowed to come for supper, Mamoon ate all his venison sausage and lentil salad. After he laid his knife and fork neatly across his plate, he thanked Mum and Dad. "Everything was delicious."

Shell should learn to be Muslim: gentle and polite and pleasing to adults. Girl Muslims must be super pretty if Mamoon is and he's a boy, and they probably don't lie or steal or dig holes in the backyard with their dads. Shell checked, but none of the makeup in her shoebox would turn her skin darker, so instead she lies out in the sun and brushes her teeth extra hard so they look white against her deepening tan.

Saturday morning Mamoon is usually allowed to play, so it's early when Shell goes to wait on his apartment steps. When the church bells chime for eight o'clock, Shell presses the buzzer that says *Sandra and Mamoon Dardenne*.

His mum says it's okay, so all three walk down to Shell's. Mamoon's mum talks with Shell's mum for a while. She knows Barb Nutt because she teaches French and is also a mature student at the university. Mum nods and crosses her arms: "I would love to go back to school." Mamoon's mother smiles and touches Mum's shoulder. Her answer is like Barb Nutt's: "It will change your life."

SHELL AND MAMOON sit out front so that if Vicki walks by, she'll see them together.

"Is it your mother's?" he asks of the makeup in the shoebox.

"I traded a girl for some antiques me and my dad dug up in the garden."

"Like my green bottle?" Mamoon takes the mascara from the box and slowly unscrews the wand.

"Our house was built on a dump that's called a midden." Shell explains it exactly like Mum: "That's where people in olden times buried their garbage because there were no trucks to come for it." And she tells Mamoon that the girl's mum's boyfriend is dumb and says it's all garbage and that she has to give the stuff back even though they traded fair and square.

"He is not thoughtful, this man," Mamoon says.

"He calls me a hillbilly." The word is so ugly to say out loud, but Mamoon doesn't get it, so Shell tells him hillbillies have buckteeth and no running water and eat animals they find dead on the road. If he wants to know more, he should watch *Hee Haw*. Shell saw it once at Vicki's.

Mamoon thumbs through one of Vicki's Archie comics. Shell is not a hillbilly. He says that he would rather have the antiques than this strange blue shampoo or this kind of American *bande dessinée*.

"Your antiques have stories in them," he says, untwisting the coral lipstick. "But this is nice too."

Mamoon leans over and touches the lipstick to Shell's mouth. Shell stiffens at first and then relaxes while Mamoon traces her lips. The warm day softens the makeup, so it glides on easily. Then Shell takes the lipstick from Mamoon. He closes his eyes—lids quivering—while Shell makes his lips match hers, only sometimes straying outside the line.

"When you get your antiques back, we can make a museum for them." Mamoon tells Shell about one museum in England he saw that is full of Egyptian mummies.

"Like King Tut." Is Mamoon from Egypt too?

No, from Brussels.

"Huh? Like sprouts?"

When Mamoon smiles, his teeth are as Chiclets against his bright lips. "It's in Belgium." He says he misses it.

Mamoon's mum comes right at noon. She is wearing jeans and sandals and her loose hair flows to her waist. She must get lots of strays stuck in her bum crack.

Shell's wiping the lipstick off on the inside of her arm, but his mum, Sandra, says, oh, Shell's so pretty with her lips like a cupid's bow. Shell badly wants to see inside Mamoon's apartment, and she's got a million questions for him and his mum bubbling inside her, but they won't come out.

And while they are standing there in the driveway making plans for next Saturday, when — yes! — Mamoon can come back, Shell sees Vicki crouching on the boulevard across the street, under the big oak tree with brown, diseased leaves. She's holding tight to her Strawberry Shortcake. Her flip-flops have thick rainbow soles, and the same yellow halter top she always wears is drooping down so her nipple shows.

Mamoon and his mum are already a few houses up the street when Vicki starts crossing over.

"Hi, Shell."

Shell puts the lid on her shoebox and goes inside. She shuts the door and the curtains so Vicki, now standing in front of the house, can't see in.

THE NEXT SATURDAY, Mamoon can stay all afternoon and even have lunch.

Dad takes him on a tour of the garden, stepping around the bag of sheep manure spilled over near the runner beans. Dad says the Latin names for all the tangled-up plants and Mamoon nods. Mamoon calls Dad by his first name like Dad said he could and then he says the garden is very sympathetic. In Brussels his grandparents have a garden out in the country where a large apple tree grows.

Are they his mother's parents?

Mamoon nods.

Dad doesn't ask where Mamoon's Muslim grandparents are.

They have grilled cheese outside. The white cheddar is

almost spicy, but Mamoon likes it—as well as the home-made bread, dills, and chili sauce instead of ketchup. Mamoon is so careful eating he does not need the napkin Mum included for him on their tray.

"Did you get your antiques back?"

Shell shakes her head. "That girl doesn't care about some makeup. And Clarke's always saying ugly things, so she doesn't deserve it."

"But, I think, you are not like your parents always," Mamoon says.

"How?"

"That's what my mother tells me about my father. I don't have to be like him. Even though I love him."

Shell doesn't ask why Mamoon's father doesn't live with them like Vicki's dad too. But she does say, "How do you know if your mum and dad don't love each other anymore?"

Mamoon scratches his curls. "They never meet each other's eyes."

"Oh," says Shell. "And is the air always cold?"

Mamoon nods as he and Shell get into the hammock, head to foot. They are very still, their arms crossed over their chests like King Tut in his sarcophagus. Mamoon's mum will be there in less than an hour. After he goes, Dad and Shell will drive out to Wild Oat Country Market to buy enough tomatoes to make a full batch of spaghetti sauce. The squirrels ate so many of Dad's, the yield is not nearly enough. They make the drive every other day now, but it's not just to buy tomatoes—it's to get rid of another squirrel. Dad takes the back roads and the Dodge

Dart smells of peanut butter and fear. Above the bumpity-bump and the constant ping of loose gravel, the squirrel in the live-animal trap wedged behind Dad's seat natters and throws itself against the sides of the cage.

"What if it gets out while we're driving, Dad?"

Dad really laughed at that.

When Dad ran out of ball bearings, he phoned the city's pest control and two men in cop uniforms delivered a cage. Natural crunchy peanut butter from the co-op store lures the squirrels inside. Once, he caught a cat and another time a possum, but other than that it is squirrel after squirrel after squirrel. There's got to be a million of them.

Dad and Shell have it down pat: they park in the ditch out front of a feral apple orchard and climb over the wooden fence rotting into the ground. Shell will go off to pee if she has to and Dad will lift the cage by the carrier handle. Inside, the squirrel will be shivering, its flat black eyes full of fear. And it hasn't even touched the peanut butter it had wanted so badly in the first place. When they've gone some twenty paces into the orchard, ducking twisted branches and slipping on fermenting fruit, Dad puts down the cage. Shell stands back while Dad opens the latch. The squirrel sprints away, deep into the orchard. That's when Dad says what number they're at so far since getting the trap. When they take the one in the cage behind the shed, it will be twenty.

"So cute," Mamoon says.

There must be a nest of squirrels in the black walnut above the hammock. Shell counts eight, or maybe ten, jumping from one thick branch to another.

"What is?" says Shell.

"How are they in English? You know, with the tails."

"Squirrels?"

The way Mamoon says it makes Shell laugh. "You think they're cute?"

"Of course. We don't have them in Belgium, but there are so many here." Mamoon especially likes the way they sit back on their haunches and wipe their faces with their tiny paws. "Shell! Look!" A grey one goes dashing up the trunk, an apple core gripped in its teeth.

"Rats with fluffy tails," Shell says.

Mamoon looks over at Shell. Deep lines crease his wide forehead. "Rats?"

"Well, just imagine them without the fluff. Like if you shaved the tail and saw it's just a bone." Shell is talking loud. "Then you'd see how ugly they are." And Shell is talking fast. "They tear up gardens and they've got no natural predators here, so that's why it's okay to kill them, because nothing else will kill 'em so they just go on and on getting worse and eating all my dad's tomatoes."

"Kill?" Mamoon says. "They are alive creatures."

"No"—what did Dad call them?—"they're rodents."

"A rodent is a creature. So are birds and fish and—"

Shell twists out of the hammock. Both she and Mamoon fall, capsized, on the hosta beds below.

Mamoon scrambles after Shell, who cuts through the garden and climbs back behind the woodshed. Brambles, tall and sharp, scratch their bare arms and faces. A stretch of chain-link fence runs alongside the shed. Two black dogs with clattery chains and flat faces live on the other side. It's some time since Dad's been back here with the clippers, so the dogs aren't visible through the bramble and maybe aren't even there. But then they come barking, the fencing bowing against the throw of their weight. Mamoon freezes, his back pressed against the shed. After a man shouts, "Candy! Royal!" the animals quiet down, chains settling with a final shake.

Mamoon's hand sweats in Shell's. His slim fingers squeeze hers in return.

Shell waits, but neither Mum nor Dad come to check. Shell tries to get Mamoon to smile, or at least to look different than he does right now: like he does not know Shell anymore, or want to either. Shell pulls Mamoon further along the side of the shed. A rough wool blanket covers what might be a coffin, but one small enough for a pet or a baby. Shell drops Mamoon's hand as she kneels down before it. When she throws back the blanket, Mamoon's face pales. The hair lining his forehead seems to recede. A squirrel—pure black but for a bright white shock at the tip of its twitching tail—shivers at the back of the animal trap.

"Hello, Mr. Squirrel," Mamoon whispers. He crouches beside Shell and shifts his weight so that his nose is but a few inches from the cage's front panel. "Wow." As he leans in, his hand presses into Shell's back, dampening her T-shirt. "Shell, you and your dad won't eat it?"

"No!" Shell whispers that she and Dad will drive it out to the country so it can run off and be happy.

"But what if its family is here? Shell? If it has a nest of little ones?"

Shell shrugs. "Well, it doesn't matter anyway—they just keep coming back. See that?" She points a finger at the white-tipped tail. "We call this one Susan, after some smart lady writer Mum likes." Dad and Shell don't know how many times they've caught her and driven her out, and in a few days she's back eating the tomatoes.

"She is clever, Soo-san," Mamoon whispers. "Soo-san." Mamoon leans in. "Look how she is shaking, so scared... Soo-san." Mamoon sticks his right pointer finger into the cage, gives it a wriggle. Whistling low, he makes a nattering noise. "Soo-san." That's when the squirrel goes crazy, rushing Mamoon's finger. Mamoon pulls back. He falls hard, landing against the fence. Caught in the thick nest of brambles, he looks at Shell and they don't know if they should laugh. Shell smiles, and Mamoon is getting there too, but the dogs break out barking and the squirrel starts flinging its body against the sides of the cage. Shell throws the blanket over the cage. Finding Mamoon's hand, she yanks him up.

Thorns tear their skin and clothes as they clamber back along the shed. Mamoon's mum is at the top of the driveway. Then she is jogging into the back. Dad steps out from the studio and dumps a bucket of murky water into a planter of rosemary. He waves hello at Mamoon's mum. His beard is white with dust, clogs broken down, and he's wearing his overalls without a shirt, chest hair matted.

But Mamoon's mum isn't looking at Dad. Before Shell can wipe the blood from the scratches on Mamoon's face or tell him the squirrel cage is a secret, he's got his arms around his mum, her long hair draped over him like a curtain.

Shell pulls leaves from her hair. Mamoon's mum pinches her eyes at Shell and turns away. By the time they walk back to their apartment, she will know that Shell and Mum and Dad are hillbillies.

IT'S SATURDAY, SO Clarke's two-door is in the driveway, still sleek and reflective from the wash he gave it earlier. With "Start Me Up" blaring from a ghetto blaster, Clarke, in cut-off jean shorts, had soaped the car, concentrating on the front grille. Shell, crouched behind the honeysuckle on the porch, prayed to God that the stubby cigarette clamped between his lips would set his moustache on fire. In a frilled bikini Shell had never seen before, Vicki grooved on the front lawn, squealing each time Clarke turned the hose on her.

Shell sucks in her breath and knocks on the aluminum frame of Vicki's screen door. She's got her quilted purse and the shell pasta necklace is draped around her neck. The shoebox is tucked under her arm like a football. Inside the bungalow, the TV is so loud Shell has to wait for a pause before knocking again.

Five Labatt's Blue bottles are lined up on the sill beneath the living room window and the crayons in the Cool Whip tub have dried into a lump. Garbage cans line the boulevards up and down Cashel Street. There are two cans in front of Vicki's, plus a kitchen chair without a seat. Down the block, Dad is putting out a bundle of cracked two-by-fours. He leans the bundle next to a rubber bin; a pair of dead squirrels are buried inside, concealed in black garbage bags. Mamoon's mum had said Mamoon was busy today, so Shell gardened with Dad. She dug up a crystal medicine bottle and gave it to Mum, and when Mum went to work at the co-op, Shell and Dad took care of the squirrels. But they don't drive them out to the country anymore. The first to go was Susan, who'd found her way back from Wild Oat's and took out so much of Dad's basil bed Mum can't make pesto.

Shell had held the garbage bag while Dad slid the trap inside. Then he tied the bag's opening around the Dart's muffler, tight so no fumes would get out. The Dart was pulled right up to the top of the driveway, and while Dad idled the car, it was Shell's job to signal when the squirrel in the bag stopped making that horrible banging sound.

"Bye, Soo-san," Shell had whispered.

Vicki's front window strobes blue. The TV is so loud with shouts and gunfire that one of the beer bottles topples off the sill, landing with a thud in the dirt patch where some petunias have wilted. Then all is quiet. Vicki's voice comes first, then her mum's. There is talk of Doritos and a new container of dip.

Shell sets the shoebox next to the crayons. When Vicki finds the box in the morning, she will bring Shell her antiques. Mamoon can have his pick from Shell's treasures, and everything will be fair and square again.

Shell's already down the steps when the screen door squeaks open. She smells cigarette. "Hey." Behind her, Clarke steps onto the porch, a Silverhorn T-shirt tucked into beltless jean shorts. Timmy the dog pants at his side. "What're ya snooping after now?"

"Is Vicki home?"

"She's busy," Clarke tells her. "And it's late to be coming to play."

Shell's not there to play. She only wants to trade Vicki some stuff back. "Vicki had asked for it."

"That it?" Clarke glances down at the shoebox.

Shell nods.

"Just leave it there, then." With his arm holding out the screen door and one foot still on the porch, he calls for Vicki. "Your hillbilly friend is here."

The television sounds again, but with the volume lower. In the window, Vicki's mum's boobs and chins are sharply outlined. Vicki's Garfield T-shirt hangs to her knees. Once, she wore it on the tire swing and had no underwear on beneath. She peeks out from behind Clarke. The knots in her hair have grown into tumbleweeds and she's blinking like crazy. When Clarke tells her to, she steps onto the porch and checks that everything is inside the box.

"Yes," she answers, replacing the lid.

"Now," Clarke says to Vicki, "you tell her where she can find her junk."

Vicki hugs the box into her Garfield chest and looks down. Together, she and Shell watch her toes curling up tight against the concrete porch, chipped nails of candy-apple red.

"Go on," Clarke says again. "I don't have all day." He stares hard at the back of Vicki's head.

Vicki closes her eyes and takes a breath. She points past Shell.

"In the garbage," she whispers.

Then Clarke grabs Vicki under the arm and pulls her inside. The screen door slams and Timmy yelps as Vicki backs onto the dog's lovely soft tail.

The television starts up even louder. Shell stays rooted at the bottom of the steps, swallowing visions of kicking the crayons across the porch or smashing the beer bottles over Clarke's head.

There are hot tears in her eyes as Shell lifts the lid from the first garbage can. The smell of sour milk hits the back of her throat as does the warm ferment of rotting fruit, because Vicki's family's never even heard of compost. With a dirty chopstick, Shell pokes among sacks of dirty Kleenex, pizza boxes, and about fifty spaghetti cans. The street lights are coming on. Soon Dad will let loose one of his famous whistles that can he heard three blocks away at least.

Shell lifts the lid from the second can. Under a crumby Purina sack and a stack of *Rolling Stone*, Shell finds her lost treasures. One by one, she picks them out, wipes them on her pants, and tucks them into her purse. What doesn't fit she sets on the dewy grass. When everything is accounted for—teacup, coins, glass bottles, the little crocheted pouch with the brass ring inside—Shell replaces the lid, bundles the trades in her T-shirt, and walks home. Clarke is in the window, the bamboo shades pushed back.

SHELL'S UNDER THE mountain ash reading *Asterix* from the library. Mamoon said that's his favourite comic. And he's right, it's about a million times better than *Archie*. Across the street, a grey squirrel chases a brown squirrel around the base of a shady maple. The brown one clutches a flower bulb in its mouth. The grey one natters at the brown, backing it into the tree trunk, tail twitching like it's electric. Only when the brown drops the flower bulb does the grey let it dash away. The bulb is probably one of Dad's. They're going for the irises now. All week Shell prayed for God to make the squirrels go away so she wouldn't have to help kill them anymore. Usually she falls asleep after such long prayers, but last night Shell tiptoed downstairs. Mum was listening to the radio in the sweaty kitchen, the counter lined with jars of gooseberry jam. The lights in the studio were bright through the back window. The top of Dad's head moved from window to window. Shell missed Mamoon. He understood about Mum and Dad without even knowing it.

Mum gave Shell milk and a muffin with warm jam.

When Shell said, "Mum, are we hillbillies?" Mum didn't laugh. Mum's glasses had clay on them and her lips were sticky from licking the spatula.

"Dad's from a farm, Shell. That's why he's always digging holes and collecting old wood and saving things."

"Like he's a squirrel? Kind of?"

"Well, maybe. But don't tell him that."

Shell said no, she wouldn't tell. And she won't tell Mum about the gassed squirrels either. "I don't have to be like Dad, do I?"

"No," Mum said, surprised. "You don't have to be like either of us, but you still have to obey our rules."

The mountain ash produces a deep dark shade. Lying beneath it in the long grass, Shell dozes off. Cars go past, swooshing in and out of waking dreams. And then there comes the flip-flipping of thong sandals—near, but not quite loud enough to be on Shell's side of the street.

With knotted head lifted high and Shell's old shoebox under her arm, Vicki walks down Cashel Street in the direction of the church.

Shell follows, well back, but never far enough away she can't hear Vicki's shoes snapping up and down or see her sharp back bones poking out above her tube top. Vicki passes Cashel Street United, trots up to Mamoon's apartment building, finds the right buzzer, and rings the bell. Mamoon's mum opens the door. She smiles at Vicki, who looks up, shading her eyes. She holds out Shell's shoebox. Mamoon's mum nods and retreats. Then Mamoon comes to the door. The church steps where Shell huddles are warm from the morning sun. Mamoon smiles at Vicki but keeps looking back to where his mum has gone. Vicki grabs his hand and leads him over to the apartment steps. They sit, knees falling open. Vicki holds out the shoebox like it is Pot of Gold chocolates. Mamoon selects a bottle of polish. Then Vicki rummages around and takes out a nail file. She picks up Mamoon's hand and places it on her knee. One by one, she cleans and files his fingernails. Mamoon closes his eyes. His shoulders relax.

Vicki and Mamoon are laughing. Shell's legs cramp from crouching, and her stomach feels sick. It's not right that Vicki does up Mamoon's nails pretending like Clarke didn't call him Baboon. Mamoon needs to know what Clarke said and so does his mum.

Shell finds her balance and steps away from the church. She goes slow, pretending to read her comic. At the bottom of the apartment steps, she lifts her eyes.

"Hi, Shell," Mamoon says, waving with his free hand.

Shell uses *Asterix* to shade her eyes. Vicki and Mamoon smile down at her.

Vicki says: "Come up." She says: "My mum gave me some nail files and stuff, so now I can give a real manicure. Want one?"

Shell looks down at her dirty nails and scratched fingers, the palms calloused from shovelling. "Okay."

Mamoon and Vicki move over and Mamoon pats the spot between them. While Vicki picks up Shell's right hand and puts it on her knee, Mamoon does the same with Shell's left. Then Vicki gives Mamoon a nail file and scrounges in the shoebox for a second. They go to work cleaning the dirt from beneath Shell's nails and filing down the snagged edges. Shell chooses the same purple polish that Mamoon has on. She shivers with calm as her friends coat her nails with thick globs of colour, one finger at a time.

DAD'S IN THE back putting in more basil. A cup of coffee is getting hotter on an old black walnut stump.

"Look, Dad," Shell says, holding out her fingernails.

Dad's eyes behind his glasses are blanked by the sun. He drops his shovel instead of jabbing it upright into the ground. Dad takes both of Shell's hands in one of his and, without looking at the purple polish, squeezes her fingers together.

Mum comes out of the studio and walks down the path towards the house. She doesn't look over at Shell because then she would have to look at Dad.

Behind the studio, the neighbour's dogs bark, chains rattling. Then comes the clatter and snap of the animal trap.

Dad smiles. Shell smiles.

"We got another squirrel."

Frozen Fish

The summer before Dad and Mum get separated, Dad digs Shell a fish pond for her eleventh birthday. Dad picks just the right spot out back—in the shade of the overgrown gooseberry bush, where Mum's rotten thyme planter used to be. They start early, right after porridge and scrambled eggs. Dad takes a final sip of coffee, tucks in his T-shirt, and jabs his pitchfork into the yard's one remaining plot of grass. Shell uses the pointy red spade with the short handle because it's not too heavy. As the sun creeps high beside them, they rip away at the squeaky sod, hunks of which they toss—underhand, like scruffed cats—towards a mound by the compost. And then, when the grass is finally out—all of it—Dad pushes his foggy glasses up his nose and says Monday the lawn mower is going in the *Penny Saver*. Twenty bucks or best offer.

Dad switches to the coal shovel. Between high school

and art college he worked a year in a gold mine up in Yellowknife. Head down, elbows in, Dad's shoulder blades pump in concentrated rhythm, torso twisting at the hips. Shell, ducking his spray, carries spadefuls of dirt over to the compost pile, careful not to spill. By the time Shell gets Mum to make some lemonade, there's a pair of nickel-sized blisters rubbed into her palm and she's sweated right through her once-good Mexican blouse with puffed sleeves and bluebell embroidery. Dad's tape measure sizes the hole at two feet down and four across: they can stop. While Shell stamps the bottom down so it's level—picking out two long nails, crumbly with rust— Dad wrestles the sun-bleached wading pool out of the shed. They brush the pool of dead bees and sticky webs, line it with black plastic, and sink it into the hole.

"How's that, kiddo?" says Dad of the perfect fit.

To hide the pool's ugly edge, Dad makes a collar of smooth, flat-topped slate; Shell seeds the cracks with creeping thyme. Before turning on the hose, they make a tower of rocks in the middle of the pool, which Dad crowns with a pot of tiny blue water irises that he and Kremski scooped from a bog in the north end of town. Shell crouches as the cool water gushes from the hose; when the rim of the iris pot vanishes, she calls out and Dad shuts off the tap.

"We finished the pond," Shell says, washing her hands at the kitchen sink. Mum is coring slender Cubanelle peppers; stems and pods overflow the compost bucket. Dad picked almost two full bushels—before the glossy green skin gets too red. The big spaghetti pot is steaming on the stove, lid dancing, and Mason jars crowd the countertop.

Mum glances at the back-door window. Under the walnut tree, Dad's going at the lawn mower with the oil can. She turns down the boiling water and sniffs up the droplet of sweat clinging to the tip of her nose. "Don't go anywhere," she says to Shell. "I need a hand with all this bloody canning."

After supper it's too hot to stay in the house, so Dad and Shell drive down to the coves while Mum's jellying the gooseberries the birds didn't get. The lot is empty. They fill their buckets with water plants. In only a few weeks lily pads crowd the pond's still surface, as do bulbous water hyacinths, each morning spawning new pods of crisp, waxy leaves. And then on a Saturday when Mum doesn't need the car, they take Highway 7 out to Gord's Water Garden. Dad drives home in the slow lane; all colours and sizes of Japanese carp and goldfish slosh wide-eyed inside ballooned plastic bags on the back seat. Like comets in a night sky—red and silver, yellow and black—Shell's new pets, her first, dart through the pond's silver water. She crouches at the water's edge with food flakes, tapped from a cylinder like Mum with the salt, and at dusk covers the pond with the mesh dome Dad made; the heavy rock that goes on top keeps the raccoons out. School starts up. The leaves turn, and when they start to fall, Dad begins to toss handfuls of dirt into the pond. The mud will settle at the bottom and keep the fish warm. "So they can survive the winter," he says. It's going to be a hard one.

DAD MOVES OUT before the first frost. The Dodge Dart—with smoky engine and dragging tailpipe—stays in the driveway, and he doesn't take much more than a suitcase because the room he's rented in Toronto is already furnished. But he does take the wool rug his grandmother wove and which has always—always—hung behind the couch in the living room. He wraps it in a garbage bag, fading borscht stains and all. The ghost of its shape stands out crisp and white against the wall's yellowed paint. In its place Shell helps Mum hang up a pen-and-ink drawing of two men boxing. Mum and Dad's friend from art school did it. He's gotten pretty big now and Mum thinks she's going to have to sell it.

The snow comes early and hard. Overnight, six inches fall, blanketing the backyard before Shell can dig up Dad's iris bulbs or pick the last of the squash or throw more dirt in the pond. The freezer and cold storage are almost empty, and Shell failed her math test at school, and for weeks in a row she can't sleep without a light on even though Mum says isn't she too old for that and it's a shameful waste, just wait until they get the bill.

Then Mum finds a cooking job at a nursing home that specializes in the disease Dad used to joke of as Old-Timers'. But the place really is called Memory Lane, no kidding.

"We can keep the pen-and-ink now," Mum says.

But if she went ahead and sold it, she could buy Shell a pair of those brown Cougar lace-ups with sticking-out tongues and fuzzy red insides the big girls wear. Shell mentions this as she and Mum drag pieces of thick metal caging from Dad's stash under the back porch. Mum laughs. "You'll wear the boots you've got."

The caging is to bar the basement windows and back door. "Because no one's home during the day now," Mum says. She calls a handyman to do it. And she posts an advert at a business college within walking distance offering room and board for a female in a quiet house with a working mother and school-age daughter. Shell's room is the one advertised. The "board" means they'll feed her, this female. Debbie is the first one to come look. She is taking the hospitality course and her snug jeans are tucked into shiny brown Cougars. She pays cash up to the end of the school term and Shell moves into the basement. Shell's bed goes under the windows, right where the foster boys slept, side by side like in a graveyard, or Snow White with the dwarves. Shell blinks big into the fall of first grey sun, missing Mum and Dad both because Mum's away so much now.

Dad had been building a carpentry workshop next to the furnace room. He and Kremski got the drywall up and even hung a door. But now his tools are all packed away and the sawhorses hidden in the cold storage. Like the walls, the concrete floor is raw and unpainted. Mum unrolls the hooked rugs her mother made and arranges them to seal out the cold ground. Shell has never seen these rugs before. The biggest one shows a tiger lounging beneath a palm tree. Also, there is a family of swans and another of a brown girl with flowers braided into her long black hair. They are like giant postcards, or the beach towels sold at gas stations.

Mum switches on the pot-bellied Filter Queen. Tugging on the wand, she attacks each of the rugs and then switches to the nozzle attachment, sucking cobwebs from the edges of the ceiling and baseboards. Her hair is cropped short now—to fit under a hairnet at work. It's gone steel wool in both colour and texture, and because her glasses are old, she squints like a Beatrix Potter mole and she won't take Aspirin for the headaches. By the thin grey light glazing the room's pair of small windows, Shell unfolds clean flannel sheets and makes up the roll-away bed dragged out from its hiding place under the stairs.

Mum works extra shifts—lunches and dinners both—so she's pretty much full-time. Plus she's taking Introduction to Anthropology at the university that's two mornings a week. The kitchen, when Shell comes home from school, is cold and unlit. On the sill above the sink, the glass medicine bottles are drained of their emerald and amber glows. At five o'clock the furnace will whir to life. That's thirty minutes before Debbie's boyfriend drops her off. Shell keeps her parka on. Underneath, Dad's Montreal Canadiens jersey is fitting her better and better—or maybe worse and worse. Shell shoves real, store-bought Fig Newtons in her mouth, one after the other—eight, nine, ten Fig Newtons—swallowing hard. She wants the biscuits to be gone so that she can stop eating them. Then they are gone. A glass of milk washes down the clumps in her teeth and the lumps in her chest. The empty package goes to the bottom of the garbage, beneath wet tissue and soup cans and dirty bottles and balls of tinfoil peeled from the tops of frozen meals.

Mum brings home a thirteen-inch RCA with bleeding colour and bent rabbit ears she got from an ad on the

Community Board at the Thrifty Mart where she buys bread rather than bake it herself all Saturday. The canning jars and yogurt maker are packed away too. "No more pioneering," she'd said, replacing Dad's meat grinder with a *Penny Saver* microwave. Mum never thought she'd agree with her own mother, but Betty Crocker truly was a revolutionary. There's Cheerios on top of the fridge too, canned soup in the cupboard, and even Kraft Dinner, about which Shell sometimes dreams at night: the way the creamy noodles slide down her throat and how just the right amount of ketchup turns their orange glow into a salmon-pink sunset and how the ketchup's sweetness and the tangy cheese and a bite of garlic pickle mix up into a thick, salty paste which she holds in her mouth for an extra bit of savour. Shell's started sneaking home for Kraft Dinner during school lunch. Alone at the table, she eats the whole pot. She can't even read her book while she's doing it, the taste and texture of the macaroni is so total. Then she carefully scrubs and dries and replaces the dishes and walks back to school, her peanut butter sandwich for dessert.

Mum's note says she's serving supper at Memory Lane tonight. *Get something from the freezer for you and Debbie.* Shell's okay making dinners on her own: some kind of battered or breaded meat with a side of fries and, because Mum insists, a vegetable. The freezer in the basement broke down, so, shopping bag by shopping bag, Mum and Shell moved the contents out to the chest freezer in the woodshed—fries, margarine tubs of frozen chicken stock, boysenberries Dad was saving for a January pie.

Kremski salvaged the freezer from a demolition and traded it to Dad for some perfectly good window glass the neighbours two doors down put out. The freezer's body is pocked with rust, and even when the corroded latch agrees to open, the lid's so heavy Shell can hardly lift it up. Plus, the coolant's leaking. Inside the tight-wrapped garbage bags are dead squirrels. Shell doesn't always remember to put one out each garbage day. Debbie doesn't know about the chest freezer because she doesn't stray beyond the back porch, where she smokes her skinny peppermint cigarettes. And she doesn't come home for dinners much anymore either.

"Isn't there some salad?" Debbie had said to Shell one night when Shell served Swanson beef pies again. She's been packing on weight since moving in.

"Don't you want it?"

Debbie huffed and took the plate. They ate in front of the local news and when Debbie got up to answer the phone — "That'll be Greg!" — she did a little dance to get the denim out of her crotch.

Through the barred glass of the back-door window, the low sky is the same thin white as the skim milk Shell pours into her cup, and the snow on the ground is old and grey. A few crisp leaves cling to remaining plant stalks, and far at the back the shed's broad window shines dark.

Shell jams on her Ski-Doo boots without unzipping them. The back porch stinks of cigarette butts, and black ash peppers the packed snow around the steps. She shoves her hands into her pockets as she clumps through the yard. Fish sticks for tonight: three each, done in the oven along with shoestring fries. Green peas for Debbie, if she's even home. When she's not home, Shell eats Debbie's fries and chicken pie or whatever along with her own. Then she crawls into her roll-away bed, clutching at the lead balloon in her belly. When Mum comes back, Shell cries at the soft footsteps on the ceiling — back and forth between table and stove — and the smell of soft brown toast and the *wheee* of the kettle whistling.

The shed's light bulb is dusty and the towering pile of two-by-fours and broken hockey sticks and other cuts of oddball wood almost touches the rafters. With an overturned bucket as a stool, Shell leans into the dank freezer. The flat cardboard box of High Liner fish sticks is unopened, but the bag of fries is down to a third. There are no peas or spring medley or anything else. A can of Habitant minestrone will have to do. At the bang of the freezer lid, chunks of wood tumble from Dad's neat pile, a chipped table leg nearly knocking Shell on the head. Shell shuts the door gently. But a rumble follows and then a loud crash.

Through a receding crust of gritty snow, the skeleton of Dad's garden shows. The bricked tiers of the iris beds have sunk, the bashed-up tomato cages have fallen over, and the cardinal bush under which Shell used to imagine no one could see her is broken down with ice. Save for the blue box of fish sticks under her arm, there is no colour: not a drop. And the chill of that scoops at Shell, hollowing her insides. What's left is a hunger, ever deepening, for salty, oil-slicked, oven-warmed food; processed, preserved, store-bought. It's so hard to get enough.

From across the yard, the back of the house is dark, the stillness of it unfamiliar. With three channels to choose from on the RCA, Shell doesn't go to the library much anymore, or anywhere else. All she wants is to preheat the oven, close the living room curtains, and lie on the couch. It's almost time for *The Price Is Right*. But it is all so weary inside Shell. The corporate, American-junk-food fish sticks she clutches make her sick. Imagine if Dad could see her.

Salt water blurs Shell's eyes. The house and the flatland of the yard look like the channels the TV antennas can't pick up. But then: a spark of green rises just above the snow. As Shell clumps towards it, the green takes its true shape, becoming the rim of a plastic flowerpot.

Shell rushes the flowerpot. Fish sticks and fries fall to the ground. With her thick mitts she claws at the crusted snow until a crunchy tug releases the pot from winter's hold. The plastic is cracked. Inside are rock and dirt and a bundle of shrivelled iris roots.

At the crisp wind, Shell tightens her hood. Her knees warm the cold ground, making them wet. She digs deeper into the snow, the discards mounding up around her. She sweats, her nose drips. Finally, she stands. The circle of frosty, opaque glass at her feet is the exact same size as a child's wading pool.

Shell's leather mitts only smear the tears. Chin to chest, the weight of the low sky climbs up onto her shoulders.

Let Mum find her frozen, like Dad did that drunk in a snowbank last winter on Clayton Street, right across from his painting studio. But then Shell won't see it if the Canadiens win the Stanley Cup this year. And who'd get

Shell's horsehair button box? She doesn't want anyone rifling through her memories, so real you can hold them in your hand.

At the call of a bird, Shell looks up: a plump cardinal has landed in the bush named just for it. The pond ice is less opaque now, more crystal and reflective. Beneath the surface, bright dots of red and gold and silver blink bright as Christmas lights.

Trapped, frozen in time past as much as in thick ice, goldfish and rainbowed carp cry for Shell to get them out — and please, please, hurry.

DAD'S AXE HANGS in the shed, above the woodpile that is now more like a heap. Shell's snub-nosed boots weigh heavy as she crests the wobbly summit and, balanced on one knee, stretches out, her bare fingertips nudging the axe's smooth wooden shaft. It clatters to the floor. Shell jumps down after it, riding a further avalanche of wood.

Crouched as a frog, Shell leans in with the axe and takes a first crack at the frozen water. The fish are trapped at different depths, so she starts with those closest to the surface.

Her fists choke up on the axe blade, the long handle wedged under her armpit. Dad always says there is a right and a wrong way to handle a tool — broom, darning needle, canoe paddle, cheese grater, egg beater, clothes peg, or toothbrush — and Shell's short fingers have no strength and no grace, and she knows that until she herself mines gold in Yellowknife, she'll never do it right.

Shell gets right onto the ice, plants her boots firm and

wide, and throws all her weight behind the axe. The ice cracks. Day dwindles into an early evening the same colour iron as Mum's hair. Shell takes another swing. Some of the fish are clumped up so close together Shell's afraid she's going to chop one in half. She pushes back her hood and unzips her parka, wipes her nose on the sleeve. There's that smell again—the one everyone calls BO. Mixed in with the mothball of Dad's rubbery hockey jersey in which she now lives is her own sour odour, which Debbie says a stick of Secret Powder Fresh would make go away. Can't Mum buy her some?

She hits the ice. A loud crack echoes across the empty sky. Shell throws down the axe. She picks up a brick-sized hunk of crystal; inside a bright orange goldfish hangs suspended. "Don't die, please," Shell whispers to the ice.

The kitchen is still dark, but the furnace is on. Shell fills a bucket with warm tap water and, switching on the porch light against the darkening sky, lugs it back to the pond, boots flapping.

Plop!

It takes only a minute for the fish to thaw. The sleek two-inch goldfish thus released darts around the bucket—eyes wide and body wriggling—not just alive but risen from the dead.

By the yellow of the porch light, Shell chops away at the pond, releasing her fish one at a time. Hot and sweating and feeling like an athlete, Shell extracts each fish cube and melts it in one of a series of warm-water buckets. A nice big carp gets axed in half, and a few small goldfish don't make it, their white-bellied corpses floating to the surface — Shell swears they'll get buried come spring.

The sky has stars when Shell's axe cracks into the pond's plastic bottom. The fish — rescued, reborn — number a dozen. Slopping the buckets up the porch and into the house, Shell finds the kitchen warm but still dark. Debbie would have been back by now, so Shell has only herself to feed. And the fish.

They are out of fish food, so while her cheese sandwich is heating in the microwave, Shell crushes Corn Flakes into a fine dust. Bucket by bucket, Shell feeds her fish, whispering how proud she is of them, how magical they are, and how sorry she is to have left them so cold and lonely. Shell dips her finger in among the Corn Flakes floating on the water and the boldest of her fish takes a nibble.

When the news comes on, Shell arranges the buckets in front of the TV, blue light flashing upon each one's surface. The smallest of the goldfish died when Shell was washing the dishes and is now in a margarine tub on the porch. But the other eleven are swimming strong. Their wide eyes are far wiser, for now they have, like in Mum's Joni Mitchell song, seen life from both sides.

White headlights pass over the front curtains. Then there's the rumble of the Dart in the drive. A door slams. Footsteps sound on the back porch. Through the barred window, Mum is flooded in yellow light. She gropes in her purse, distracted by the margarine tub and Dad's axe leaning against the railing. Shell opens the door. Behind her glasses, Mum's eyes spring wide, half angry already.

"Guess what?" Shell says before Mum can step inside, out of the frozen winter.

Snow Tire

Vicki's jean jacket is pink with rainbow trim. When Shell steps onto the porch in the morning, it's easy to see if she's already out front of her house waiting to walk to school. If she's not, like today, Shell will knock on the door—very softly, because Clarke might be sleeping off his night shift. But the windows of her bungalow are never this dark, plus the driveway is empty. Shell just goes on up Cashel Street to school. Maybe Vicki's at the doctor's again; she's always having trouble with her tonsils. But at recess Vicki's not in the area where the younger grades play. While the rest of the school screams and teachers blow whistles, Shell squats behind an oak tree and for ten allotted minutes reads her favourite part of *Tiger Eyes*—where Davey first meets Sal at the Grand Canyon and, though he is older, he sees something in Davey that is special.

Vicki's gone a second day, though Clarke's car is back in the drive. Shell tells Mum and Mum says just wait. It's probably nothing. Shell tells her diary what she can't admit to Mum: she misses Vicki and she never thought of her as a best friend but now she does.

The next day, Vicki is on her porch waiting. For a minute, though, she tricked Shell with a new jacket: black satin with bedazzled trim. Her mum is in the hospital getting her stomach stapled.

"Huh?" Shell pictures rubber gloves and raw pizza dough and then how Dad stretches canvas with one of those guns.

Vicki says the staples go on the inside. "So she won't eat very much." In no time at all her mum is going to be as skinny as she was before she had Vicki. Also, Clarke is working overtime at Silverhorn to pay for the operation, which means — hooray — that he won't be home much.

"But the hospital was really neat." Vicki got to watch TV in one of those sit-up beds and eat Jell-O from a tray.

Vicki's mum comes home with a talking scale, new bed sheets, and a TV for her room. She lies on the waterbed playing along with game shows and drinking juice glasses full of chocolate milk that Vicki carefully measures.

"That's all her stomach has room for," Vicki says, holding up a Weight Watchers measuring cup, the eight-ounce line marked with orange nail polish.

With Clarke always working, Shell and Vicki watch a lot of music videos on tape. After school, Vicki pours diet root beer while Shell finds the Ritz crackers and Kraft peanut butter, so salty and sweet she could live on it. Cyndi

Lauper's new video is on when Vicki's mum comes out. She's in white jeans; just one leg is as big as Shell's whole sleeping bag, and her underwear lines show. As she twirls around in front of the TV, the freckled meat of her arms quivers. These jeans have not fit her for five years. Vicki glances up from the video she's trying to sing along to, though she's never heard the song before.

"Move it, Mum, you're in the way."

Shell stays for supper. Vicki heats chicken cacciatore TV dinners while her mum microwaves leftover Chicken McNuggets. They eat in the lopsided kitchen where Vicki and Shell used to run marbles down the sloped floor. Vicki's mum spreads a napkin over her lap and, dipping her nuggets in honey-mustard sauce, tells them about how, before she met Clarke, she was dating Luis Duarte, the lead singer from Abacus.

"You see their video, Shell?"

Shell nods. It's the one where the band are slaves on some kind of island with ladies in chains and bikinis and feeding the slaves meat bones.

"Well, they're big now." So big they're going to open for Van Halen at Maple Leaf Gardens in the spring.

Shell is thinking Vicki's mum probably wore those white jeans when she was dating Luis Duarte, and then she, Vicki's mum, wriggles out of her chair and thumps to the bathroom, which is right on the other side of the wall. Shell and Vicki keep eating while Vicki's mum is throwing up. When her mum comes back, she says she should have measured the McNuggets with the scale but she only ate five and that seems like not much.

"Right?"

Vicki shrugs. Vicki's mum puts the two leftover McNuggets back in the fridge, pours a cup of diet root beer, and goes into her bedroom. The waterbed sloshes. The music for *Taxi* comes on and after Shell and Vicki have ice cream sandwiches on the tire swing, Shell says she had better go.

VICKI'S MUM STARTS doing things like raking the leaves and walking slowly up to the store to get small bags of chips, or she picks Vicki up from school and walks back with her and Shell. She goes from the white jeans to a new pair of stonewash that don't show her underwear lines and she cuts her hair so it's feathery like Princess Di's. And then, more and more, when Clarke is at work, a black Trans Am is parked in the drive.

Monday morning, Vicki's house is dark. It's cold, but Shell waits around. There's all kinds of stuff to tell Vicki about visiting Dad in Toronto on the weekend. Like how she took the Greyhound all by herself, and she and Dad bought cheese in Little Italy — there's a whole street of places to eat real chicken cacciatore! Oh, and the man Dad rents a room from is kind of weird but nice and gave Shell a roll-on deodorant that was his mother's. Shell bounces from foot to foot and shifts her bag from one shoulder to the other. The warning bell rings. Shell steps up the front walk. Where are the bamboo blinds? She creeps onto the lawn and, on her tiptoes, cups her eyes to see in through the window's reflective glare. The TV is gone, as are the lamps and the Chinese fans and Stones posters. Timmy is asleep on the La-Z-Boy that was known as "Clarke's." The final bell rings. Shell cries all the way up Cashel Street, and when she gets to school, all the kids are already in from the yard.

A For Rent sign goes up on Vicki's front lawn and soon Clarke's gone too. The only thing left is the tire swing. Some Chinese people move in, five adults and only one baby to go around. Many on Shell's street believe the Chinese people talk too loud when they sit out on the porch.

"Well," Mum says, "it's better than Vicki's what's-his-head with no shirt and the goddamn Stones."

THOMAS ANSWERS THE phone when Vicki calls.

"Was that your dad?" she asks Shell.

"No," Shell says. "Just a guy who lives in my room now."

"Oh?" says Vicki. "Is he cute?"

Thomas has been their boarder since September. Thomas is taking the hospitality course and, like Debbie, eats out at restaurants a lot, though he pays Mum for board.

"Oh, I had a late lunch," he will say to Shell, patting his belly, when she asks what kind of toast he'd like to go with the canned pea soup.

Thomas is never there when Shell gets home from school. She will creep into her old room, dark with denim curtains and smelling of cologne and Aqua Net. Thomas used to keep dill pickle–flavoured chip dip between the windows where it's cool, a bag of plain Ruffles in his desk drawer. Because Shell couldn't stop eating the dip and Ruffles until both were almost gone, Thomas moved his private snacks somewhere else.

"No, he's not at all," Shell says. Thomas is at the harvest table, bending over his binder of hospitality notes. "He's ugly."

"Well, there's cute boys out here, Shell." Vicki sounds older.

When Shell says, "I thought you were going to marry Bruce Springsteen?" Vicki laughs.

"Oh, Shell."

Vicki is living out in Railton with her mum and her mum's new boyfriend, whose name is Scott. Scott has a black Trans Am, satellite that picks up MTV, and a cousin with an in-ground pool. "There's a pool party every weekend." Shell should come out for a swim.

"I'll ask," says Shell.

"It's pretty far in the country out here," Vicki goes on. She has to go to grade six on a bus. "Some kids my age drive already. And girls are getting periods." She wants to know how grade seven is for Shell. "Any new kids at school?"

There is silence. Vicki is saying, "Okay, well, I better go," when Shell blurts out that Mamoon wrote from Brussels. His grandparents cut down the apple tree in their garden and there's something there called Nutella that Vicki and Shell would love. Mamoon bets Shell's dad could catch more squirrels with Nutella than with peanut butter. Shell lies and tells Vicki she wrote back to Mamoon. But really, the unanswered letter is tucked inside the musty horsehair button box, along with the spare key for the studio, the pasta-shell necklace Mamoon made her, a bullet from Schwartz's sausage meat, the jagged piece of Mountain Dew glass that left her with a row of stitches. When Vicki gives Shell her number, Shell repeats it back, pretending to write it down.

MUM SAYS SHELL should make some friends her own age for a change. Like what about that Wendy? Wendy's mum bought a whole whack of pottery from Mum and Dad. She is smart, has large green-grape eyes and clothes from stores even better than Eaton's.

When they're checking out library books, Shell says to Wendy, "Oh, you like Judy Blume. You ever read *Tiger Eyes*?"

But all Wendy wants to know about is how Shell's dad doesn't live with her anymore. Is it true strangers pay rent to live in Shell's old bedroom while Shell sleeps in the basement like a hobbit?

Shell says, "No, well, yes. I guess."

Then Mum brings home a garbage bag full of hand-me-downs.

"Where'd ya get 'em?"

Mum doesn't say. She's too excited about this blue Beaver Canoe sweatshirt with a hood. "Oh, Shell, isn't that a good label?"

Shell shrugs, but she keeps it because it's long enough to cover her bum. She wears it to school with some corduroy pants that were also in the garbage bag. Five minutes after she files out of the cloakroom, everyone knows Shell is wearing the old clothes of Wendy's big brother.

Shell puts her parka back on and walks out of class. She's halfway across the deserted schoolyard when a teacher stops her and makes her go back.

Some of the other girls in Shell's grade seven class are like Shell in that they have only mums at home. Instead of reading books, they have babysitting jobs and many have boyfriends who are in high school. These girls wear jean jackets and jelly shoes even though it's cold. At recess they stay in the bathroom putting on lip gloss and talking about Tampax and Platinum Blonde. Vicki with her jean skirts and Lip Smackers is like them already and someday won't call Shell anymore. And in not too many years Shell will be in high school, and what will happen to her then? So Shell reads. Sometimes she walks and reads at the same time, or reads in class, a paperback hidden inside her textbook.

Shell wakes up Mum one night and gets in next to her. Shell tells her about Wendy and the girls in the bathroom and asks if they can move to another city. Or how about just letting Shell switch schools? But then Mum gets it all wrong and buys Shell a Platinum Blonde LP for an early Christmas gift. She stands there as Shell listens to it, twisting her hair around her fingers and studying the skinny men on the pastel cover. Shell doesn't want to turn thirteen in the summer. She cries, tears falling on the shiny men. Mum flies across the living room and shuts off the player. The needle goes screeching along the vinyl surface.

"What *do* you want, Shell? I can't always guess!"

"Bob Marley," Shell chokes.

Shell falls asleep on the couch listening to *Uprising*, a rough pioneer blanket pulled over her head.

THE CHINESE PEOPLE in Vicki's house move away after only a few months, leaving the boulevard out front piled high with old furniture and bundles of flattened cardboard boxes that all kinds of new stuff came in: a baby stroller, high chair, box fan, ghetto blaster, digital alarm clock, sixteen-piece pot and pan set, colour TV, VCR, electric kettle, and a deluxe rice cooker. Mum says the young man of them must have been promoted. Before the For Rent sign can even go up, some Native Indians move in. No one on Shell's street says anything about them. But Shell can feel the air shift, locking down in tense anticipation. There seems to be four of them, three women and a man, plus a Ford station wagon, but no kids.

Twice a day — four times if she sneaks home for lunch — Shell walks by Vicki's. The tire swing in the backyard is still up. Sometimes, like now, it seems to sway, as if someone has just been for a ride. Without anyone to push them, Shell or Vicki could usually give themselves a pretty good start just by leaning backwards and running as fast as they could. Shell watches the swing. She sits in the grey velveteen armchair that's been on the boulevard since the Chinese people moved out. The seat cushion is missing and now, after two weeks of cold autumn rain, the wooden arms are splitting and the fabric is growing mould, a smear of which Shell now wipes from her pants.

Shell is at the top of Vicki's driveway staring at the

swing in the back when the bungalow's screen door squeaks opens. A Native woman with short side-parted hair and long legs steps onto the porch. She hitches up her faded jeans, sits on an aluminum lawn chair bowed by Vicki's mum. She lights a cigarette, crossing her legs at the ankle.

"Hey," the woman calls out, "what's so interesting back there?"

Shell turns away from the driveway, pretending to be contemplating the armchair on the boulevard. She peers at the hulk of mouldy velveteen through the bottom of her glasses, like Dad when he's sorting the good stuff from the junk.

"It's the swing you want, isn't it?"

Shell frowns and makes her brows touch above her nose.

"Go have a blast on that thing, if you want to. I don't care."

Shell says thanks. Then she walks quickly away.

MUM'S AT NIGHT school, so Shell calls Dad to see if he is watching the Habs game, but really she wants him to say it's okay to go into Vicki's backyard if the people who live there say she can. Like, that's not weird or anything?

Jonathan answers. Dad is out at some kind of pot-thing.

"A potluck?" Shell asks. She's going to ask what dish Dad made — garlic eggplant, stuffed grape leaves, the kind of hearty goulash he ate on the farm as a boy. But then Jonathan asks Shell about Odin — you know, the god whose wife was Frigg — and that leads to Leonard Cohen and space shuttles, and finally Jonathan starts to cough so violently he has to cover his face with his oxygen mask.

When Jonathan's breathing eases, Shell blurts out, "So I just wanted to know about this tire swing, you know, and it's in a stranger's yard, but she said I can use it."

"She?" Jonathan wheezes.

"A lady. Yeah. Is that okay to do?"

"That's fine with me, dear," Jonathan growls, just like Dad's Tom Waits.

"Thanks," says Shell.

"Oh, sure. And who's this I am talking to again?"

"No one," Shell says, hanging up the phone.

THERE'S NO LIGHTS on at Vicki's and someone has tipped the armchair onto its side. Mum says rentals often have that big kind of garbage. Shell kneels down as if to look at the chair's ripped underside and stubby wooden feet, then pulls her hood down as far as it will go and follows the empty driveway into the backyard.

The grass is long and wet. On the back stoop under which Timmy used to hide, there's a large cage with two big brown rabbits twitching inside. They are quiet and still and smell of fresh wood chips. Through the cage's mesh, Shell touches their soft, silky fur. The slender vertical troughs under their noses really do look like harelip scars. Shell calls both of them Kremski and wishes for a rabbit of her own. Maybe Mum will agree to that since she doesn't like cats.

The tire swing hangs low; its yellow rope is starting to fray and the walnut branch to which it is tied is as crooked as a boomerang. One leg a time, as if testing frigid water, she climbs into the swing. Shell pulls *Firestarter* from her pocket and finds her page, her back to Vicki's bungalow.

Shell's really got to pee and the light in the low sky is no longer enough to read by. The bungalow is lit now: a blue fluorescence in the add-on that was Vicki's bedroom as well as a flickering in the kitchen. Shell is halfway up the driveway when she smells cigarettes. The Native woman is on the porch, caught in the spotlight of the bare bulb over the door.

"Nice and quiet back there," the Native woman says.

She looks at Shell over her bifocal glasses, tucking back her wavy hair. Her face is long and thin. So are her limbs and hands, which are wired tight with muscle and bumps of bone. Short fingernails are painted the limiest green. Shell stands up straight and tries to be as confident and strong as the woman on the porch.

The woman says, "Glad you're helping yourself to the swing, honey." Her cousins won't care, but if Shell sees them around, "Just tell them Wanda said it's okay. Okay?"

Shell nods. Her wet nose drips.

"Let me hear you say it."

Shell clears her throat. "Okay."

The lawn chair groans as Wanda gets up. The door closes with a click.

SHELL CUTS THROUGH Vicki's yard for the swing. Each time Shell climbs into the cold rubber tire, the branch sinks lower and the old yellow rope further frays.

Sometimes she will hurry down at recess time. Pulling up her hood, she ducks through the staff parking lot and is late getting back only a few times. Wanda's cousin might be out feeding the rabbits. He is tall and thin like Wanda, with a ponytail and hands so big they could palm Shell's head. He nods at Shell, Shell at him. Then there are two older girls who might be twins. Shell never sees them except when they are driving the Ford station wagon up or down Cashel Street.

It snows—wet, melty flakes the size of teabags. The rabbits disappear from the back stoop and Wanda's not outside smoking as much. With the cold, the creaking rope grows brittle and the yellow coating flakes off, leaving not much more than a twist of dirty grey fibre. Her back aches if she sits for too long and the cold rubber rim cuts lines into the backs of her thighs or bum, depending on her position. But it is quiet back here and with her feet suspended above the ground Shell can drift far away.

Shell's halfway through *Gone with the Wind* when the swing breaks. The rope emits a creaking groan followed by a decisive snap. She tries to free herself from the tire as it is falling, but her body is too firmly wedged in. She lands on her back, legs up in the air. Stuck as a pig, she lies there for a long time holding tight to her novel. Above her is white winter sky; below her, the melting snow makes her bum wet.

Wanda answers Shell's knock. Shell says she's sorry the rope broke. There is a hard chunk in her throat and her lips tremble.

Wanda points to Shell's bulging pocket. "Maybe it's your big book that broke the camel's back."

The chunk dissolves enough Shell can swallow.

"Hey, I got something for you." Wanda opens the door wide.

It smells like spaghetti and tomato sauce. Shell thinks she'll make that for her and Thomas tonight. Clarke's La-Z-Boy is still there, as is his oak grandfather clock, the kind that might be showcased on *The Price Is Right*. The picture above the couch is that French one like in Mum's art history book, haystacks glowing red in a low sun, and there are about a million Polaroids stuck to the walls — mostly close-ups. Cross-stitched fabric drapes the long corridor all the way to the kitchen, which is covered with more Polaroids plus pieces of paper with words and dates and pencil drawings. The rabbits are not inside either, unless they're lost among the piles of cardboard boxes everywhere — *living room, dining room, Wanda's, den* — bursting with dishes and books and balled-up newspaper. A tape gun and scissors are on the kitchen table.

"Hey, what's your name, anyway?"

"Shell."

"Nice," Wanda says, squinting at Shell over her bifocals. "Well, Shell, you got a cassette player?" Shell says yes even though all they've got at home is Dad's turntable.

Shell lifts her arms as Wanda stuffs her parka pockets with cassette tapes.

"You take these, then. They need someone to listen to them." She catches Shell's eyes and says square into her face: "That old rope was bound to break someday, Shell. And so it did."

148

THE CASSETTES ARE by Patti Smith, Blondie, one called *Sandinista!*, as well as T. Rex and the Police. The Men at Work tape makes Shell think they were all in fact Clarke's. Well, whoever's they were, they listened to T. Rex and the Police so much some of the song titles are rubbed off the cartridges and the brown magnetic ribbon is crinkled from jamming in the machine. Shell studies how it is that Patti and Blondie look back at her so brave, so unafraid. She can't imagine what the songs will sound like, but Clarke didn't think they were very good because the hinges on the cases are stiff and the spools wound right to the beginning. Shell hides the tapes in her horsehair button box, right on top.

Then the boulevard in front of Wanda's is full of cardboard boxes, a deflated waterbed mattress, Vicki's kitchen table, and the lawn chair from the porch. Shell doesn't see Wanda again. The landlord comes with a For Sale sign and a pickup. A teenager in earmuffs helps him load. As the pickup trundles away up Cashel Street, the tire swing teeters on top, the length of frayed yellow rope still knotted in place.

AT CHRISTMAS, MUM works extra time at Memory Lane. Shell goes along to help serve suppers, and every time the elevator doors open, the old people are gathered around so tightly Shell has to push her way through. The scrum then follows her down the hall towards the damp kitchen, where Mum stands over a big pot, her glasses steamed. They writhe, cling, beg Shell for such things as cigars, hairbrushes, kisses, and in various accents and languages tell Shell she is lovely and a pretty girl. To some, though, she is a boy. Their skin, when they touch her, is soft and women's knobby wrists burst with tangled veins—red and blue and black veins, just like C-3PO's stomach.

Dad sends Shell a Seasons Greetings card with an invitation to Toronto for New Year's. A bus ticket falls out along with a crisp fifty-dollar bill from Jonathan. Dad writes he's going to have Salvadoran Christmas dinner with some friends from school. Thomas is going back east for the holidays so Shell and Mum will work December 25 at Memory Lane. That way they don't need a tree or a turkey, plus Mum earns time and a half, from which Shell can have thirty dollars to spend on Boxing Day. With the thirty from Mum and the fifty from Jonathan Shell buys a cassette player at Mister Sound's annual Boxing Day sale and still has enough left over to buy Mum the Bob Dylan LP with the "Oh, Sister" duet that Mum sings but forgets the words to.

"What about you, Shell?" Mum wants to know why Shell doesn't buy cassettes to play on her new machine.

"Got some already, Mum," Shell says. "I'm okay."

It's only five o'clock, but the light through the basement windows is charcoal. On the other side of the wall behind Shell's bed, the furnace whirs to life. Cross-legged, cassette player resting on top of the pillow on her lap, Shell sorts through the tapes in her box. Patti Smith is going first. She slides the tape into the door marked A, clicks it shut, and presses Play. A red light blinks on and there is the hiss of static. The first song has an ugly word in it, which is of course why Clarke bought the tape. But the song is about something else. Shell listens to Patti's tape once, twice, three times, then four, and soon she's singing along about feeling like a stranger among people and finding peace and strength in that.

And Shell smiles and Shell swings, back and forth on her bed, and then she sheds her blanket and her socks and starts dancing barefoot, just like Patti Smith sings in the song she's got now in her head. All on her own, ready for something new now. Her now. Then Bob Dylan singing with Emmylou comes on upstairs and the ceiling starts squeaking. Mum's in the kitchen dancing and cutting up squash for soup. So Shell turns her cassette player up higher, highest, drowning out Mum, up there, dancing all alone too.

Hole in the Wall

Dad calls on Friday. The evening before Shell is to make her monthly trip to Toronto. Her Greyhound ticket—return, child's fare—arrived in the mail a week ago and she's not heard about it since.

"Shell! Listen!" Dad's on a pay phone. The line crackles and a streetcar—*ding, ding*—jangles by.

"Dad? Did Jonathan not pay the bill again?"

Dad's rent at Jonathan's is discounted because Jonathan's got a personality disorder. Also, he smokes three packs of Exports a day and told Dad up front that he swallows things—coins, kitchen spoons, rocks from the garden. So when Jonathan gets a certain pinched look in his eyes, Dad calls for an ambulance.

Mum turns down the radio in the kitchen. There's a tea towel over her shoulder and a wet spot on her abdomen where she's been leaning against the sink.

Mum's thinking and Shell's thinking that Dad's going to cancel tomorrow's trip, but all he wants is some camping gear from the basement. Can Shell bring it with her?

"Sleeping bag, cutlery sets, tin cups, air mattress, and whatever freeze-dried food is left."

"You're not going camping, are you, Dad?" Shell shouts so he'll hear over the zip of traffic and his own competing voice. Dad goes lots of places on his own now—Ottawa, North Bay, Hamilton—but he would never go to Algonquin Park without Shell.

"What's that?" Dad cries into the phone. He adds the blue tarp to Shell's list, and the steel Thermos. The operator cuts in warning his funds are going to expire. And then they do expire.

"Dad?" Shell says to the pulsing busy signal.

"HE EXPECTS YOU to carry all that by yourself?" Mum pauses on the basement stairs with a basket of laundry. Shell, cross-legged on the concrete floor, attaches the blue goose-down sleeping bag to the aluminum frame camp pack.

"Who cares? We'll never use it again."

With the toe of her clog, Mum prods Shell's mess of tin plates, maps, bottles of bug spray, tubes of biodegradable soap, tent pegs, and coils of rope. The smell of wood ash and wet feathers is sharp, and with it comes the call of loon, the slap of beaver tail, the taste of potatoes slow roasted in hot ashes for the whole afternoon.

"Well, then," Mum says, "take as much as you can tomorrow and don't ever bring it back."

Shell sticks her thumbs under the straps of Dad's pack and leans forward, against the weight of the gear inside. Shell and Mum arrived at the bus station early enough that they are near the beginning of the Toronto-bound line. Shell keeps a full step apart from Mum so that anyone looking will think she's travelling solo.

"Well? You do have them, don't you?"

Shell looks away.

A group of Mennonites gather around the baggage hold of the coach. While the men among them organize their heap of Adidas duffle bags and leather steamer trunks tied up with rope, the women clutch at black bundles of infant or hold the hands of kids dressed up like midget versions of themselves. All are scrubbed and properly tucked in, faces tight against the bus exhaust. They could be standing on a train platform during the Industrial Revolution, like in that picture from the first movie ever made — Shell's reading about that in grade eight. It would be great to wear one of those long black dresses; then no one has to know how you're shaped underneath. Shell's camouflage army coat does that in its own way; in her head that's the real reason it's called camouflage. She saved up and bought it from the army surplus store along with a pair of red canvas high-tops that were made in Czechoslovakia. But the lace-up Mennonite boots look even better than her Cold War sneakers, and those old-fashioned Anne of Green Gables glasses one Mennonite mother is wearing are way better than the jumbo plastic pair she's got jammed in her pocket.

Mum grips Shell's elbow. "Can you even see that this is the right bus?"

"Says Toronto right there," Shell says, squinting. "I'm not blind, you know."

"And you have some money in your pocket, in case?"

"You think he won't show up, don't you?" Shell is sure Mum secretly hopes for that.

Mum and now Shell don't say "Dad" out loud anymore. It's to stop Mum's neck from shrinking up like someone's poked her.

Mum passes Shell a ten-dollar bill even though Shell earns enough for cassette tapes and used clothes from her Monday afternoon *Penny Saver* route. She also gets a few bucks sweeping out the studio for the watercolour painter who is renting it, and by stealing some bills from Mum's purse or from the purse of any pottery collector or gallery curator who comes to take away more of Mum and Dad's artwork.

"You don't have to spend it," Mum says.

The line starts to move. Dad's pack goes under the bus in the luggage hold while her own canvas shoulder bag—stuffed with books, toothbrush, pyjamas, and a bottle of apple juice—will make a good pillow. Mum looks back at the line. Shell's to sit beside a woman and not to leave the station if for any reason Dad's not there.

"And you have Bernadette's number?" That's Mum and Dad's old friend—now Mum's friend—who lives in some suburb that's really not close to Toronto at all. "She knows you're coming, Shell, okay?"

Shell gives the driver her ticket. Mum pats her back.

Right here on this same butt-ridden Greyhound platform Shell saw Mum and Dad kiss for the one and only time she can remember. Mum and Shell were taking a three-day bus ride to the Prairies; they'd be gone a whole month. Dad knelt down and drew Shell into the tuck of his firm chest. He said he wouldn't get lonely. He said Kremski would be around almost every day helping rebuild the shed out back. Then he stood and looked at Mum. Mum looked back. Glasses to glasses. They both pinched their lips and banged their faces together like bighorn sheep on *The Nature of Things*. At Dad's insistence the driver let Dad settle them on the coach. Shell wondered: if it were not for Shell, would Mum just stay in the Prairies and never come back to Dad ever again?

DAD'S NOT WAITING on the platform. Shell's stomach drops. There is a crush as the driver pulls baggage out from the hold. The Mennonites lead the way, piling their trunks into a taxi. Oh my God, what if she *does* have to call Bernadette for help? There's a pair of pay phones across the street on Bay — outside the Swiss Chalet where she and Dad have once or twice had lunch. She could sit in there for a while and read. Or what if she walked up Yonge Street? Sam the Record Man is only a block away.

Across the platform, a man is laughing at her, his arms crossed over his chest. Shell frowns, her forehead collapsing. But then he ducks through the crowd, scooping up the camp pack just as the driver flings it out.

Dad's beard is gone. He has just a moustache now, no

ball cap, and he looks small. Instead of his plaid work coat, Dad wears a corduroy suit jacket with a T-shirt underneath. He asks how the irises are. The black one called Licorice Spice was Shell and Dad's favourite.

"It must be coming out?"

Shell says sure, "It's a beaut, Dad," even though the iris, like most of the others, died in the winter. Any remainders were dug up when Mum called around and invited friends to come take what they could.

Then Dad grabs hold of Shell and pulls her in. He squeezes her so hard she can't breathe and the glasses in her pocket might break. Dad smells of smoke: not just Jonathan's cigarettes but like he spent the night before poking at a rugged campfire, seeing it through to smouldering dawn. He releases her.

"Hey, new coat, eh?"

Dad's anti-Reagan, so Shell made sure the jacket was not American issue. It's East German. Dad looks through the bottom of his glasses at the patch she's sewn on the breast pocket: a white circle with two black and red hammers crossed like an X. When she bought the patch at Mister Sound, the guy said, "Cool. Floyd." Shell just handed him over five dollars from her *Penny Saver* money and pretended to know what he meant.

The camp pack goes in a locker, as well as Shell's pyjamas and hardcover books, which Dad says look heavy to cart around.

Shell says, "What about Jonathan's?"

There's a Portuguese bakery between the subway and Jonathan's that makes savoury cod tarts Jonathan loves.

He swallows them whole, a cigarette in each hand. Shell and Dad will usually get him a bag of those or some cheese croissants. Then Jonathan gives Shell some money to spend—as much as ten tightly rolled five-dollar bills once. In the horsehair button box under Shell's bed there's a very soft two-dollar bill upon which—back and front—Jonathan drew a tiny ancient Greek village with blue ballpoint pen.

Dad shuts the locker door, releases the key, and tucks it into his wallet.

"Oh," he says. "Didn't I tell you? Jonathan's house burned down two weeks ago."

DAD COULD REALLY use a coffee. How about Shell? A Beanery just opened in an underground mall near the station. Dad orders Costa Rican in a mug, Shell a steamed milk, and they split a cheese Danish which Dad gets for the protein content even though Shell would rather have raspberry.

Dad tells Shell about his MFA. Some of the instructors he calls egomaniacs, but he likes his colleagues. Pavel comes up a lot.

"See that?" Dad holds open his jacket so Shell can read his T-shirt. *S.U.N.S.* is written inside a cartoon yellow sun: "Students United for Nuclear Sanity." A quote from George Orwell runs across the bottom: "History is a race between education and catastrophe."

"Oh, yeah." Shell knows all about George Orwell. She's read *Animal Farm, 1984,* and *Down and Out in Paris*

158

and London. She also read *A Clockwork Orange* and got an A on the book report she wrote for it. The teacher liked it so much he asked her to read it to the class.

"Now I'm on to Camus, though," she says. She shows Dad a library copy of *The Outsider*. "In French it is *L'Étranger*. The Cure has a song about it called 'Killing an Arab,' which is what happens in the book, so it's about racism but existentialism too because you don't know why the guy, Meursault, shoots the Arab. Maybe he just had the sun in his eyes. And, oh, to quit smoking in jail, he, Meursault, chews on a splinter of wood he breaks off his bed. Well, anyway, I'm not done it yet."

Irina gave Shell the Camus. Irina is living in Shell's old room while she's acting in a play at the Somerset Playhouse. Mum's been to see it and says it's very weird.

"Technically, Irina is a billeter," Shell explains. She's from Yugoslavia and spent a whole afternoon making Mum and Shell spinach *böreks* with sour cream. "You would have loved it."

Dad fans through the book. Camus is on the cover in black-and-white. His hair is rock-and-roll like Elvis and his coat collar is turned up; a cigarette dangles from his mouth because, unlike Meursault, Camus did not have the will to quit. Dad puts down the book. Shell stares at the photograph the way she used to stare at the pictures of hockey players she'd clipped from sports pages and tucked under her pillow. Mike Bossy from the Islanders was her favourite.

"This MFA, though, it's worth the sacrifice. It'll really set my CV apart." Maybe he can get a teaching job with it. He bites into his half of the Danish. Hopefully he can stay in Toronto. "It feels like home now," says Dad. He chews, chews, and talks; his naked jawline, cheekbones, and snub of chin are those of a stranger. He still clicks his denture plate and pushes his glasses up his nose, but he is quicker and more wiry. Shell is sure she is bigger than Dad now, in width and in height. Because of that, she's not going to take her coat off until she's back home with Mum.

DAD POINTS AT the CN Tower. "What's the direction?"

"South?"

Then he points behind them.

"North."

Shell passes the test for east and west too.

They go west down Dundas, past the big art gallery and into Chinatown. Dad's fast, darting between Chinese people pulling wheelie carts or walking slow with hands clasped behind their backs. Shell, one or two steps behind, closes her throat against the smell of dried mushrooms and fermenting fruit. Dad's woven shoulder bag goes diagonally across his chest, just like Shell's. His bag is new too—a gift from a friend who went to Greece. It's the same kind fishermen there use.

It is past noon. Any chill of morning has burned away. Shell's sweating under her jacket and her feet are on fire. Ahead, Dad passes a bandana over his glistening face and shaven neck. He squints back at her; a toss of his head tells her to hurry.

They cross Spadina, dodging more Chinese people and U-turning cars, clanging red streetcars that Shell has yet to ride because Jonathan's place is on the subway line. When the smell of fish hits, they're in Kensington Market. She waits outside World Cheese because the reek inside is worse than on the street. There's Rasta guys on rickety bikes, bloody butchers out for a smoke, hippies with guitars on their backs, and Jewish men with black coats and beards sort of like the Mennonites. Best, though, is a pack of big meaty men and stick-thin women wearing leather boots and the same studded collars as their mottled dogs. Barb Nutt's son Soren is a punk too. He bleaches his mohawk and his girlfriend paints her face to look like old silent movies, and both go to the high school Shell will attend next year. But these Kensington Market punks are dirty and old and have no colour to them — their clothes and hair and faces are just grey. A few carry buckets of black water with squeegees for cleaning windows, like chimney sweeps in *Oliver Twist*.

The parkette is full of dog poo and beer cans and loitering punks, but Dad manages to find a clean, quiet bench. While Shell was watching the punks and gazing at the fronts of stores selling studded belts and old-fashioned ball gowns, Dad had shopped for lunch: Italian buns, sharp cheddar, almonds, halvah, and for a centrepiece these yellow patties from Jamaica filled with beef. Dad got the most mild ones. The patties are flaky and warm, the meat minced to a pulp — almost as good as a *börek*. Dad slices the cheese with a Swiss Army knife and gives them each a Beanery napkin. They eat with their fingers because Dad doesn't like to take the plastic forks the beef patties usually come with. The punks organize some kind of dog-wrestling contest.

Dad says not to look at them. "It's exactly what they want. That's why they dress like that."

"Like what?" Shell's army coat looks just like the ones that some of the skinny girls in ripped nylons and buckle boots have tossed down on the grass.

"Oh, come on, Shell."

They eat. Dad's finishing up his mango nectar—droplets hanging from his moustache.

"So Jonathan's always lighting a cigarette, putting it down. Go away, light another. Sometimes there would be five or six going. It was bound to happen."

"Is he okay?"

Yes, but he is in intensive care from smoke inhalation.

"Poor Jonathan." Shell says she'll send a card to the hospital but doesn't write down the name.

Dad was coming up from the subway station and saw the flashing lights across the park. He knew right away. Dad's books and clothes got burned or smoke-damaged.

"But nothing too valuable. Like, these jeans were okay." Pavel and some people at school gave him these new Toronto clothes.

Dad crosses his legs and folds his napkin. "Could be worse." He nods at a thin woman too old and wrinkled to be in a bikini top. Her belly button is tattooed with a bleeding yin-yang she might have done herself and the fringes on her shoulder bag nearly touch the ground. She is on tiptoes, salvaging pop bottles from a trash can.

Her withered breasts fall forward, zigzagged with pale stretch marks.

"Be thankful you have a place to lay your head," Dad says.

IT'S TOO HOT for this early in spring. Shell's pants are sticky at the waist, damp at the crotch, and the wetness of her armpits has soaked through to the thick material of her jacket. She follows Dad way down Queen Street past a park where more punks and dogs sit up on picnic tables. There's a diner Dad likes called Elvis, plus antique shops whose owners all know him by name, and second-hand bookstores they can stop in on the way back.

The gallery where Dad works organizing slides is called Data Darling. The only pictures up are two large paintings of soldiers with naked bums. An old, thin woman in a sleeveless black dress is sitting at a desk with a glass top, surrounded by oversized art books that Mum would probably love. She looks too old for her clothes, like the one in the bikini top at the park. Dad and Shell clomp across the glossy pine floor. The old woman takes off her tiny square spectacles. Her frizzy hair is bright Florida orange and about two dozen gold bangles extend from elbow to wrists. The style could be African — Maasai — like in Mum's anthropology textbooks.

The woman, Jackie, likes Shell's army jacket. But that can't be the truth. The camouflage is heavy with damp. Standing there in the cool of the bare white gallery that should smell only of the lilacs on Jackie's desk, Shell detects the sour odour of the East German soldier who wore the jacket before her as well as of the smoke lingering on Dad's jeans.

Down a narrow hall and beyond the toilet there is a beaded curtain concealing an overflowing file room. Dad and Shell sit at a tiny desk and sort through slides sent to Data Darling by people who want Jackie to exhibit their art. Dad writes each applicant's name on a plastic folder and hangs it in a metal cabinet. Most of the slides show paintings and photos combining nudity and war. Shell wishes she hadn't looked.

"Would you send your work here, Dad?" Shell glances up from the slide viewer.

Dad shakes his head. He pokes his finger in the direction of Jackie's crackled old voice coming from the front of the gallery. Then he leans over and whispers something about not being Jackie's cup of tea.

Jackie has an envelope for Dad. Oh, and a poster for Shell. It's a white square of cheap paper with lines and lines of upper-case sentences she can't stop reading. "'Abuse of power comes as no surprise,'" Shell whispers. It's the kind of poetry Shell wants to write.

"The artist is a woman." Jackie wriggles her arms so her bangles chime like on storybook records when you're supposed to turn the page. "Jenny Holzer. She's magnificent." Shell can hardly wait to show Mum and Barb Nutt the next time Barb comes over to proofread one of Mum's essays. Over coffee and bran muffins at the harvest table, they talk about women artists and writers and politicians. "Good for her," they are always saying.

"Abuse of power comes as no surprise." Shell thinks

about that all the way up Queen. By the time they get to Bathurst, she's concluded that Jenny Holzer is an existentialist like her and Camus.

Shell's swollen feet burst the glue holding her sneakers' canvas uppers to rubber bottoms. Stones and grit keep getting in; especially bad is the right. A million streetcars ding by as Dad leads Shell up past the shops and parks and punks they saw on the way down. The CN Tower creeps up alongside on their right, and then around the corner is the Greyhound station.

Stopped at a light, Shell asks Dad where they are going to stay tonight, and Dad just says, "What? Are you worried?"

"No," Shell lies.

Dad said that same thing to her and Mum and Kremski when they were late getting to Algonquin Park their last summer there, and they canoed into the park anyway instead of camping near the park ranger's cabin like Mum had practically begged. They'd been on the water for at least an hour when Dad whistled for them to stop. He lifted up his glasses and squinted at his map, comparing it with the needle of the compass strung around his neck. Shell was curled up among the packs and Thermos cooler, and she got to drag her fingertips in the water so long as she didn't cause a lean. Mum's hair was in pigtails. She was looking all around, her face straining to find a clearing in the dense tree-lined shores where they might pull over and pitch their tent. Kremski sighed a lot, asking Shell if there was time for a cigarette, and when she shrugged, he pulled out matches and a pouch of Drum. Loons were gliding along the horizon and the water was a deep navy blue beneath a rosy orange sky. The hollow rocking of the boat and the rich scent of Kremski's tobacco made Shell sleepy.

"Well, now where to?" Mum had said. "Can you at least tell us where you *think* you're going?"

They eat trail mix in front of Sam the Record Man before going inside. It's already seven. Dad says let's look here until eight.

It's good to be alone in the immensity of Sam's and with a sense of purpose. She heads for Rock and fills her arms with so many tapes she might not have enough money to pay for them. There's tapes by people she knows, like Patti Smith and The Clash, as well as one she chose based on the cover—Talking Heads' *Speaking in Tongues*—and also she's got a tape called *Bad Moon Rising*. It was playing over the stereo and she heard the guy at the counter tell someone else he could find it under *S* for Sonic Youth. Shell followed the guy over and got one too. She had fallen in love with its wrenching, low-strung mood.

Shell's looking through Blues LPs now. Dad's nearby in Jazz. She's lost within the rhythm of people flipping through the tapes and records, as lost as Mum when she's typing an art history paper on the old Smith-Corona.

L is for Lead Belly. Dad used to sing her those songs, "Goodnight Irene" and "Take This Hammer," but now the record's gone from the shelf in the living room at home. A man comes up and starts to flip through Lightnin' Hopkins, so Shell moves over. He says, "Oh, pardon." He has an accent. With a sharp, trim beard and an overcoat with the cuffs rolled up to the elbow, he inches closer. Then, very quickly—like a mosquito in the ear—he says he's a photographer. Would Shell like to come with him to have her picture taken?

Shell dreams that Camus might have done this too: seen something special in her that no one else can. Shell is sure it is in her, deep down. Like kids with big teacup ears or when the teacher wrote on Shell's *A Clockwork Orange* book report that she had so much "potential"—she just has to grow into that something she's got.

"Me?" Shell says.

The man nods, running his thin fingers up and down the LPs. Somehow his accent makes it okay that he does not smile.

"I live in a hotel nearby," he says. "Could be quick."

"Okay. Hold on." Shell grabs her tapes. "I just gotta ask my dad."

Shell squints. Five or so rows over, Dad's got his notebook out, discussing something with a clerk.

"Hey Dad!"

Dad looks up, frowning. "What?" he mouths.

Shell waves then turns around to speak to the photographer who is now, so suddenly, gone.

IT'S ALMOST NINE when they get back to the Greyhound station. Dad took forever getting the clerk to find the Miles Davis recording from Massey Hall that Dad himself had attended. A block down from Sam's they passed a store whose front was hung with T-shirts for Bob Marley,

Mötley Crüe, hammers and sickles, and marijuana leaves, all of which were grey with the pollution of Yonge Street. There was a Ramones T-shirt too, so Shell went inside and bought it. Dad asked the Pakistani woman behind the counter if she had any shirts like his. He opened his jacket and explained the meaning of "nuclear sanity" while Shell, beside him, looked at buttons with ugly expressions on them about boobs and butts and farts and smelling like fish but tasting like chicken.

The bus locker smells of the basement back home and, more than that, of Mum and Dad and Kremski and Algonquin Park. Dad won't let Shell carry the camp pack. He says they'll get on the subway now and go have some supper. They share the last Italian bun and a slice of cheese before going out to the street.

"What'll we eat, Dad?"

They're on the Yonge line going north.

Bengali. Dad knows this great little hole in the wall up near campus. "I've not been there myself, but people leave leftovers in the studio fridge and those're quite nice."

They make two transfers: to the westbound Bloor line and then at Keele they get a bus that trundles north. Dad reads the *Toronto Star* that was on his seat and Shell looks at her tapes. After a bit, Dad starts looking out the dark windows for something that the driver says they've already gone past. They get out at the next light and Shell follows Dad south down Keele, then turn onto another street which, like Keele, is more of a highway. But it's a highway loaded on both sides with strip malls full of Jamaican, Korean, and Indian restaurants and grocery stores, and also there should be a certain Bengali hole in the wall, the name of which Dad doesn't know.

"You mean Bangladeshi?" Shell calls out when they pass a place with that in its name.

Dad keeps going, the camp pack strapped to his back.

"How about Sri Lankan?" Shell says, squinting.

"I was sure it was Bengali," Dad calls over his shoulder. The traffic whizzes past, white lights blinding whenever Shell tries to find the eyes of drivers.

Dad finally stops out front of a South Indian place called House of Fire.

"This must be it," he says, looking around at the landscape of signs written in languages from everywhere in the world that's had a war or flood or famine recent enough Shell knows about it.

"Are you sure, Dad, it's not an omen?"

"Omen?" Dad opens the door. *House of Fire* is written in gold on the frosted glass.

"Well, like with Jonathan."

He hesitates for a second. Then he ducks through a bamboo curtain. Shell's being silly. "There's no such thing as omens."

As Shell passes into House of Fire, she has to admit Camus would probably agree with Dad.

The place is empty. But there is cheerful clangy-type music and a spicy onion smell, so they stay. A tall waiter, very brown and in shirt and tie, welcomes them to sit where they wish. There are thick menus on the table, from which Dad orders chicken *biryani*, potato *dosa*, tomato *rasam* soup, and *banji banji* crispy snack. The waiter goes away and they don't see him again for about an hour, it seems. The kitchen is the source of much laughter and music but not, Dad says, of food. Dad drums his fingers and scrounges in his fisherman bag for stray morsels of trail mix. Then the waiter comes with the water they asked for, half of which he spills. His eyes are red and droopy, his shirt unbuttoned and tie loosened; even Shell knows the man is drunk.

Another waiter, also hazy-looking and unsure of his footing, brings their food. It comes all at once. Shell's mouth burns at the first bite and right away Dad starts to sweat. Though they agree the food has a lot of heat, they are hungry and continue to eat, engaging forks, thumbs, few words, and lots of napkins. Dad takes off his glasses because they keep sliding way down his nose. He has his jacket off too, and his napkin is a damp ball by his plate.

"Wow," he keeps saying as he wipes his head and chews.

They're out of water and the waiters are in the kitchen, where the party is really going now. Shell fills their glasses in the basement bathroom. There are cases of Coke and Sprite and some bottles of Indian malt under the stairs, and if she had her shoulder bag with her she might just snatch something. Dad chugs his water and sends Shell for more. His T-shirt is drenched, but he keeps eating, shaking his head.

When the *dosa* and *biryani* are gone, Dad purses his red lips and lets go with one of those sharp whistles that would always bring Shell back home from playing, in time for bed. There is silence. The cook comes out, his shirt unbuttoned to the belly button. He wipes Dad's moist face with the greasy towel he has slung over his shoulder and laughs in his own language. Then he leaves Dad with some candied fennel seeds and a bill badly miscalculated in Dad's favour. Shell says, "Right on," but Dad takes out the envelope Jackie gave him and pays what he thinks the full amount should be—but doesn't leave a tip.

They have to catch another bus. On the way to the stop they pass a Chinese bakery, where Dad buys hot lotus balls. There's a Tim Hortons across from the stop. Dad takes the Thermos from the camp pack and runs across the road. A bus goes by while he's gone, so they wait fifteen minutes for another, watching the cars, the cars, the cars. The air is chill with damp. Shell pulls her jacket around her, crosses her arms over her chest to keep her warmth to herself.

Dad's standing rigid against the bus shelter, the camp pack at his feet. His watch says eleven. They get on the bus and Dad promises that after a few more stops they can go to bed.

"What's the next stop?"

"Campus."

Shell yawns. Dad yawns. The black man beside them yawns, then the turbaned man beside him yawns, and the Chinese girl standing up with a big suitcase yawns, and then Dad pulls the bell and he and Shell get off the bus.

A sharp wind greets them as they step out onto the student commons, a roundabout where a lineup of empty, brightly lit buses wait for no one, really, to come. There are few shadows. Mostly the campus is as empty as House of Fire; and like House of Fire, there is the distant noise of music and laughter.

Dad brought Shell to his campus studio the first time she came to Toronto. The ceilings of the second-floor fine art wing where Dad's cohort are assigned their own small work spaces are just as high as she remembers. The smell is the same too—Varsol, acrylic paint, warm wood chips, fresh-ground dust, and coffee. Fluorescent lights hum overhead and somewhere a rattling boiler keeps the air warm if not hot. The walls are painted a flat gesso white so every scuff and bit of graffiti, poster, splash of spilt paint, or jotted phone number stands out.

Dad leads Shell down a wide, empty corridor. Each studio is self-contained with its own door, but the high walls don't reach the ceiling, such that someone with a ten-foot ladder could climb up and, leaning over, look right in.

They stop in the communal kitchen, where Dad scrounges for a couple of clean cups and plates. Dad forgot to get Shell milk at Tim Hortons, so he helps himself to what's in the fridge, ignoring several notes saying not to.

"I'll replace it tomorrow. He never comes in on Sunday," Dad says of Ken Carroll, whose name is marked on the carton.

Dad's studio is full of wood. He says his thesis project is going to be fully three-dimensional and mobile, not painted flat and lifeless on canvas as he'd been doing all those years before. Along with a drill and saw and several sizes of chisel, Dad's got coffee cups, maps, notebooks, pens, pencils, and cassette tapes strewn about. Dad pulls up a stool for Shell and they both sit at his work table, drinking coffee and milk, slurping the sweet, mealy paste out of the lotus balls.

"That food was really hot," Dad says. "*Gad*. I can still feel it in the back of my throat."

Dad has Shell help him move the work table away from the wall. Then Dad pulls away some leaning sheets of plywood, behind which a neat circle has been cut in the drywall—about four feet in circumference, near to the floor. The circle becomes a hole when Dad pulls along the bottom and, as if removing a manhole cover, lifts out the drywall.

"Look. It's hollow inside."

The wall dividing Dad's studio from the one beside it is indeed empty, top to bottom, the recess yielding about three feet of wiggle room. An air mattress and sleeping bag occupy the floor inside, plus Dad's Braun alarm clock, a few charred books, a flashlight, and a pair of scorched leather slippers.

"Plenty of room, Shell," Dad says. He's blowing up the narrow air mattress Shell brought from home; the sleeping bag's already unrolled.

"Quiet, warm, and free," Dad goes on. "But don't tell your mother or anyone else, otherwise my goose is cooked. Okay?"

In the washroom down the hall, Shell takes off her jacket, letting her skin breathe. She ducks into a stall to change into her flannel nightgown but then puts the jacket back overtop for a robe. The water she splashes on her face and neck is cold. She dries with brown paper towel then brushes her teeth with no paste because she thought she'd just use Dad's or Jonathan's.

In Czech sneakers, East German army coat, flannel

nightgown, and giant glasses, Shell hurries back to Dad's studio—the only one with light coming out the top and from under the door. Dad's wearing a pair of donated pyjamas—he hates plaid—and drinking the rest of his coffee.

"Ready, Shell? You go first."

Shell peels the Cellophane from her new tapes. She takes these, plus Camus with the Jenny poster and the Ramones T-shirt, into the hole in the wall. She wriggles into her sleeping bag, elbows banging into the drywall on either side, and, sitting up, takes off her jacket.

Dad leaves his glasses and denture plate on the work table and climbs in too. While Shell holds the flashlight, Dad lifts the circle of drywall back into place, sealing them up until morning, when Dad says they'll go back downtown and have *huevos rancheros*. Then they'll go to a photography show for one of Dad's friends and hit Little Italy for a late lunch before Shell catches her bus. If security comes, Shell's to hush. They make the rounds about one and again at three o'clock.

"Just a formality," he says.

Dad and Shell lay foot to foot in their sleeping bags. Shadows flicker in the skylight above. Dad snores before long, his arms crossed over his chest like always. Shell stays up with the flashlight, reading Camus and memorizing the lyric sheets from her tapes. A door creaks open down the hall. Shell switches out the light then holds tight to her breath—one, two, three—letting go only when the heavy, deliberate footsteps of the security guards are gone and she and Dad are home free.

MUM'S WAITING IN the very same spot on the platform. How quiet the house must be when Shell goes to Toronto. Does Mum think she hears burglars like Shell does when Mum is working late? She doesn't want Dad to feel lonely either, but she also hopes that he is thinking about Shell and missing her too.

Shell's army coat smells of sawdust now. She has only her shoulder bag, no luggage underneath. Mum smiles but waits for Shell to reach for a hug before pulling her in. Mum's leaner now that she's been reading *Diet for a Small Planet* and going with Barb Nutt to tai chi.

"Did you have supper?" Mum asks in the car. The Greyhound lot is crowded. Mum gets honked at trying to back up.

"Gnocchi," Shell says. "You know what that is?"

Mum sighs. "Yes."

Sunday evening in Somerset passes by the Dart windows: mums and dads pushing strollers, joggers with silky dogs, people struggling into sweatshirts as the sun disappears. The group of jelly-shoe girls lighting cigarettes in front of the doughnut shop used to go to Shell's school but are at Somerset Central Tech now.

Mum and Shell don't say anything. Shell's trip to Toronto never happened. Shell doesn't say she wants to move to Toronto just like Dad, that Dad's thesis project is so smart and great, or how *huevos rancheros* is her new favourite breakfast and something you'd never get in boring old Somerset. Shell doesn't show Mum her Ramones T-shirt, her new tapes, the poster from Jackie either.

Mum's typewriter is clattering upstairs. When the

fullness of the gnocchi wears off, Shell grills a cheese sandwich and finishes Camus, ketchup dripping on the pages she has worn thin with thinking and fingerprints and a few salt tears. Shell goes down to the basement without saying good night. By the light of the stars barely falling in the basement windows, Shell rereads the last page of *The Outsider*. Then, like Meursault, she opens her heart to those basement stars, and what for Meursault is "the benign indifference of the universe." Shell finds that, like Meursault, despite all her sadness, she is happy and has been happy all along.

She Will Make Music
Wherever She Goes

Shell reaches for another of Mum's Women's Studies flash cards then crams a digestive in her mouth.

"Patriarchy," she says, reading Mum's neat printing on the back of the card.

They are down to the twenty-five definitions sure to be on Mum's summer school exam next week.

Mum closes her eyes and whispers, "Patriarchy. Patriarchy...A societal organization where men are taken as naturally having power and authority over women, property etc., and females are subordinate and men are always favoured."

"Yup. Pretty much." Shell reaches for another card. "Okay. How about *gynocriticism?*"

Fiddling with the crumbs gathered in the grooves

of her placemat, Mum begins: "Gynocriticism...what the hell..." She looks up at the ceiling. "That's the, um, study of books by women about women and the history of those books and writers as a tradition."

"Good." Shell passes Mum the cookies.

"See you got something in the mail?" Mum asks, nodding at the silver envelope propped against the pepper mill upon which Shell's and Mum's names are written out in someone's neatest cursive.

Shell licks dark stickiness from her fingers. Inside the thick envelope, the embossed wedding invitation is also silver. Written out in fancy calligraphy — so curly it has a perm — are the names of Vicki's mum and her mum's boyfriend, Scott: first, last, middle. Their wedding, to which Mum and Shell are cordially invited, will take place on the *twentieth of June, nineteen hundred and eighty-five at one p.m.* at the Good Shepherd Chapel located at *five thousand eight hundred and thirty-three Euston Avenue North.*

Shell slides the card across to Mum.

There's no map or directions — that far north on Euston seems a hell of a long way out — and "June! That's only three weeks."

Mum gets up for the calendar, brushing crumbs from her shirt.

"Don't bother," says Shell. "I'm not going."

Mum frowns. "But Vicki's your friend."

"No." Shell looks up. "She was a dumb little girl who lived down the street. Besides, I'm in high school now and she's still in grade eight."

"So?" Mum reminds Shell that Barb Nutt is younger than Mum and it makes no difference.

"Well, when's the last time Vicki called me?" Shell wants to know.

"When's the last time you called her?"

"That's because all she talks about is satellite MTV crap. And what the hell would I wear?"

"Not that coat, for starters." Mum sits down and opens *The Politics of Reality: Essays in Feminist Theory.* "Or those revolting jeans."

It's been eight weeks since Shell washed the men's Levi's she wears every day to school. It's like with her hair — now a month without shampoo: after a time the fabric will stop being oily and itchy and just sort of clean itself.

Whatever Mum just copied from textbook to loose-leaf gets underlined about five times.

"So do you think her mum will be thin now?" she says. It's been a while since Vicki's mum had her stomach stapled. Three years already?

"We won't ever know, because of course we're not going."

"Well, then, you call Vicki's mum and tell her that."

Shell shuffles through the flash cards. "What's next — 'Other,' Oedipal complex, or, your favourite, male gaze?"

"Oedipal," says Mum.

APART FROM CREAKY wooden floors and squeaky scissors and the expert ripping of fabric — *zip!* — right along the grain, Adelard Textiles is quiet. Mum licks the tip of her index finger and flips through thick plasticized pattern books from Butterick, Simplicity, McCall's, and Vogue, pointing out high-waisted princess gowns, tunics with wide-legged trousers, and A-line jumpers.

Shell shakes her head. She pulls a photocopy from her pocket. "Like this. Like Patti Smith." Shell smooths out the inky black-and-white image in which Patti Smith prances barefoot across an empty studio loft in what just has to be New York City. Rayed light falls through floor-to-ceiling windows, catching her from behind — an aura. Her overalls are of something black and very flowy that Mum says must be silk, and she's not wearing a shirt underneath. Wide straps with big silver buckles hold up the bib, her chest caving in beneath. Arms, pale and so thin, twist upward towards a beam of light, her long fingers catching tendrils of her own messy hair.

Mum's in a hurry. Her exam is at six. She flags down a lady in an Adelard smock and homemade blouse. Is there a pattern that looks anything like Shell's photocopy?

"Let's see." The lady's name tag reads *Gladys*. Long, unpolished nails filed into triangles pluck at Patti Smith. "Well, that's a different look, isn't it?"

At the opposite end of the pattern table, Gladys pulls out a *McCall's*, and with a wave of her triangles flips to the overalls, a subsection of uniforms.

They settle on #9203. The overalls have a chunky zipper down the front and long sleeves, which means Shell doesn't have to bother getting a blouse to go underneath. Gladys says to use crepe instead of the heavy cotton suggested in the book.

"It will achieve a similar look" — she points to Patti

Smith—"but, I warn you, it's not very breathable."

There's a table of crepes beyond the craft fabrics. Mum thinks the sky blue is nice and will go with Shell's eyes, eyes which Shell then rolls. As everything else is pastel or patterned—tiny flowers, polka dots, sailboats—Shell grabs a bolt of bright grape. Mum says the price is right at $1.99 a yard.

"You're sure?"

Shell nods.

The cutting tables are at the back. The warm, unwashed air is clouded with fine fibrous particles and glue from spray-on sizing. A team of smocked ladies with sharp, tooled fingernails like Gladys's measures out lengths of fabric against the yardsticks embedded right in the tabletops. Rather than actually snipping, they just give the fabric an initial clip, put down their scissors, and rip it, perfectly straight, down the grain.

Gladys and her co-workers agree Shell's purple is quite stunning. It is also a good value as it's been sitting around since the Somerset Snow Owls hockey team switched their colours to emerald, and that was some three or four years ago. Shell doesn't know her size, so she has to take off her army jacket while Gladys embraces her with a measuring tape, announcing for all of Adelard the size of Shell's hips, waist, bust, and thighs. Maybe Gladys can't smell Shell's armpits or her stale jeans or see the ice cream spilled down the front of her oversized Shell Oil T-shirt, but Mum can, because she looks away. Gladys cuts three yards of grape crepe and wishes Mum happy sewing.

"Promise you'll eat something proper for dinner."

Mum unlocks the Dart's passenger door because the driver's side doesn't open anymore. "There's spaghetti sauce thawed out."

The muffler chokes and growls as Mum pulls away. Shell leans up against the rough brick wall behind Adelard. In the crumpled photocopy in her hand, Patti Smith's sooty eyes look right through the camera and into Shell's soul, telling her to be brave, to be free of the chains of conformity and stop worrying all the time about what other people think. And standing there behind the fabric store watching Mum drive away, Shell shrinks up. Because she should have her own ideas about dressing and not just steal Patti's. She's doing what Patti never would: being a copycat, not thinking for herself.

The Dart has stopped at a light up ahead. Shell wants to run up through the intersection, grab the Adelard bag out of the back, and, though the cashier stamped the bill No Refund, make her take back all that purple crepe. She's never going to look like Patti Smith and it's not brave of her to even want to, and Mum spent all that money and Shell wants out of this wedding and to forget about the overalls and she's tired of the effort of being her, Shell. Make it stop, even just for a minute —

"Mum!"

But now the light changes and the Dart trundles off and it is too late.

MUM'S GUNNING FOR an "A" in Women's Studies while cooking full time at Memory Lane, so it takes forever to finish the overalls. Plus, when Shell finally tries them on for size, she closes her eyes and won't look at her big fat purple reflection in the hall mirror.

"Who cares, Mum? Just make them fit."

It was the same with the eyeglasses. She wouldn't look in the mirror, so the optician picked them out and now she's stuck with giant pink frames for another year until OHIP chips in for a new prescription.

"They'll be very comfortable," Mum says of the overalls, pinning up the pant cuffs. It's the night before the *twentieth of June, nineteen hundred and eighty-five.* "And if you want them to look slightly more tailored, just cinch the waist with a belt. You can borrow one of mine."

Shell is already borrowing plenty from Mum: pointy black flats Mum bought for some event twenty years ago that might have been her and Dad's wedding; saggy beaded handbag and black crocheted gloves; and a selection of silver jewellery, including eleven Navajo bangles, her turquoise ring from California, and the long silver earrings with ivory balls on the ends that her art school roommate made. Maybe with all the jewels and stuff no one will see the overalls.

"Come on, Shell, have a look."

The purple crepe is brighter now that Mum has washed away the sizing and dust. It swathes Shell's entire body, head and hands and feet excepted. The purple blob in the mirror looks a lot like that cartoon, Barbapapa. *Clickety-click: Barba Trick.* Or is it Mr. Grumpy she's thinking of? Shell closes her eyes and turns away.

"That's not too long? You don't want them dragging."

"And I don't want to look like I'm from Bangladesh either."

Mum's brows cross, pins clamped between her lips.

"Floods," Shell says. "You know?"

"How're the shoes?"

"Too big." Shell will stuff the toes with toilet paper.

Downstairs, the sewing machine whirs full blast. Shell falls asleep with the light on, Mum's brittle copy of *On the Road* open on her chest.

SHELL COMES DOWN from her room, dripping with accessories.

Mum starts clapping two fingers against a cupped palm, singing what was once Shell's nursery rhyme:

Ride a cock-horse to Banbury Cross,
To see a fine lady upon a white horse,
Rings on her fingers and bells on her toes,
And she will make music wherever she goes.

"Mum, please shut up," Shell snaps. Mum's knee had made the best horse and until now she had thought nothing of the "cock" part.

"Don't you dare speak to me like that." Mum fixes her nylons. "Where's the present?"

"I dunno." Shell looks away as she passes the hall mirror. "I thought you were going to wrap it."

"Jesus Murphy." Mum kicks off her clogs, polished to gleaming, and heads upstairs for the wrapping paper. "Now we're late."

Shell signs the card while Mum conceals a set of heavy ceramic wine goblets that Dad made in white tissue and ties the bundle with silver ribbon.

Hurrying down the porch steps, Mum trips on the hem of her long, embroidered Mexican dress, which she got by sewing curtains for the owner of Siddhartha, the ethnic store downtown. The air is thick with humidity. Mum gropes for her prescription sunglasses—big black goggles like those for welders or blind men—and unlocks Shell's door. The black vinyl seats inside the Dodge Dart are soft with heat. Mum raps on the driver's window— her door is broken—and Shell leans over and lifts the button, recoiling from the burning seat.

"Shit, it's an oven in here." Mum unrolls her window. Does Shell have the map and the wedding invitation? "The last thing we need is to get lost."

"Let's just get this over with," Shell says, looking away from her reflection in the side mirror. "Please"—a whisper now—"make this day end."

SHELL PAINTS HER mouth Rojo red. The mirror clipped to the pull-down visor is rusty at the edges.

"Shell, will you get your glasses on and help me look for that goddamn chapel?"

Shell has never been this far north on Euston. The speed limit climbs to seventy kilometres per hour and the lanes go from four wide to six. Truck traffic is heavy with freight heading south to the border, and also there's plenty of rough-hewn pickups zipping up and down between the Build-All centre, Zellers, and the outlying farms that aren't really farms anymore so much as feral fields used for breeding puppies and hosting auto swaps. The Canada Post sorting depot is out this way too — coming up on the left.

"What the hell is the address?" Mum slows to grab hold of the street numbers flying past. A pickup with three heads in the cab tailgates behind.

"Five thousand eight hundred and thirty-three." Shell smooths damp red over her top lip.

As the Dart drifts over into the next lane, the pickup, now creeping up alongside, honks. Mum jerks the car back into its lane, and Shell gives herself a full-on Rojo moustache.

"Look, Shell, please!" Mum shouts above the bluster of wind resistance and the whir of engines.

"Oh, all right!" Shell screams. Then she goes on screaming. It feels really good — so, so, so good that she can't stop — "all right, all right, all right!"

"Stop it!" Mum grabs Shell's arm and pulls, hard, her nails digging into flesh.

"Ow!" Shell's throat is ripped up from screaming. Her eyes tear. The pickup is within spitting distance now. Three guys in sunglasses shout through a lowered window that they're crazy bitches.

"Assholes!" Shell screams back as Mum changes lanes.

Mum slows, pulling the Dart into the empty parking lot of a small-appliance repair centre — *blenders, microwaves, hair dryers, and more!* Her head falls forward onto the steering wheel and then she wipes her face with a Kleenex.

"So where's this bloody Good Shepherd?" Mum says. "I mean, am I crazy?"

She wrenches her head around, wiping sweat from her upper lip. Between here and the T-intersection about a quarter kilometre ahead that marks the end of Euston, there's no sign of a chapel or church. The only thing is a pristine green lawn ahead. It is edged in trees and bright pink petunia beds and it's on the odd side of the road, like Good Shepherd should be.

"What's that?"

Mum says no, "It's the SPH."

"Somerset Psychiatric Hospital? Really?"

Mum looks at her watch: twelve-fifty.

Shell's back is wet, so are her pits, and her Rojo lips are melting.

As they pass the Somerset Psychiatric Hospital, Shell strains to see the street number. The lush lawn that flashes by twinkles with sprays of irrigated water while the driveway up the hill to a looming grey concrete edifice is lined with flowering trees and a bright patchwork of red and white bedding plants. But the SPH's sign itself is set back from the road, concealed by fronds of Japanese maples.

Mum turns left at the T. They curve back around, heading south. The Dart rattles, straining to keep up with the seventy-kilometre-per-hour limit.

"Look, look, look." Mum squints into the sun despite her goggles.

The cashiers at Zellers don't know where five thousand eight hundred and thirty-three Euston Avenue North is, but the guy selling hot dogs out front says to ask at the SPH.

"You think that's okay?" Mum says. "I mean, to drive up there?"

The man, chest hair showing through his damp white T-shirt, shrugs and reaches his bare hand into a giant jar of sliced olives.

"Why not?"

THIS IS CRAZY, Mum says, turning in at the green lawn and bright petunias.

Maximum twenty. The Dart crawls up the sloping hill towards the main building. The lot is full of cars, but Mum finds a shady space near a set of sliding doors marked Receiving.

And they are received. The heat barrier breaks as they step inside. All is silence and cool, and the smell of hand soap permeates. Leaning against one of a cluster of puffy leather couches, they allow the air conditioning to solidify their melting bodies and cool their fizzy brains. Mum struggles to find her regular glasses in her purse, while Shell peels damp crepe from the backs of her legs.

The receptionist looks extra brown in her snow-white uniform. She's got a fragile gold crucifix around her neck, which seems weird because she must be from India. She takes the invitation card from Mum and smiles, showing off how well her teeth match her uniform.

"We've been up and down and up and down," Mum says. "I mean, what the hell?"

The nurse glances at the card and passes it back. With a few graceful hand gestures, she says they can follow the lane back around to the rear of the main building then proceed down the hill; at the copse of lilac trees, turn right.

"Good Shepherd Chapel will be straight ahead."

Mum looks down at the damp invitation.

"But you better hurry." The nurse smiles and holds up her gold watch, also delicate. "You're already a touch late."

GOOD SHEPHERD CHAPEL is surrounded by flowering lilacs; a decorative bridge arcs over a narrow stream twinkling behind.

"Maybe Scott's a patient here," Shell says as the Dart noses down a steep, twisting descent.

Mum is hunched up over the wheel so it grazes her stiff chin. "I bet this place offers very good rates. They were smart to have it here."

Two guys with feathered blond hair and baggy tuxedos preside over a gravel parking lot crammed full of pickups, motorcycles, and a few hot rods. They flag down the Dart.

"Lot's full," they say. "Gotta go back up to visitors' parking."

"Shit," Mum says again and again. "We just came from there."

She cranks the wheel— "Shell, you help me"—looking from mirror to mirror, squeezing the Dart's boxy girth back up the lane. The tuxedos, hands in their pockets, watch the operation while Shell—face flushed—leans out her window and calls out: "A little to the left,

189

easy, easy. Nope. Stop. Now to the right." Mum's doing okay—at the fourth point of what's going to be an eight-point turn—but then a long white limo comes twisting down the hill behind them. The limo's front grille is laden with flowers, streamers cascade from the antennas, and the radio is pumping something a little too loud.

"Gosh, is that Vicki's mum?"

"Shit!" Mum says, shifting the gear lever from forward to reverse.

The tuxedos forget Mum and Shell and the rusty Dart, so Mum just reverses really hard and—with a couple of grinds and scrapes to the undercoating—pulls up on the lawn beside the chapel, cutting deep furrows into the grass. Mum grabs her purse and pushes Shell out the passenger side, practically climbing over her to get into the chapel before the limo doors open and they're officially late.

"HOW DID ALL these people not get lost?" Mum says loud enough that people sitting on the aisle turn around.

Mum and Shell take the last two seats, right near the front. There are plenty of long-hair guys in the pews, and over there is that one with the bum-chin and lion's mane perm who drove to the beach once with Shell and Vicki and Vicki's mum. All day he kept singing "Everybody Working for the Weekend" and another about going for a soda. Shell came home so sunburned her shoulders turned purple and Mum almost called Vicki's mum, but Shell, crying, begged her not to: "No, she already thinks

190

we're weird." Mum just drove to the co-op store for raw aloe instead.

White lilies and red roses frame the doors and windows of the chapel. Light, tinkly music leaks from the speakers at the front, where some guy in a suit is fiddling with the sound system. Shell starts telling Mum this is her very first wedding, did she know that? But Mum, she's groping in her purse and muttering, "Shit."

"What?"

Mum's sunglasses blank out half her face.

"Where's your real glasses?"

Mum looks around. "Do I still have time to run out to the car?"

Cut the tinkly music. A hush falls over the chapel. A woman Mum's age wearing a white and gold tunic comes out of a shiny oak door behind one of the speakers and steps up to the podium. Shell finds her glasses in the pocket of her overalls just as Mum finally stops rummaging for her own. Mum leans over and whispers that the woman up there is the minister.

"Good for her." She nods. "We need more strong women like that."

Silence, complete and utter, is broken only by an involuntary dry rasp. The minister lifts her arms like an orchestra conductor. Everyone stands. Behind them, the tuxedos from the parking lot step through the flowered archway. Then a guy with a red rose in his lapel. Scott's dark hair is parted down the middle and tied back in a ponytail. The three come up the aisle. Then Vicki appears. She's taller now and slim, her hair redder than before and her skin more freckled. Her long silver dress is cut straight and narrow; a cropped jacket of matching silver covers her otherwise bare arms and shoulders. The red roses she clutches are just like the ones stuck in her upswept hair. Shell shrinks up in her overalls. Even if she stopped eating grilled cheeses before bed and washed her hair more, Shell would never look like Vicki does now — a soft, creamy girl a boy would want to touch and have a picture of in his locker.

Vicki's dress rustles as she takes a few tiny tightrope-type steps forward. Then a "click" comes over the sound system, followed by the tempered, raspy notes of a drum machine. The electric guitar sounds like it's from India. Then keyboard plucks — also one-two slow — join in. Vicki's mum enters the archway next. She is still chunky and plump. Maybe her stomach staples gave out, like the spine of a book read too many times. Her sleeveless white dress shows off her freckled shoulders, and the smooth humps of cleavage are squeezed into her bustier. Her bouquet matches Vicki's; and like Vicki, her red hair is swept up and pinned high on her head. The music gets louder as Vicki and her mum — arms linked — head up the aisle. Then a chorus of backup singers on the stereo startles everyone with a shout — "Hey" — repeated a few times before Tom Petty's whiny mono-voice cuts in, layering with the wispy drums and Indian-from-India guitar. They can't stop playing "Don't Come Around Here No More" on MuchMusic or CJYG. Even in Shell's English class, Miss Jabara discussed the video's *Alice in Wonderland* references.

Vicki's mum's face is exploding in smile. The music

slowly unfolds, keyboards and drums coalescing, up, up, up, picking up the pace and sounding more rock and roll than what they play at the Siddhartha store.

At the altar, Scott is grabbing his head like the Snow Owls just scored big, and as Vicki and her mum are getting closer, Shell sees Vicki's got a really big zit on her nose. Her eyes, seeing Shell, fill with juicy tears; behind her scratched lenses, so do Shell's.

"Don't Come Around Here No More" booms for Shell alone. She wants to be in the backyard with Vicki and Timmy—putting on dried-out lipstick and tracing pictures on each other's backs.

Mum leans over. "Is this really Bob Dylan?" she asks as Tom Petty says again and again for someone not to come around here no more, whatever she's looking for.

With her dark sunglasses on and rusty old Dart hulked on the chapel lawn, it's Mum who looks like she knows something about rock and roll—more than Shell in her purple jumpsuit, baggier than the coveralls Dad used to wear to sweep the studio.

"Tom Petty and the Heartbreakers."

Mum frowns.

The song bursts open: the guitar becomes more rock, drums roll, backups get shrill and Tom Petty's voice frantic.

Right when the music cuts and it's silent enough to hear the palming of Kleenex, a dark-haired woman clomps in. She gives a thumbs-up to those—practically everyone—who turn to look. Even without the heeled booties, she'd be taller than every man or woman in Good

Shepherd. She's at least as old as Vicki's mum. Her red silk blouse is tucked into a short leather skirt and a fringed leather purse dangles from a solid shoulder. And with her hair cut shaggy, sooty raccoon eyes, skinny legs in a wide-legged stance, she might as well be Joan Jett. Or, no, she *is* Joan Jett. She stands at the back during the ceremony — Shell turns to look — and then at the end, when everyone stands up, she leads the hooting and whistling.

Out on the lawn, Joan Jett leans up against the Dart and lights a cigarette.

Shell says, "Excuse me," and Joan Jett — "Oh, sure" — moves away from the car, her blackened eyes following the handfuls of rice skimming high in the air and landing on Vicki's laughing mum.

Mum and Shell wait until the parking lot is empty of tooting cars. Then Mum backs off the lawn and drives slowly up the hill and back down Euston Avenue.

THE BANQUET HALL of the Candlestick Inn is air-conditioned. It is also dark, apart from strobe lights, and smells of meatballs and chlorine. There's a DJ and lots of requests for Led Zeppelin but no sit-down dinner as Mum had thought. Shell heads for the food tables. She promised Mum to stay for at least two hours and try to have fun. Then she'll call from the pay phone in the lobby and, though the inn is way out in Railton, Mum will take a study break and drive out to get her.

Metal stacking chairs line the periphery of the room, opening up the floor so that just about everyone but Shell can dance. Instead of dancing, Shell fills her plate with toothpicked meatballs, ham and cheddar roll-ups, celery sticks, and Ruffles, and finds a corner near the speakers where it's loud enough no one is going to join her. Hunching over her lap, Shell empties her plate and goes for another. This time it's triangles of tuna sandwich, Ritz topped with cheddar, a scoop of potato salad, and a brownie. Across the dance floor, Vicki is talking to some teenage guy with his hair gelled into spikes. His skinny tie is made of leather and the tongues of his high-top basketball shoes are hanging out. Vicki pulls out a compact mirror and the guy holds on to her bouquet while she powders her zit.

When Shell goes for thirds—carrot sticks and ranch dip, a rum ball, and a cup of Sprite—the dance floor is throbbing and the speakers are so loud her bum quivers against the metal chair. Billy Idol's "Dancing with Myself" comes on. Just as Shell jams the rum ball into her mouth, Joan Jett marches into the banquet hall, lets out a war whoop, throws her cigarette into an abandoned cup of beer, and races onto the dance floor. While everyone forms a circle around her and goes "woo-woo," Joan kicks out her legs, her shaggy hair flying. Then she starts looking around at people, singing right to them. She grabs a guy in tux and ball cap to dance with her, but he pulls away. So does the next guy, and a lady after that.

Shell slouches forward, pretending to look for something in Mum's beaded purse. The clapping and singing get close, and then Shell is pulled out of her chair—"Hey, no, I can't do this!"—and she's dancing with Joan Jett in the middle of the banquet hall. Shell closes her eyes and channels the Patti Smith of her photocopy: tough and graceful at the same time. But really, her body's just jiggling—not dancing, jiggling—the purple crepe of her outfit clinging to her sweaty form and, despite its roominess, getting caught in her bum.

Something slow comes on. Joan Jett, panting, skin shiny, pats Shell on the head and teeters off towards the bar.

"GUESS HOW I got home after I dropped you off?"

Shell plugs her left ear so she can hear Mum through the pay phone.

"No." Shell gulps. "Can't guess."

"In a tow truck."

Out on the dance floor, wedding guests are hopping to "The Wild Boys." Alone in a corner, Joan Jett looms above the crowd, smoking another cigarette—a skyscraper swathed in her own blue cloud—and while everyone else has plastic cups, she's drinking beer right from the bottle.

The Dart, Mum says, overheated on Ealing, just after the Railton exit. A tow truck came by after thirty minutes of sitting in the middle of traffic. Mum's voice breaks up. She takes a breath. Only one of the emergency lights worked, so everyone was honking and swearing out their windows that it wasn't a turning lane.

"Okay, so I'll come home in a taxi."

"Shell, that will cost a small fortune." Besides, Mum spent all her money on the tow truck and has to cough up more when she goes back to the mechanic tomorrow.

"I don't have any money either, Mum." Now Joan Jett is bobbing her head and prowling the edge of the dance floor, waiting to swoop in. "Mum, please, I just want to come home."

After a heavy silence, Mum says, "It's that bloody old car. I just—it shouldn't even be on the road, Shell. It's dangerous to drive you around in it. I should have asked the guy to tow it right to the dump."

One, two, three plump tears run down Shell's hot cheeks.

"After all these years... and why am I still driving your dad's bloody horrible Dart—"

"It's not Dad's fault," Shell sputters through a spit bubble.

Mum breathes through her nose. "Can't you ask someone there for a ride? Put Vicki's mother on. Don't they live right nearby?"

Shell's words are filtered through gritted teeth. "Mum, everyone here is drunk. If I ask for a ride, I am going to get in an accident and die. You want that for me, Mum? Huh? You want me to die?"

Mum's going, "Oh, Shell, be reasonable," when Shell hangs up. Very properly and gently, the receiver—click—goes back onto the hook. Then, fists at her sides—like rocks, like hammers—Shell returns to the reception.

THE CAKE LINEUP is a mile long. People push up behind her, but Shell doesn't turn around. There's a tap on her shoulder. Shell shrinks away.

"Hi, Shell! My mum said she invited you." Vicki's with that gel boy and one of the tuxedos from the parking lot.

Shell smiles. The overalls coating her body feel acidic.

"Hey Vicki."

Gel boy drapes his arm around Vicki. Vicki says, "This is Ryan." Then she glances around. "Where's your mum? She here too?"

"She's out with her new boyfriend," Shell lies. "Some fancy dinner thing."

"Wow, that's great!" Vicki squeezes Shell's arm. "I miss you, Shell. And when I have a dream that's set in a house, it's always yours."

Shell smiles. "You look pretty, Vicki. So does your mum."

Vicki doesn't say anything about how Shell looks. She just asks a million questions: how's Shell's dad, who lives in Vicki's old house now, and isn't Shell in high school? "I can hardly wait."

"Yeah, it's fine," Shell says.

The line moves up. "Brown Eyed Girl" comes on and the dance floor starts to groove. Vicki says, "Oh, I just love this song. Shell, don't you?"

Vicki grabs Shell by the elbow and says when the next Duran Duran song comes on, they just have to get out there and dance.

"Okay?"

That's when Ryan leans over and, scuppering his own laugh, says: "Sorry to interrupt, ladies, but hey — uh, Shell — my friends and myself, we were talking, and we're wondering if you're a representative of McDonald's."

Shell can only blink. Around her the music starts melting, the room spins.

"Because, you know, your costume, which is great, really does look like Grimace."

"Who?" Shell swallows. She had thought it was Barbapapa.

"*Grimace,*" Gel boy repeats. "Ronald McDonald's sidekick?"

The tuxedo pipes up, shaking his blond hair. "Kind of fat and doesn't do anything but dance around and be purple."

"Especially when Idol's on."

Shell's stomach lurches. Ryan laughs and ducks away. Tuxedo realizes he should go too. The cake line shifts ahead of Shell, leaving her behind. She fights to keep her face from crumpling.

Vicki throws her arms around Shell. Vicki smells like the red bottle of perfume they always snuck squirts of until her mum hid it. "I'm so sorry, Shell!"

Shell hugs Vicki back. Her hair is chemical sweet like a beauty parlour and her body is small and thin but without being bony. Shell wishes she knew how to even start to be pretty. It must be all the cheese Shell eats.

"That asshole your boyfriend?" Shell says, and Vicki laughs.

"Ryan's not my boyfriend!" He's Scott's nephew, so that makes him Vicki's step-cousin. "Anyway, his sense of humour is kind of weird."

Shell lets go of Vicki.

"You better get some cake, Shell." Vicki ushers Shell

to the front of the line, the guests nodding and smiling as they butt ahead. Then Vicki steps away.

"You don't want any?" Shell asks, grabbing two Styrofoam plates with cubes of cake — white with about an inch of chocolate icing and a sprinkle of silver balls.

Vicki just clutches her handbag. "I am so happy you came, and don't mind Ryan, he didn't mean that about your purple suit."

Shell promises she won't leave without a goodbye hug. She sits on a folding chair and, as strobe lights sweep over her, eats both pieces of cake. When the cake is gone and the line is shorter, Shell goes back for more.

THE PICNIC TABLES out by the parking lot are damp with humidity, but it's better than sitting on concrete or the wet grass. And it is shadowed here. Traffic on the country highway cuts through the muffled boom and cry of the reception, and the crickets are many; must be a stream nearby. Shell wishes for a book. Her quilts and bed. The gleam of the Dart's headlights coming towards her through the dark, airless night.

With a whoosh, Joan Jett pushes out the Candlestick's front doors. She wobbles around the parking lot, smoking hard, sucking night through her teeth. Throwing down a cigarette, she lights another. The moon above is almost full, as is the spill of stars — like the Minute Rice on the black asphalt out front of the psychiatric chapel. Joan Jett lets her head fall back.

"Star light, star bright, the first star I see tonight. I wish

I may, I wish I might, have the wish I wish tonight." Then she shuts her eyes—lids blackened—and whispers fast, under her breath. She finishes her cigarette.

Flick.

The butt lands on the back of Shell's hand.

"Jeez!" Shell sucks in.

Joan Jett squints into the shadows. "Hey."

She teeters over in her booties, knees rubbing together in her narrow leather skirt. "Like a Virgin" begins to thump. Maybe it's Vicki who lets out that squeal.

Joan Jett steadies herself against Shell's picnic table, finding Shell's face in the dark.

"God," she drawls. "Don't you just totally hate Madonna?"

"Yes," says Shell. "Yes. I hate her." Shell says she loves Patti Smith.

Joan Jett goes: "Her? Really? God, that's a boring name." Joan Jett loves Heart and Girl School, the Pretenders. "Chick bands," she says. Lita Ford, Eurythmics too. "Hey." She leans in close. "Why so glum?"

Black makeup clogs the corners of her eyes, and her red lips are cracked. Beer and smoke waft from her mouth, while the spice of Obsession clings to her body. The girls in Shell's class who tease their hair wear that perfume too.

"Come on, kid. You look sad."

When Shell tells Joan Jett about Vicki's cousin calling her Grimace from McDonald's, Joan Jett doesn't laugh.

"Fuck those assholes, honey," she says. "They don't understand. You just go on being yourself. And I will too, okay?"

Shell nods, drinking in the tears running down her face.

Joan Jett finds a cocktail napkin in her fringed leather purse.

"Here." She sits down right on the tabletop, crosses her long, skinny legs, and leans back, eyes to the moon. "You waiting on a ride?"

Shell says no, her mum's car broke down.

"Oh, yeah, the old beat-up yellow one. What kind's it, anyway?"

"A Dart," Shell sighs.

"Good old Dodgeball Dart, eh? Well, if you can wait a few hours for me to sober up, I'll take you." Joan Jett points down the road. "You see those lights there, up the road and back a bit?"

Shell does.

"Well, that's Scottie's place and that's where my car's at. Just a sec." Joan Jett comes back from the Candlestick with her leather jacket slung over her shoulder. Her purse is stuffed with neat tinfoil packages tied with ribbon. A sticker on each announces the names of the newlyweds and their wedding date.

"Cake."

Joan gives a couple of pieces to Shell. Then: "Grimace, eh? Those dumb fucks." Joan Jett spits, but it doesn't go very far.

Shell follows Joan Jett down the highway's gravel shoulder. The lights ahead are their guides. Joan Jett says the Candlestick is Scott's drinking hole now he's moved out to the country.

"Which is okay, except I prefer live music, you know?"

Not some crap DJ." Clouds drift across the moon. Joan Jett tries her cigarette lighter, but the flame keeps blowing back and burning her fingers. "Frig!"

They stop and unwrap one of the tinfoil packs.

"But wasn't that just a beautiful wedding?" Joan Jett's mouth is full of cake.

Shell braces herself as a car goes thundering by, spraying stone. "Vicki looked pretty."

"Vicki, yeah. She's a good girl, but like I say, she's too pretty for her own sake. Just like Bonita. Like, look how fat she is and still men're always drooling over her. It's the giant tits, don't you think, honey?"

Another car comes whizzing by. Joan Jett looks away from the blinding white and squeezes Shell's shoulder for balance.

"Shitheads."

Shell says she likes Vicki's mum's freckles and she does have a nice smile.

"Really?" says Joan Jett. "A nice smile . . . ?" She skids a bit over the loose gravel. "Guess that's why I'm here with you and she's getting married. Even if it's to my jerk-off brother."

Shell frowns. "Huh? So Vicki—"

"Yeah. You believe it? Your friend back there turned me into a goddamn aunt."

SCOTT'S RANCH HOUSE is set back from the road. The pickups and motorbikes and cars that were parked out front of the chapel fill the driveway and the sloping front lawn. The lone

Honda among them—a blue station wagon—is Joan Jett's.

"This place's been party central, honey," she says as they cut across the grass.

A half-dozen BMX bikes lie discarded among lawn ornaments—swans, gnomes, a family of deer—and a dozen or so aluminum chairs cluster around a bug tent, partly collapsed.

Plastic lanterns are strung above the back deck, cluttered with cases of empty beer bottles, patio sets, and a big silver barbecue from which Joan Jett retrieves a spare key. She unlocks a set of sliding glass doors. Dogs howl. Shell freezes as Joan Jett steps inside.

"Penny, Gremlin, T-Bone! Shut it!"

Three sleek Dobermans come barking down a long hall, their nails clicking against the tile floor. But it's just Joan Jett—their barks turn to panting whines. Joan Jett kicks off her boots.

"I gotta piss," she says, leaving the dogs to sniff Shell's purple crotch.

Shell goes to the bathroom after Joan Jett—black towels, candles, bowls of spicy potpourri. She has to unzip her overalls and practically get naked just to pee. She shivers on the toilet, leafing through a BMX magazine.

Joan Jett is rummaging in the kitchen. The island, topped with some kind of stone, is piled with tubs of sour cream and cartons of juice.

"Hey." There's a cigarette in her mouth and ash on her blouse. "You want some pizza?"

"Sure. It's big, eh?" Shell says of the house.

Joan Jett pops a plate into a microwave that's as wide

as Mum's regular oven. Appliances clutter the counters; there's even a bread maker and something mechanical for squeezing oranges.

"Yeah. Well. Scottie's got a business, you know, like some kind of construction thing."

The pizza is ham and pineapple. They pull up high stools and lean over the island. The only sound is their steady chewing and the sawing of crickets through the kitchen windows. Shell and Joan Jett finish off most of what was a large pizza then eat strawberry ice cream right out of the tub. They wander around the darkened house looking for a place to sleep. Scott's room is off limits, of course, and there's already people snoring on the couches in the living room, and in the den there's a figure sprawled on the pool table. The guest room contains the rough heap of someone Joan Jett calls Grandpa.

"Frig." Joan Jett says they might have to sleep in her station wagon, and then she remembers that Vicki got a waterbed for her birthday — a double. "She won't mind."

Vicki's room is dark. They keep it that way because Joan Jett has a killer headache. The moonlight coming through the window is generous enough to make out the shape of the bed as well as the posters looming above it: Madonna is flanked by Prince on a motorcycle on the right and Wham! on the left.

"Christ, friggin' Madonna," Joan Jett groans. She crawls onto the jiggly sack that is the bed and sort of rolls over to the wall. Then Shell climbs in. The mattress sloshes around worse than stepping into a drifting canoe.

"Now you just lie still or I'm gonna get seasick." Joan Jet pulls Vicki's bedding over her head.

Shell stretches out. The covers are oily with what must be Vicki, but there's still a smell of laundry soap. Shell just hopes the sheets don't give her any zits. When Joan Jett starts to snore, Shell shifts and pulls out the lump from under her back: a brand new Wrinkles dog with red fur and paisley bone tucked in the pocket of its overalls. Shell holds the Wrinkles close. The mattress beneath her stills and, conforming to her shape, she pretends she's lying in warm sand, sunk on a beach, a million miles away from here but not nearly that far from Mum.

Shell cries a bit, uses the paisley bone for a tissue. Then voices approach from down on the road. The Dobermans bark, music goes on, and the microwave starts to whir. When the bedroom door opens, Shell pretends to be asleep, the Wrinkles concealing a good portion of her face. Vicki whispers and then so does a boy. The door closes with a click, and Shell and Joan Jett are alone again.

Shell's half sleep is broken up with laughter and car doors slamming—engine flare. When Vicki comes to bed, the house is quiet. Moonlight catches her profile. She lets down her hair, steps out of her dress, and lets it fall—crinkling—to the floor. Then she pulls a long T-shirt over her head and crawls between Shell and Joan Jett.

"Shell, you awake?"

Shell mumbles like asleep people should.

"Shell, I'm so happy you came," Vicki whispers. "Thank you, thank you."

Shell makes her breaths rumble into something like a snore.

"Mum's making everyone brunch in the morning. Then you can meet my new family, okay?"

Shell is quiet. Then Vicki's nose starts to whistle. Shell blinks against dark, the only one in the waterbed not yet sleeping.

THE WATERBED SLOSHES. Morning is grey enough that Madonna — in black lace and jelly bracelets — is fully visible. Joan Jett picks her jacket off the floor; under it is her purse. Shell rolls out of the bed very gently, jewellery tinkling, bracing herself against the velvet frame. She tucks the Wrinkles dog next to Vicki, whose soft, curly hair is splayed out across her pillow. Even with her mouth slack and cheeks crusty, Vicki looks pretty. Shell opens the door without a sound, leaving Vicki alone in the waterbed.

Again Shell finds Joan Jett in the kitchen. They stand over the sink, guzzling from various containers — orange juice, Clamato, 7 Up — and cut chunks of wedding cake from a slab left uncovered on the island. The Dobermans lie in a mass by the patio doors. As Joan Jett steps over them, they raise their heads and sniff her fingers.

The grey-blue yard is dewy — both Shell and Joan Jett slip — and the air humid and warm. The windows of the vehicles are opaque with condensation. Shell and Joan Jett wipe the Honda's front and back windshields with napkins and their sleeves. In the driver's seat, Joan Jett lights a cigarette, shakes her hair, and turns on the ignition. They lumber across the lawn towards the road, crushing drink cans and rubber dog toys. Looking left and right between inhales, Joan Jett pulls out onto the empty morning highway.

At first Shell doesn't recognize the house without the Dart in the driveway. Joan Jett idles out front.

"Good thing I had that snooze," she says. "Feel like a million bucks now."

Under her leather jacket, the red silk blouse is dirty and untucked. Her hair is limp and the darkness around her eyes is less from makeup than deep wrinkles; the sun, up full now, highlights the silver in her hair.

"Gosh," she says, shaking her head. "I still can't believe my little brother's married."

Shell wants to ask her in. Mum will be up soon and there will be porridge and coffee. But Shell is quiet and so too is her driver. The smell of car exhaust enfolds them in the either-or of hello and goodbye, of neither staying nor going.

"Well, maybe we'll see you at Scottie's, then—after they get back from the honeymoon."

"Sure, okay." Shell finds her purse and package of cake. "Thanks for the ride."

Joan Jett's nicotine smile is big and bright, and her swollen eyes shine.

THE SPARE KEY is under the porch. Shell lets herself in but is too tired to put it back. The house is quiet, the curtains still drawn.

She climbs the stairs. Mum's bedroom door is closed. In the bathroom, Shell takes off her purple overalls and lets them fall to the floor. Her skin is stained violet. As hot water fills the tub, Shell stands before the mirror, and each time she looks away, she makes herself look back.

Shell wakes in a tub of lukewarm water. She tosses her dirty clothes on the floor of her room and, shivering, exchanges beach towel for her velvety robe.

Mum's up. Porridge bubbles on the stove. Coffee drips in the pot. Shell takes the cake and a mug of coffee out to Mum, who sits at the harvest table, leaning over a Women's Studies textbook. She looks up.

"Check the porridge doesn't boil over."

Shell serves them each a bowl, topped with milk. They eat. They read. Then Mum shoves her textbook away and finds the Wheels section of the *Somerset Times*. She says she has to get another car. "It's insane to put more money into that Dart."

"But isn't a car a lot?" Shell slurps her porridge.

"I've got to have a reliable way to get to school and work, Shell." Mum says she can get a small loan. "Besides, it'll just be a used one anyway."

"I hear Hondas are good."

Mum pushes away her empty bowl and reaches for the cake. It's mostly just crumbs and hunks of icing, so she eats it with her spoon.

"Vicki's mum drove you home?"

Shell shakes her head. "Joan Jett."

"Oh? She nice?"

"Not nice. But I liked her."

Mum says she can't take any more studying. While Shell washes the dishes, Mum gets on the phone and makes appointments to see some cars. Barb Nutt will take her around. Barb wants Mum to buy a Volvo. Shell asks if she can come too, then goes down to the basement to change. She tucks the silver wedding invitation into the horsehair button box beneath her bed and puts on her soft, baggy Levi's.

Jesse

Shell and Carla grab their bags and link arms and half stomp, half stroll down the narrow, butt-strewn laneway that is the smoking pit, chins high and sun in their eyes, heading for the road. Passing through the entrance gates, they turn left towards downtown, away from grade ten homerooms and the polished oak doors of Somerset Central Tech. Who cares if the secretaries call Mum at work again? After all, it's Friday.

Shell's got Mum's old cowboy boots on: heavy hand-stitched burdens and more than a size too big. The hunks of turquoise hanging from her ears are Mum's too, same as her silver bangles and those broadening hips she tries to hide under oversized plaid button-downs. The *Essential Rimbaud* she carries around like a tourist does a phrasebook is the same one Mum bought in Paris when she was only three years older than Shell is now. But while Mum at Shell's age might have favoured a peasant blouse or Nehru-collared tunic, Shell's got Patti Smith's silhouette stretched wide and loud and distorted across her going-on-D-sized chest.

Carla lights a cigarette. Shell says, hey, she saw that guy Darren. He's the one in real leather pants whom Carla loves though she's never talked to him before — but, oh, Carla can tell a lot from his eyes, his silver rings, and of course from those leather pants he's never not wearing, and they look so good with his Chuck Taylor high-tops — red, just like Carla's, and that's a sign if anything.

"He was in the coffee shop during first," Shell says.

"Really? What'd he get?"

"Um." Shell thinks it was a coffee. "And, oh yeah, and a cookie." But she didn't see what kind.

"Really? And then what?"

"Then he went out and turned right. Maybe back towards the pit."

"Well, I am totally jealous. Where the hell was I?"

Carla lays a stick of powdery gum in her mouth; Shell gets to finish the cigarette. They pass Wizard's — blank cinema marquee topping the arcade's double doors. There's no one inside or leaning against the wall out front, and except for Moses, the Stroller's Alley food court is empty too. His tray is loaded with sweet and sour chicken balls, always with an extra side of fortune cookies. Moses nods them over.

"Hey Moses, what's going on tonight?"

Moses shakes his head and passes them each a strip of codeine tabs: the white 747 ones that still the bowels for days and make Shell's eyeballs as numb as her limbs. Moses's long nails are orange with sauce, as is the end of his bib-like beard.

"Peace," he says as they walk away from his rolling eyes.

Carla gets an Orange Julius and sucks it in fast, shivering at the ice cream headache.

"Let's just go to the park," Carla says. She's got to work soon anyways. But at Clayton and White, Carla sees this guy across the street. She grabs Shell's hand. "Jesse'll know if there's a party."

Jesse is standing right smack in front of a phone booth, skateboard under his arm. No one is getting in those saloon-style doors.

Jesse waves Carla over, and Shell and Carla almost get hit by a car crossing Clayton. Carla laughs and gives the car the finger.

"Fuck off," Jesse is saying to some kid scrounging in his pocket for a quarter. "Got a call coming in."

"Hey Jesse," Carla says.

Jesse snarls. Lips pulled back, his small, sharp teeth are porridge grey. Or, no, he's not snarling. He can't help the way his mouth twists like that. It's just the deep split pulling his top lip right up into his nostril that makes him look like an attack dog.

Shell tries not to stare at Jesse's harelip. He does look like a rabbit—the wild spirit kind of hare, all bone, tough muscle, with half-closed eyes and tight blossoms of cartilage for ears.

Jesse's eyes pass over Shell, falling again on Carla. There's no chance he would ever recognize Shell, if this is even the same kid.

"You got a smoke?" he says.

Carla reaches for her Belmont Milds. "You know what's going on tonight?"

Jesse props his skateboard against the phone booth. His thin fingers are as dirt-stained and cracked as a gardener's. He pokes the cigarette in the far left corner of his mouth, where his cloven lips can fully close. Carla's Zippo flames.

Cleft lip, tobacco hit.

"Don't know," he says.

Beneath his backwards ball cap, his brown hair is thin, dry stuff. The T-shirt under his jean jacket, from which the arms have been torn, is for the band DRI — Dirty Rotten Imbeciles. Mosquito bites popple his bare arms and face, several scratched to bleeding. Plus, his nails are black and his jacket and army pants smell of campfire. Does Carla know that Jesse spends nights camped in some brush by the river, with a makeshift fire and sipping something hard to stay warm? And his eyes are restless, darting from Shell to Carla to the cigarette receding between his wishbone fingers.

"Who's calling ya, Jesse?" Carla nods at the phone booth.

Jesse says, oh, he's just taking a message for some guy. Then, inhaling deep on his cigarette, he says, yeah, there's a party at Dan and Maček's. "You guys could come to that."

The phone rings. Jesse throws down his cigarette butt, pushes through the booth's doors.

"Yeah?" he says, practically swallowing the receiver. And then he listens, his eyes flicking back and forth like crazy.

Carla and Shell guard Jesse's skateboard. Then Kremski

comes riding up the sidewalk, scanning the ground for cigarettes. Shell pulls Carla—quick—around the corner.

"I bet you-know-who will be there," Carla gushes, less to Shell than to the spring sky above.

Outside the phone booth, Kremski toes Jesse's smoking butt, shoulders hunched and neck flesh hanging loose over his collar. Dad doesn't look that old yet. Not even close. Kremski's bald spot has taken over his entire head. Or else it's the yellow of his beard or the clouded eyes behind his glasses—the same metal frames he's had since he was giving Shell Soviet Barbie dolls and buying lemonade at her stands.

"No. Who?" Shell ducks behind Carla as Kremski pushes on towards the bus stop, a gold mine of half-smoked butts.

Carla links Shell's arm. "Walk me to work?"

The phone booth, when they pass it, is empty now and Jesse's skateboard is gone.

AT THE BACK of Harvey's hamburgers, Shell and Carla sit on overturned milk crates next to a pile of juicy garbage bags. A sack of pre-cut french-fried potatoes props open a bent metal door; fatty meat sizzles inside and boiling grease smokes. Shell unhooks a safety pin from the cuff of her jacket and bends it open. She smears deep green hash oil on a cigarette paper, which she then rolls into a slim joint. Carla lights her Zippo. Shell leans in. The joint comes alive with an earthy, comforting reek.

"Christ, I look hideous."

Carla always says that before a shift. Her short-sleeved Harvey's blouse is held at the bust with safety pins while the regulation polyester pants are fuzzy and too tight, so she's always checking her reflection in the chrome fridge to make sure she does not have what her sister Jasmine calls "hungry buns." But Carla jangles her big silver hoop earrings anyway, insists on her red Chuck Taylor high-tops though they're against the rules, and always gives extra pickles to any cool guy who comes in.

"So what about that guy Jesse?" Shell tucks her vial into the secret pocket sewn inside her backpack.

"Who? Lipper?" Carla wrinkles her nose but is too nice to imitate that snarling lip. "You into him?"

Carla's sister Jasmine is twenty-one and already lives on her own, and from her Carla knows about boys, as well as how to skip school, apply eyeliner, get into bars without ID, and smoke. And also Carla shaves her legs, buys her own specialty shampoo, and wears tampons not pads, because pads are like diapers. The first time Carla slept over, she ate a bag of cookies then threw up in the basement toilet. Throwing up works for Jasmine; she is tall and slender and wears tight jeans in a way Shell and Carla long to do—without shirttails hanging down to conceal bulges and rolls.

"No," Shell says. "Not into. He's just kinda familiar."

Carla holds in her toke until the smoke seeps out her nostrils. "He's older. A little intense. Oh, and he loves that frickin' skateboard."

"So what's with the lip?" Shell takes her turn on the joint.

"Heard Maček say it's from a fight." Carla sips from

her Harvey's cup of icy fountain Pepsi. "Like the other guy had a knife."

"Really? Oww." Shell burns her fingers on the paper.

Carla unhooks a roach clip from her key chain. "I mean, that's what Maček said. Who knows? But imagine kissing that guy? Very weird."

Shell shrinks up and looks at the toes of her boots.

"Yeah. Weird."

The door behind them opens wide.

"Heads up!"

A wet garbage bag comes flying, missing the Dumpster and spilling its guts on the pavement.

"Jackasses." Carla sucks in the final toke. She crushes the roach under her sneaker then puts on her orange sun visor with the hamburger on the brim. "I'm pretty high."

"Me too," Shell says. "Stay away from the deep fryers, buddy."

When Carla laughs, her chestnut eyes twinkle like stars are supposed to.

Shell promises to be back at nine-thirty. "I'll help you mop up."

SHELL TAKES OFF her boots and gets into her sour basement bed. The floor is stacked with banker's boxes Mum brought home from school. Now that the last boarder has finally moved out, Shell's old room just needs to be painted and then Shell can move back in. But the paint has to be something creamy white; the deep dark Sugar Plum that Shell circled on the colour wheel is out of the question. Shell clicks the tape player on the floor: the Doors. If she had been born back when Mum was, she would have gone to see Jim Morrison and Janis Joplin and Black Sabbath. Above all else, she'd have found her way to the Chelsea Hotel and made friends with Patti Smith.

Shell tries a poem about Jesse—his snarl, his smoke, the darting eyes, how time works backwards as much as forwards, and the way things in your past you thought you were moving away from are actually coming up ahead. But the poem succumbs to some kind of dark Dr. Seuss rhyme, so she flips the page and starts a letter to good old Patti Smith.

Dear Patti, I met this skater today. I know him, Patti. I know it's him from before. What does that mean, Patti? Because it means something—a secret something, like fate. Don't you think?

DINNER IS WHOLE wheat spaghetti with lean chicken meatballs and green salad—all homemade except the noodles. Now that it's just the two of them, Mum's back to cooking from scratch again; both she and Shell could slim down a bit. "Enough with the Fig Newtons and frozen junk," she said. The radio in the kitchen has the news on loud, otherwise it'll be a whole lot of silence. Mum's hungry; her eyes—the grey drained to merest silver—do not look up from her plate.

"How's the rich-bastard Sumac Valley kids?" Shell asks of the high school near her and Dad's fiddlehead ravine.

The first day Mum supplied there, she stopped at Consumers Distributing on the way home and bought an electric razor. Now she keeps her legs hair free: smooth white bone caught in a net of fine purple veins. And she doesn't wear as many handmade clothes, and also she parks the brown Datsun station wagon on a side street where the kids can't get at it with their keys; she's still paying off the paint job to hide the pentagram scratched on the door.

"Oh, just a joy," Mum says, swallowing. "Only one girl fainted from hunger and no angry calls from parents. Where you going tonight, anyway?" Mum reaches for Shell's dirty plate, stacks it beneath her own.

"Nowhere. Just over to watch TV with Carla."

SHELL PAINTS HER lips Morocco brown. The piece of rope she ties around her plaid shirt turns it into a dress. A couple of beers clatter in her backpack.

Cross-legged on the damp floor of her bedroom, she waits—eyes to the ceiling—for Mum's footsteps to recede up to the second floor and an early night to bed. Splayed on her stomach, Shell reaches under her bed, drawing out the horsehair button box from behind dusty shoeboxes and a garbage bag of sweaters. Shell sneezes. She runs her fingers over the bits and pieces nestled inside the box's silk interior: a necklace made of pasta shells, a crinkled wedding invitation, the key for her old strap-on roller skates, medicine bottles she and Dad dug up from the backyard. There's a broken hair comb made of tortoiseshell, a scallop of cracked soap, and also a jagged piece of green glass, the broken bottom of a Mountain Dew bottle. The glass's serrated edge corresponds to the thick white scar that spans the length and width of Shell's right foot, cutting clear across the meaty ball. She peels back her sock and holds the glass against the scar; the two seal-like lips, a broken plate, a letter torn in two.

Mum finally treads up the stairs to the second floor, dragging her fatigue — *thump, thump* — behind her. It's nine-fifteen by the blush of the clock radio by Shell's bed. She replaces the jagged glass and closes the box. Then she carries her boots up the basement stairs, grabs a pocketful of cookies from the pantry, and, locking the back door behind her, disappears into Friday night.

THE NUMBER TWO Clayton East smells of the greasy Harvey's bag Carla clutches on her lap. Stopped at a red light, Carla takes out her lipstick and compact and touches up her Firefly lips.

"Is it straight?" She turns to Shell, plumping out her mouth. Shell nods and Carla says, "Well, yours isn't, buddy."

Against her reflection in the dark bus window, Shell wipes the underside of her bottom lip with a thick finger.

At Wood Street, a couple of punks get on, each carrying a case of beer. One has a flopped-over bleached Mohawk and the other a shaved head with sideburns. Carla sits up and smiles. The punks don't look at her, but the guy they're with, Rollo, says hey. Shell's stomach jitters. She hunches up and feels for her *Essential Rimbaud* through her backpack. Maybe she'll just find a corner to read in until it's time for her and Carla to catch the last bus home.

The bright lights inside the bus obscure the city beyond. They pass the toasted corn of Kellogg's and the bubblegum sweet of Washko, and then—blindness, a tunnel of dark. But Carla's been out to Dan and Maček's before and knows when to pull the bell. They exit through the front doors. The punks and Rollo get off at the back. Shell starts to step into a storefront—a dry cleaner's, but with lush begonias and succulents filling the window— to let them pass. But Carla grabs her arm and pulls her ahead so they're the ones leading the way. Behind them, the punks and Rollo duck into a Korean grocery store on the corner of King and the dead end called Alberta, down which Shell and Carla have turned.

This far from the haze of downtown, the firelight from what must be Dan and Maček's place glares bright. Up and down the short street, the properties are dark and alternate with vacant lots. Dan and Maček's is right at the end. The front porch is half sunk into the ground. Beneath the glow of a bare red bulb, maybe twenty people are sitting-leaning-crouching, beer bottles in hand. Shell follows Carla up the sloped steps. To the few people who look over, Carla says, hey, they're looking for Dan and Maček and that Jesse invited them. But no one cares—not the skaters on the front walk pulling tricks; not the new wave girls in pointy boots and short skirts sitting, legs crossed, on the low, sagging couch; not their boyfriends leaning up against the railing opposite, a procession of faded T-shirts for the Cramps, Misfits, Smiths, The Clash, Minor Threat, CCR, Bauhaus, the Doors.

"Hey, cool, Patti Smith," one says about Shell, and starts singing, "'So you wanna be a rock and roll star...'"

Then Rollo and the punks come up the sidewalk. Against the swell of whistles and high-fives, Carla pulls Shell inside.

MAČEK HAS BLOND hair to his shoulders, acne-scarred cheeks, and Dracula teeth when he laughs. He is quiet, never gets too high because he's the one who sells the drugs, so he's got to keep one eye open, always. Some say he was in the Czech army before he came to Canada and that he left his whole family behind. Dan, Maček's best friend and business partner, wears black—jeans, runners, raincoat, Slayer T-shirt. His long, wavy hair is dark and the moles on his cheeks are so black they look green. Shell can't be the only one who thinks Dan's thick glasses make him look like "Weird Al" Yankovic. As Carla says of guys who are nice but not hot, Dan and Maček are "sweet."

The kitchen is bright with fluorescent lights, warm with dope smoke. Dan and Maček smile big when Carla and Shell come in. The back door opens inward; one long leather leg at a time, Darren steps in from the porch. Carla stands tall, sucks in her tummy.

"Hey, hamburgers!" Dan digs into the paper bag. "Thanks, man."

"Awesome." Darren's eyes flare open. "Can I grab one?"

Carla laughs and says she can't guarantee the burgers won't have spit in them.

"Wanna hot knife?" Darren says to Carla when she passes him a wax-papered package. "This one's a double." He leans into the greasy stove, turning on the rear burner and propping a pair of blackened butter knives between the element's rings. When the knives are red-hot, Darren uses one to pick up a pebble of dark brown hash from a plate on the counter. He squeezes the two blades together and a thick coil of hash smoke rises.

Carla leans over and with an empty toilet paper roll inhales the sweet hash smoke deep into her lungs. She holds the toke, her nostrils flaring, allowing the warm wave of narcotic to wash over her brain. She opens her eyes. Smoke escapes from her lips and nose. And she coughs, good and stoned.

"Now one for Shell," Maček tells Darren. His voice is flat. Shell says thanks and Maček gives her his vampire smile. "Here's to nuclear sanity," he says, lifting his beer.

Shell drank too much to remember a lot from the time when, under the Clayton Street Bridge, she and Maček talked about war and disarmament. Shell must have gone on and on about Chomsky again, because now Maček tells everyone she's pretty smart.

Shell takes the toilet paper roll from Carla and when the knives are hot, she leans into her toke: a fiery wash of full-body nourishment. In the glow of the smoky kitchen, hot knives brewing and beer and burgers, Carla and Shell are making all kinds of jokes and everyone's laughing, even Rollo and the punks, who've come in with their cases. The fridge is jam-packed, so they start emptying it of beer in cans and bottles, ketchup and spaghetti sauce, a murky jar with a stem of dill weed in the bottom, cramming in their own drinks instead.

Dan stands up from the sticky table.

"That's not cool."

Maček, hunching over a marijuana joint, turns around. His voice is gruff from Czech and filterless cigarettes: "Hey man, that's our stuff."

The punks say, "Oh, sorry, man. We'll get ours chilled and then switch it back, cool?"

"No," Maček says, his pale eyes narrowing.

Then someone calls someone else an asshole. Shell and Carla back away from the gathering scrum. Darren turns off the stove and gathers up his hash. The blackened knives sizzle as he releases them into a dirty pot in the sink. Then the girls from the porch come in to put something on the ghetto blaster and one starts moaning because—what the fuck, man—her beer is sitting out, and that's when Darren slips out the screen door into the back. Carla follows him and Shell after that.

IN THE MIDDLE of the narrow yard and towards the back, a campfire rages. While everyone else has found a chair, jacket, milk crate, skateboard, or lap to sit on, Jesse is on his feet, circling the flames, fists full of snapped branches and thin maple switches. Like a matador goading his rival bull, Jesse twists each piece of wood upon inserting it into the fire, challenging the flames to rise and meet his stature. And then, when his fists are empty—the sticks devoured—he picks up a thick arm of crooked maple and shoves it with grit force into the fiery swell. A roar, sparks fly; Jesse's eyes enlarge along with the broadening flames. But though every other body leans away or otherwise reacts, Jesse does not move. And so he is singed. Hot, popping embers touch down on his bare arms and live there for a moment before they die, extinguished.

One of a cluster of girls sitting close and passing around a mickey of rum and a bottle of Diet Coke goes: "Hey, watch it, Lipper!" Black ash streaks their faded jeans and there are bits of dry leaves caught in their ponytails. Tomorrow, late morning or afternoon, everyone around this fire will wake to the deep dark smoke still infusing the oils of their hair and skin, the fibres of their denim. And they will think of the kid with that cloven lip who smells the same as they do, only he does not know it or care, and that will make them soap themselves harder, scrubbing the night's fire from their scalps and eyes, between the legs.

Shell fishes the beers from her backpack — warm, labels worn, dark European lagers pinched the last time Carla's sister had a party. Darren opens the bottles against the edge of the rusted barbecue collapsed in a corner beside the back stoop. They drink — Shell, Carla, and then Darren from Carla's bottle — and then Darren retrieves a moulded plastic lawn chair from among the junk on the neighbouring porch, ripping the knee of his leather pants climbing back over the saggy chain-link fencing. He wipes the dirty seat with his shirt cuff and offers the chair to Carla while Shell steps backwards into the shadows where she can just watch the party come and go and also, by penlight, read her Rimbaud. But Carla calls her over.

"Why not talk to Jesse?" she whispers so Darren, on whose lap she is now sitting, will not hear. His hand, on Carla's thigh just above her knee, has a thick silver ring and the wrist is lopped with a bracelet, which Shell agrees is totally like Jim Morrison.

"Why?" Shell hisses. "And what the hell about?"

Carla removes the plastic wrap and protective foil from a fresh pack of Belmont Milds. She holds it out to Shell — twenty-five pristine white cigarettes, as inviting and comforting to consider as a full sheet of cookies just pulled from the oven, as uncut cake, a crisp, clean bed. Shell takes one, another.

"Go!" Carla says, nodding her away.

A DISEASED MAPLE behind the place next door leans over into Dan and Maček's yard, showering it with misshapen castoffs. Jesse is in the shadows, drinking 50. The bread-knife with which he strips leaves from a bundle of fallen wood is rusty and dull.

"Hey. Jesse?"

Jesse glances over, his eyes round and his thin face warm with flush.

Shell takes a Belmont from behind her ear. "Got a light?"

Jesse pulls a book of matches from the breast pocket of his jean jacket and tosses them over.

"I remember you," Shell says, striking-lighting-inhaling.

Jesse grabs the matches from the palm of her hand, held flat, like feeding an apple to a horse. "Me too."

"Really?" Shell smiles. "It was a long time ago."

"Huh?" he says. "It was just this afternoon." He stabs the knife into the earth and wipes his hands on his pants. "You're that chick Carla's friend..." His voice is shallow and his words are slurred—not with alcohol but with the cleft that so wholly pinches away what might otherwise be an upper lip.

"Shell."

He considers the word and then turns his attention back to the flames.

"And you're Jesse." Shell offers him her cigarette. Jesse's fingers are chicken feet compared with her own, thick with abundant food and Nivea cream. Jesse is not much taller than Shell, either, and while her clothes cannot disguise her wide hips and broad shoulders and thick legs, it is not clear just exactly how scrawny is the body floating within the loose articles Jesse wears. The narrowness of his hands and wrists, however, suggests they are connected to a sinewy skeleton with countable ribs, a bony butterfly for a pelvis, and a chest that's caved in.

Then there is nothing more to say, so Shell picks up Jesse's bundle of sticks, divides it in half.

"I know about fires too," she says, tossing the cigarette— now a butt—into the flames, which have grown milder.

Jesse and Shell roam the fire's periphery, building the flames into a bellowing mass, the heat and spew of which force those around to move further back, to the fenceline. This includes the ponytailed girls with the rum and Diet Coke. They get up and, brushing off their damp bums, look at Shell with dirt in their eyes, with piss and stink,

and one whose bangs touch her lips calls Shell or Jesse—
or both—*freak.*

That's okay.

The flames, for Shell, are an instrument she cannot
play, the dull moan she goes to sleep with every night, the
stupid scream of having to live here in Somerset and be
ugly and fat when really, inside, she is as light and breezy
and full of poetry as the rock star on her chest. And looking at Jesse through the crackling flames, Shell hears in
their orange heat his own wail, howl, growl, which, if he
played a guitar or basketball or had a mountain to climb
or field to plant, would come out no less powerfully, but
oh so different. And maybe then he'd be free.

Maček touches Shell's arm. "Hey, fire's too big." He
says the same to Jesse, offering him a can of Blue.

The cops come not twenty minutes later anyway.
Everyone goes home.

NOW THAT IT'S spring, there's parties both nights of every
weekend and sometimes on weeknights too. Or maybe it's
just that Carla and Shell know more people now and are
themselves starting to get known as being pretty funny
and cool for fifteen-year-olds.

Shell helps Carla mop the floors at Harvey's and
together they walk over to Field Street, south of downtown and near the forks of the river. The air is chill
from recent rain. Carla borrowed a black scoop-neck
from Jasmine, showing off the moonstone pendant Shell
stole for her from Siddhartha. Over that, Carla's wearing

the corduroy blazer that was once Jasmine's, while Shell has a Salvation Army jean jacket on top of her plaid. Her Patti Smith T-shirt is the same as always, because if anything is going to give Shell luck or power tonight, it's that shirt.

"Whose place is it?"

Carla and Shell pass a cigarette back and forth, sipping from the mickey of Prince Igor vodka Shell got from the LCBO. An old guy fished it for her; she was so polite, how could he resist? *Excuse me, sir? I forgot my ID and . . .*

Carla winces. "Next time, get something smooth. Okay, dudette? Jägermeister or Bailey's, please." The only thing Carla knows about the party is that gorgeous, beautiful, sweet-hearted Darren invited her at school today. "Oh, and it's number thirty-two."

Field Street is behind the beer factory, so maybe the permanent stink of hops accounts for some of the parties and fires and fighting. Or else it's just the concentration of subsidized housing and the open flow of drugs into and out of downtown. Of the empty bungalows that line the stubby street, every other one has squatters inside. The smell of their fires is toxic, garbagey; flashlights in the windows strobe yellow and blue as, elsewhere, TVs might. One house is burned to the ground. Shell wonders how many charred corpses are inside.

"Christ, Shell," Carla says, "you are just so morbid all the time."

"You sure you got that address right?" Shell says.

"Yeah." Carla squints at the shadowed houses. "Darren wouldn't tell me wrong. Right? Shell?"

The neat brick bungalow on the next corner has no house number. Instead, a BEWARE OF DOG sign carefully reordered as BEWARE OF GOD hangs on the door; the mailbox alongside says MALE.

Maček, Dan, and Darren are in the kitchen, near the stove, though there are, as yet, no hot knives going. One of those mint-green dinette sets from the time of ducktails and banana splits dominates the room, along with a wide window through which a back porch is visible. A circle of guys in ball caps lounge in lawn chairs; so does Moses, combing his beard with his nails, eyes rolled back and lids as fluttery as trapped moths. Jesse and his skateboard are outside too, down on the porch steps, his backpack on, turned away from the party.

Shell sits down at the table. The couple who live here are about as old as Mum and Dad. In fact, they probably know Mum and Dad. The tall, thin lady has an underbite and hair dyed Eggplant with drugstore Flirt. The guy has red hair in an army brush cut and a dimple poked deep into his chin—like a finger testing dough—and silver John Lennon glasses that make him look like the folk-singer Bruce Cockburn. They both wear black tank tops and Levi's safety-pinned at the ankles and have so many tattoos it's like the ink is part of their clothing. While the lady wears a silver ankh around her neck, the guy's is wreathed with a Polaroid camera. Of the piles and shelves of books around, most are glossy hardcovers that have to do with African tribes or samurai, but there's also tons of homemade Xeroxed cartoon books, the covers showing cone-shaped boobs and penises doing violence. Crates of records are stacked as high as the walls in the living room, and whatever Japanese-type stuff is currently on the turntable plays low enough that people can talk. The guy, Bruce Cockburn, is shooting Polaroids of a girl with about a million earrings and two hoops in her nose and her forearms covered in bloody Band-Aids.

"Nice, nice," he keeps saying as she peels back the Band-Aids.

One of Kremski's oil paintings hangs on the wall: a grizzly blowing a big pink bubble of gum. Shell always loved that one. Kremski laughed at her when she asked how much allowance she should save up to buy it.

Shell whispers to Carla she's sure her parents know that guy.

"Who? The Bruce Cockburn look-alike?"

They laugh and Carla mock-sings "If I Had a Rocket Launcher," but Shell keeps her back to him all the same and even pulls her hair over her face.

Maček gives Shell a bottle of Radeberger beer.

"Cool." It's what her dad drinks.

Maček says, "Nice." And it's too bad the cops gave them a noise fine because they won't have another party for a while. Shell's sorry about how big the fire got. Maček smiles—Dracula—and says it's cool. "That's what parties are for." But he says Carla and Shell can come over any time, it's just that things will be mellow for a while. "Okay?"

"Oh, okay," Shell says.

Carla pinches her when Maček goes to help Darren pick the right type of butter knives, singing, *"Maček likes yooooouuuu!"*

"Fuck off, does not."

Carla goes: "Don't say fuck off to me."

"Sorry. But you're scaring me with that shit, okay?"

Carla rolls her eyes and goes to stand next to Darren at the stove.

Shell finishes the beer from Maček then remembers her and Carla's Prince Igor. There's nothing else to do, so she sips. And again. And then her belly and brain get fuzzy, just enough to feel like everything's going to be okay. But after the next sip the fuzz turns dark, giving way to emptiness, homesickness, something. Shell goes outside, caps the Prince Igor, otherwise she'll wake up on the front lawn again, her bag gone and wanting to kill herself. Hash is just so much better for her and maybe the whole human race.

The handsome guy who works at Mister Sound is talking about his new drum kit. "Like, really tight, man." He has dark hair and stubble and wears the best T-shirts in Somerset. Tonight is Hüsker Dü.

Jesse is sitting on the lowest step, his skateboard propped between his knees.

"Hey Jesse."

Jesse shifts his backpack and moves over. Shell sits. It smells like maybe he washed his T-shirt, and his hands are for sure less dirty.

"Things are okay, yeah," he slurs. He's crashing at Maček and Dan's, and Dan's going to try to get him into his autobody class, too.

"Cool. At Somerset Tech?"

"Yeah."

"Well then, I'll see ya, because I go there too." Shell offers the Prince Igor to Jesse and when he takes it, their fingers meet. Shell's heart gets warm and fast. Then their knees are touching. Shell takes a long swallow when Jesse passes back the bottle.

She says: "I know where you come from, Jesse. I knew you as a kid. You remember?"

Jesse pulls his knee away from Shell's. He doesn't know what the hell she's talking about.

"On Cashel Street. That place you lived. You know, with the school buses?"

The muscles in Jesse's neck pop. He closes his eyes. "Man, I lived so many fucking places and had so many fucking parents, how can I remember them all?"

It is then that Bruce Cockburn comes out onto the porch. He's looking for the kid with the best scar of all.

"You know who I mean, right?" he says to the Mister Sound guy.

"Lipper?" says Mister Sound, pointing at the steps with his beer bottle.

From where he stands, Bruce Cockburn cannot see Jesse's face. If he could, he would retrace his steps right back into the house. And lock the door. Like you do when a growling dog comes between you and wherever it is you had intended to go.

Bruce Cockburn nods his thanks. He crosses the porch with a silent tread, then kneels down and lays his hand on Jesse's chiselled shoulder.

"Oh, hey. Hey, uh, Lipper? That's what they call you, right?"

Jesse's shoulders peak, touching the cartilage of his ears. Finally he turns.

"Wow, that's quite a scar." Bruce Cockburn speaks with tenderness. Like a doctor, his gaze fixes upon the injury and not the injured, the illness and not the one who must endure it. "Can I, uh, take your picture?" He holds up his Polaroid and asks Jesse to come inside where there's light.

"You wanna what?" Jesse says, low and quiet.

"Oh, ah" — Bruce Cockburn pushes up his glasses — "just get a shot of your lip. I mean, I research scarification and I have never seen what you have unless it's in, like, a Foster Parents Plan ad, you know? Like, it's really wild." Bruce Cockburn is talking on and on like people do on cocaine and that's probably what it is because he's not smoking or drinking or anything and something has to be making him buzz like that.

If they weren't before, everyone on the porch is looking at Jesse now. He boils, digging his nails into the underside of his skateboard. But Bruce Cockburn keeps smoothing his brush cut with his free hand, talking about scars and social transgression, and when he reaches out with his index finger going for Jesse's lip, Jesse reels back and hits him right square in the face.

Bones really do crack when they break. But there is also a wet sound. Blood explodes.

Bruce Cockburn drops his camera and falls off the steps into the forsythia bushes, his broken glasses left mangled on the porch.

"Stop!" Shell grabs for Jesse, but he is fast and focused and he knows how to hurt. With his knees straddling

Bruce Cockburn's limp form, he unloads two more cracks onto the head area before jumping back.

"Fucking creep," he shouts. "Motherfucking creep."

Bodies with beers and cigarettes flow down the steps.

"Oh my God, oh my God." The girl with the Band-Aids starts crying.

Maček yells at Jesse, something in Czech. Inside, Carla and Darren squint through the glare of the window, straining to get a view. A towel appears. Mister Sound holds it to Bruce Cockburn's face. "Stay cool, man." Bruce Cockburn's wife comes out, screams, her skin turning translucent—rice paper. She rakes her fingers through her hair and pulls it so hard it must hurt, and then a guy in a ball cap catches her from behind as she teeters, withering into a faint.

Someone says, "Police." Shell pulls back from the bodies crowding around the forsythia. Complete with striped socks, Bruce Cockburn's sneakered feet poke out from the scrum like the Wicked Witch of the East under the fallen house.

"Jesse?"

His bag is gone from the porch, alongside which a shadow crawls, shoulder blades slinking through the tall grass. Jesse grabs the Polaroid camera from the flower bed where it landed, crushing a young hosta just unfurling its leaves. As Shell steps towards him, he shoves the gleaming thing into his backpack and disappears down the narrow lane between Bruce Cockburn's and his neighbour's with all the Confederate flags for curtains.

"Jesse," Shell whispers, watching him, head low, duck out and away.

Bruce Cockburn is moaning, choking on something that might be his teeth. The crowd parts to allow his wife access to the mound in the forsythia bush.

"Where the fuck's Lipper?"

"He's a loose goddamn cannon."

"Call the cops on that kid."

"Leave him alone"—that's Maček—"me and Dan'll deal with him."

"Well, here's his board," says the girl with the Band-Aids, pointing to the forgotten skateboard leaning against the bottom porch step. Maček picks up the skateboard before anyone else and smiles as Shell steps out of the dark. A smile that falls fast and hard as Shell grabs the skateboard away from his blond hands and runs down the lane and out to the street.

KER-CLICK. JESSE SNAPS a Polaroid of Shell filling her extra-large at the Big Gulp machine. The wet photograph slides out. Jesse waves it through the air and when the image comes to life, Shell says, jeez, how awful she looks.

"Instant memories," Jesse says, handing it over.

Does Jesse want anything to eat? "I have five dollars, you know."

Jesse shakes his head. "Just some of your drink."

"Because you love pop," Shell says. "I remember: Mountain Dew."

"Huh?"

Shell pays and they pass through the front doors, setting off the buzzer.

"Mountain Dew. I thought it was your favourite."

Jesse says maybe. Once. Now he has no favourites.

THE MARION STREET Parkette is swampy with dew. Through the cracked leather of Mum's boots, the wet of grass seeps. They find a bench away from the floodlit monkey bars.

"You're cold," Jesse tells Shell when she shivers, the Big Gulp freezing her hand.

Shell says no, not really, because Jesse has fewer clothes than her, what with his bare arms and the rips in his pants.

The knuckles on Jesse's right hand are swollen and red. He opens and closes his fist to keep it from stiffening.

"I really popped the guy," he says. "But what's with that camera? He a perv or what?" Jesse turns to Shell, snarling. "Hey? You're supposed to be so smart."

Shell kind of knows or at least can guess, because she's read Mum's anthropology textbooks and she goes to art galleries in Toronto with Dad. People like that Bruce Cockburn guy think Western people are not so advanced or special and in fact we're no different from people with bones in their noses and tattooed faces— they're not weird or exotic at all, you know? It's all just relative.

"He was on cocaine, wasn't he?" Shell says.

"Shit, that's no excuse."

"So why do you let people call you that name?"

"Lipper? It's like a joke."

"Yeah. But it's just as mean."

Jesse shakes his head. "Naw, they're my friends. It's like black people now call themselves—"

"Stop!" Shell squeezes the Big Gulp between her thighs and plugs her ears. "It's ugly."

Jesse snorts. As Shell eases, he reaches over and takes the Big Gulp, brushing her leg. He inhales pop through the wide red straw, cheeks funnelled and nostrils flared.

"Can't you get it fixed?"

Jesse shrugs. "My case worker says it's too late. You know, I just turned eighteen and that means no more fostering, right? No more benefits and shit. I'm on my own." He snaps his skinny fingers. "Just like that, they cut you off: bye-bye, see ya later, done."

Out on the street, a bus goes streaking past towards downtown, to make the night's final connection. If Carla's not on that bus, mad and worried about Shell, she'll be with Darren: keeping warm, whispering secret things Carla will tell Shell tomorrow anyway.

Jesse takes her hand and pulls her to her feet, skateboard slung under his arm. Shell squeezes his cold, bruised fist.

"See if you remember where I live. From back then, before, when we first met."

THEY DON'T SAY anything all the way there. Shell's boots resound against the cold pavement, following Jesse's lead. The further south Jesse takes them, the bigger the lawns become and the further back the houses are set from the road. Bungalows, cottages, ranch-style—a car or two on guard in the driveway—all are similarly suspended in this time of gloom and blue, without birds or wind or direct light, a dim no-space, against which they move. A few times Jesse drops his skateboard to the street, shattering the stillness. He does a few tricks, then flips the board into his grip and keeps on going, Shell just behind.

Jesse turns right at Maurice Street then again at Cashel, and continues west, Shell clomping behind. He stops once, looks around before crossing over, leading Shell through this lights-out movie-set version of the street she's known almost all her life, but never this way, Jesse's way, not ever.

Jesse stops.

Mum left the porch light on, curtains drawn. The brown Datsun is at rest in the drive. Jesse points up at the dark second-floor window where Mum has her sewing machine and typewriter.

"That room yours?"

"No." Shell shakes her head.

Jesse wipes his nose. He looks so hard at Shell's house it might very well shatter, or fade away into blackness—the end of a movie, of a dream.

"You hungry?"

Jesse nods.

"Then you better come in."

THE CLOCK ON the stove reads one twenty-two. In silence and in dark, Shell makes a box of Kraft Dinner, slices of hot dog cooked right in. She seasons it with pepper and salt, then wraps the pot in a towel and takes it, as well as a canvas bag packed with bowls, spoons, knives, peanut butter, a loaf of brown bread, and a carton of milk, down to the basement. Jesse is sitting on Shell's unmade bed, surrounded by quilts her grandmother made, while the pillow he leans into is covered in one of a pair of flowered cases Mum had made to match a set of curtains, now long gone. Jesse left his skateboard in the middle of the floor, and his scent—sweat and damp cigarettes—overrides Shell's own sweet-and-sour musk.

Without looking at Jesse, Shell arranges the food on the desk.

"Sit here," she says, unfolding a chair.

Jesse pounces on the food. He emits a low hum as he eats, dialoguing with himself about the tastes and textures in his mouth. When he finishes the solids, he drinks the milk. Then he asks for a cigarette.

"Okay, but you gotta blow it out the window."

Their bodies get close as they smoke out the small square window that had once been Jesse's. Shell can almost taste his sweat, the cheese and peanut butter on his breath.

"Strange to be back here?"

"No," Jesse says. "Not really."

"Look." Shell gives Jesse the cigarette. Sitting down on her messy bed, she takes off her socks and, leaning back, holds out the bottom of her right foot. "See? Eighteen stitches. I still have the glass in my box."

Jesse ashes the cigarette on the window ledge. "What? What's in a box?"

"You know," she tells him. "It's in a keepsake box."

After a deep drag on the cigarette, Jesse blows the smoke right into the room. "Huh?"

"Yeah, like things in your life that you value because they remind you of something that happened or of a person you met."

Jesse shakes his head. "I don't keep anything for any sake."

Shell rolls over onto her stomach and stretches out, reaching beneath the bed for the horsehair button box. Her T-shirt rides up, baring her back to the cold. She wriggles and twists until she feels the rough contour of the box against her fingertips.

But then she stops. Her grasp retracts. Jesse's fingers drift along the length of her spine. And his touch is tender. He strokes the bottom of Shell's scarred foot and then his sinewy body, inch by inch, impresses itself upon her own. Shell turns to meet him, his snarling rabbit face softening, and she lets Jesse's bashed fist guide her hand down the loose waist of his army pants. He is all warmth and stickiness. And he has no underwear on. And soon neither does Shell.

Jesse rises and falls, into Shell and out of Shell, twisting among the bedding of Shell's mother and her mother's mother, breathing and expelling the same damp air of the same damp basement where he had never quite been a boy. And Shell is surprised by how much it hurts, and the whole time she keeps thinking about what will come next. Like when they see each other at Dan and Maček's or walking down Clayton, will everyone know? Of course, Shell will never tell. Maybe not even Carla, though she'd like her to know that kissing a harelip boy is not weird at all. It's just your teeth clank a lot.

They wrap up in quilts and again take their places by the window, blackening the screen with cigarette smoke. Jesse makes a peanut butter sandwich and empties the milk carton. Shell wants him to make her a sandwich too or offer her a bite, but he just sits there at her desk humming and chewing, fingering her books and pencils, clucking his tongue when the peanut butter sticks. There are burns on his arms from tending to fires and his hair is flat from wearing a cap. The quilt he's tucked around his waist falls away and he lets it, not feeling the cold though his skin is prickled and nipples go to tacks.

If Jesse would leave, Shell could have a bath and put her pyjamas on. Then she'd sleep on the couch in the living room and when Mum comes down, they could have porridge. Maybe Mum will make blueberry muffins like she does sometimes on Saturday, enough to take to school next week.

Jesse swallows the last of his sandwich, crawls into Shell's bed, and stretches out, careful not to touch her.

"What will happen tomorrow?" she whispers, stupid and naked.

"Don't know."

Jesse's breath is deep and steady, catching in the back of his throat. Between Shell's legs, it is sticky. Maybe the blood will have stained the mattress, like the first time Shell menstruated — upstairs, in this same twin bed. Stiff and careful, Shell lies down, covers pulled up to her chin. She blinks into the indigo light coming through the window, cigarettes butted on the sill, and wishes — with all her might — that it was winter: white and cold and very still. Maybe Dad will be out front shovelling the walk for Shell and Mum and the mailman, and before any of them are even out of bed. He'll put on the coffee when he comes in and he'll put the weather report on the radio.

And then she falls asleep, to the sound of Dad's shovel breaking snow crust, scraping the pavement below.

BY SEVEN, WHEN Shell's headache wakes her, Jesse is gone. She wraps up in her housecoat. The bloodstain on the sheets is in the shape of an eggplant, a paisley, or some kind of amoeba. Arms full of dishes, she climbs upstairs, ladylike, as if she is riding a horse. Really, though, she is just sore.

Morning is grey now. A cool breeze comes in the window above the sink and also through the back door, ajar by two or three inches. Jesse left the pantry doors open too — the top two shelves empty of crackers and cookies, Cheerios. Even the basmati rice and brown sugar are gone, and there is nothing in the fridge either: no block of marble cheddar, egg carton, butter, bagels, chicken meatballs wrapped in foil.

Shell cries washing the macaroni pot, wooden spoon, bowls and utensils and cups. Then, upstairs in the bathroom, she eases herself into a warm bath — bubbled with Mum's Yardley Rose — and, with soap and loofah, scrubs. The water that drains is thin pink, and bits of grass and sandy dirt float on the surface, like the stale bird bath out back.

Mum's alarm goes off. Shell runs downstairs to get breakfast on — the most important meal of the day. Even when she and Carla wake up hungover in some party house, having slept head to foot on a cat-piss couch, Shell, first thing, wants breakfast. Everyone else has a cigarette and what's left in stray drink cans, but Shell makes Carla struggle down to 7-Eleven or a doughnut shop to buy at least a hunk of something bready and a carton of milk.

Apples and walnuts will go with the porridge. Shell chops and grates, stopping to shake from her head the wet crack of Bruce Cockburn's breaking face, the look of Jesse's raised knuckles, or the throbbing between her legs.

Then Mum comes in.

"Hi, Mum!" Mum's got her runners on, XL Amnesty International T-shirt, and sweatpants with paint on the knees. She had mentioned a tai chi class first thing Saturdays, but Shell's never awake to witness it. "Up and at 'em, eh?" That's what Dad used to say. Or he'd sing "Lazy Bones."

Mum's lips are very thin. "Shell, where is my wallet?"

Shell freezes, knife poised, the tip just breaking the apple's waxy skin. "What? Why? What do you mean?"

"It was in the hall by the phone. I need to go, Shell. I looked all over. Did you take it?"

Shell moans. Her head falls, the apple, the knife. She steps over to Mum and puts her arms around her soft neck, drawing her in close.

"Mum, Mum, no."

Mum lets herself be hugged. But then she untangles herself and grabs Shell by the wrists. "Shell, my wallet.

Where is it?" Her eyes, behind her glasses, are grey, drawn tight at the corners, rimmed in red.

"Mum," Shell whispers back.

The lid on the porridge pot explodes into a clatter; grey goop spills over, sizzling on the element. Shell gathers up the length of her housecoat and thumps down the basement stairs. Her room smells of Jesse. The weight of his head is still crushed into the pillow. Shell falls to her knees, twists onto the floor, reaching under her bed. "God, God, please," she whispers, fumbling, blind. At the familiar touch of the coarse horsehair weave, she breathes easy.

Everything is inside the button box as it should be—pasta shells, tape cassettes, rusty nails, postcards, keys, hunk of serrated bottle glass. And something new: a single Polaroid. Within the glossy white frame, the photograph is gold-hued and grainy. The girl in the picture is asleep, her lips parted and breasts uncovered, hair streaming across her pillow. Because she is almost beautiful, Shell has to look closely to believe it's her.

Left Luggage

Somerset is less than two hours from the U.S. border, but Shell and Mum have never been to the States. Even before Reagan, Dad wouldn't step foot in the place. The mechanic at the high school where Mum teaches said Mum's brown Datsun station wagon is decent enough to make it down south, and with her permanent contract Mum can finally afford to do a Christmas trip.

"Now you're sixteen, Shell," Mum says, "you should see there's more to life than Somerset. Or Toronto."

"But, God, Florida is so tacky," Shell says. "Go with one of your teacher friends." Shell can take the bus to Dad's for the holidays. But Dad, when Shell calls, says,"Why don't we catch up for New Year's?"

Mum is at the harvest table stirring honey into her tea and flipping through bright Season's Greetings! grocery flyers: crackly brown turkeys with pieces of holly stuck in them, thick mugs of eggnog with candy cane stir sticks, potatoes already wrapped in gold foil.

"We'll do something special," Dad says. He'd like her to meet a new friend. Her name is Valery.

"Oh," Shell says. "Okay."

If Mum would find a boyfriend like Vicki's mum, the constant prickle of Mum's loneliness would finally go away. Then Shell could stay over at Carla's or visit Dad in Toronto without sudden flashes of Mum hunched over the kitchen sink washing her dinner plate or standing alone on the Greyhound platform. Worse is the silhouette of the back of her head when she drives away in the Datsun. Shell could just drink beer and smoke cigarettes and hash to have fun, not to drown out that sinking feeling that Mum is sad and needs Shell like Shell needs her. How will Shell ever go away to university? And she'll never go to France with Carla like they're planning instead of finishing grade eleven. Carla's already saved enough Harvey's paycheques to buy a one-way ticket to Paris. Shell's glad she only has fifty bucks so far. Then she won't have to say she can't go anywhere too far from Mum.

Mum checks the *Penny Saver* and gets a good deal on a condo in Fort Myers. The lady on the phone says Conch Lane is a little out of town yet "just steps from water."

The semester finishes on the twenty-third of December. They'll leave for Florida at five the next morning. "Pack a swimsuit, Shell," Mum says.

Shell snorts. Mum doesn't own a swimsuit either. Like last year at Lake Erie, Mum just rolls her pant legs up to her alabaster knees and carries her clogs down the beach.

Mum spends the whole week getting ready. She packs a box with dry pasta and cans of soup, beans, tomato sauce, and calls Environment Canada to ask about coming storms.

"Wow. Look, Shell." The glossy photograph in the Somerset Public Library's *Budget Guide to Florida* could be some minimalist painting: Rothko or something by Georgia O'Keeffe. On a closer look, though, the three horizontal strips—white, bottle green, and azure on top—are in fact a faultless beach. A lone figure stoops over in the distance, "shelling," as *Budget Guide* calls it.

"Let's go there," Mum breathes.

"Hmm," says Shell, cutting herself a great hunk of cheese.

Mum's new suitcase—finally, one with four wheels and a wide pulley strap—was on sale at Eaton's. She fills it with travel-sized toiletries, lightweight pyjamas, summer blouses, homemade jeans, and an array of sun hats, then test drives it around the house.

"See how civilized this is?" she says, smiling. When Mum was Shell's age and sailed to England, her luggage was the brass-hinged steamer trunk now at the end of Mum's bed. Inside are quilts and framed pictures, Shell's baby clothes, a few pieces of Mum's pottery, the wind-up clock from the farm where she grew up.

While she's packing, Mum stuffs a Goodwill bag full of old clothes. "Out with the old," she keeps saying. She tosses stained tea towels and a stack of *National Geographic*s in the garbage bag too. Does Shell have anything to add? Mum has been clearing closets and drawers all school year. Most of Dad's stuff is gone now. She hired some men to take away the appliances he'd salvaged—the extra washer and dryer and the leaking chest freezer in the back shed. And Kremski and some other artists Dad knew have been coming over and, piecemeal, taking away the wood and metal scrap Dad stored under the back porch. Shell watched through her upstairs window while Kremski rode away with his basket full of kiln bricks, a bundle of hockey sticks tucked under his arm.

CBC IS ON in the kitchen. Overnight programming from the Netherlands; the morning show doesn't start for another half-hour. Mum and Shell slurp Cheerios and coffee; outside, the world is still dark. Shell throws books and tapes, jeans, T-shirts, and cigarettes into her knapsack. She hopes the border guards won't find the twenty-sixer of Jameson wrapped up in her pyjamas. Mum keeps calling out, "Make sure all the luggage is in the car and that the bedroom windows are locked."

Shell laces her Doc Martens, bundles up in her parka, and carries her bag out to the car. The back seat is stuffed with umbrellas and food and extra shoes, but there's still room in the trunk, right on top of the Goodwill stuff Mum forgot to drop off.

"Have everything?" Mum asks again and again, locking the door behind them.

Shell says yes.

"Your bag is—?"

"In the car."

"And mine?"

"Uh, what?"

"Did you get the suitcase from my room?"

Shell yawns, last night's Jameson nightcaps throbbing in her right temple.

"Yeah. In there too."

EXCEPT FOR THE forest of fast-food signs along the freeways and warehouses selling firecrackers and ammunition, it's not so different here from their part of Canada. Maybe that's why Dad and his friends think America is so evil—because it looks so familiar. The farther south they drive, the more exotic the fast-food restaurants get: Cracker Barrel, IHOP, then Waffle House diners start popping up every fifty miles or so. Mum and Shell start counting the yellow-and-black signs and stop at the twenty-second one for lunch. They're in Ohio. Mum gets a club sandwich and tomato soup and Shell the all-day breakfast: two eggs over easy, bacon, and hash browns— which is what Waffle House is famous for rather than the waffles.

Shell flips through the glossy colour plates in the middle of the *Budget Guide* and Mum pores over the road map. After the holdup at the border, getting to their reservation in Macon, Georgia, before dark is going to involve some gunning.

"It's Sanibel you like, right?" Shell holds up a collage of local seashells.

Mum nods. "Teachers at school say it's beautiful."

Mum takes the book from Shell, wowing at the

mottled cowries and yellow cockles, conches pink as bubblegum, and tulip mussels in indigo. "Sanibel's treasure,"
Mum reads, "is a *junonia* or *Juno's volute*. At four to six
inches in length, the shell of the predatory sea snail is so
rare that shellers who find them are said to be descended
from the goddess they are named for."

Shaking her head, Mum says, "I've always wanted to
see a shell with counter-clockwise spirals. Those ones are
complete anomalies."

"Since when are you so into shells?" Shell says, reaching over to snatch back the guidebook. But Mum holds
tight. She stares across the table. Shell stares back. Finally
Mum relinquishes the book.

"Since before you were born, Shell."

SHELL AND MUM can't believe how beautiful it is in Ken-
tucky and then in Tennessee.

"It's nicer here than even Algonquin," Shell says.

As the mountains flow by—soft and blue—Shell
relaxes into daydreams. They don't say much. The music
is enough: Bob Dylan, Joni Mitchell, the Billie Holiday
tape that almost went in the Goodwill bag. Looking out
the window, Shell understands where her life's best music
was truly born, and when they're side-swiping Chatta-
nooga and "Visions of Johanna" comes on, Shell cries
behind her sunglasses.

By the time the sun starts falling—coffees and cookies
and a bag of oily peanuts later, coats off because it's getting
warm—Mum says her legs are numb.

"Okay, Mum." Shell folds the map. "Only about twenty miles to go."

"Miles or kilometres?"

"Miles. No, yes. Miles." Like Davis.

But really it's kilometres, and then they take a wrong turn and can't find the on-ramp again — "Shell, you watch for me: make sure it's east not west" — so it's dark when they get to Macon and darker still when they pull up in front of Priced-Right Inn and Suites, set back on a dark road lit only by fast-food signage and no street lights anywhere. Their room — seventy-six — is in a rear building, main floor. Mum seems to know the drill. They drive right around, parking out front of the room.

Mum says they have to carry everything inside. "Shell, what if we got broken into?"

They pile everything — cassette tapes, umbrellas, Shell's bag, rubbers, cooler, Thermos, food boxes, maps — behind the door and then Mum locks the car. The motel room, the first Shell's ever been in, smells like Waffle House hash browns, and the buzz-cut carpet is bright pumpkin. Everything else — bedspreads, wallpaper, towels — is the colour of mushroom soup, so all the cigarette burns show up.

With her boots and jean jacket still on, Shell perches on the edge of one of the two twin beds and turns on the TV.

Mum closes her eyes and bites into an Almond Joy. Shell takes a Grand Slam. They also stocked up on Whatchamacallits and Milky Ways. They've got way more kinds of candy here than in Canada.

"Ugh," Mum groans, rolling off her bed. "All I want to do

is put on my pyjamas, brush my teeth, and close my eyes."

"Yeah," Shell says. The weather guy on the local news says it's going to be eighty degrees tomorrow. "Mum, what's that in Celsius?"

Mum's not listening. "Shell," she says, "where'd you put my suitcase?"

"There. By the door."

A McDonald's commercial comes on. Shell knows from Mum and Dad's record collection that the real version of the Mac Tonight song is from Brecht. "Mum, it's Mack the Knife!"

But Mum's eyes are narrow with worry. "Shell, I don't see my suitcase. Go out and look."

THE AIR IN the parking lot is as damp and cool as wet laundry, and the sky is faded black like it's been washed a million times, and there are no stars. Somewhere, traffic rushes. The pollen of some late night bloomer sweetens the air. The familiar cold of Somerset feels far. No, it *is* far, and after just a day of driving. With a match held to her cigarette, Shell vows to both quit smoking and go on a diet right after New Year's. Maybe then Maček will finally ask her to go on a date. Then they can fall in love and take off for California, or maybe New Mexico, where they'll park a trailer in the middle of nowhere and raise a pack of dogs. Mum can move somewhere close. Pheonix, maybe.

Having been in the Czech army, Maček knows how to climb fences and pick locks, remove beer caps without a bottle opener. Because of that and his vampire smile,

Shell's started showing up for first period: if she passes by the autobody parking lot just as the first bell goes, Maček will be there, finishing his cigarette. Then she'll walk by again at lunch. He'll be leaning against whatever car he's working on, Big Gulp in one hand, cigarette in the other; the safety goggles pushing back his shaggy blond hair show off both a widow's peak and the V of his cheekbones. Three times now, Maček's waved at Shell. Each time after, Shell carries around a bright orange glow—a candle burning inside her—for days. But if Maček truly likes her, and Carla says every day when Shell asks her that he does, he would do more than lift his hand when she goes past. And when she does walk by, her neck burns and she pulls down her plaid shirt to make sure he can't see her bum.

The light comes on when Shell opens the back of the Datsun: coffee cups, Kleenex box, dirty plastic plate, cracker crumbs—oh, and the garbage bag with stuff for the Goodwill. But no brand new wheelie suitcase.

"Shit," Shell whispers.

"Well?" Mum sits facing the door, hands in her lap. "Find it?"

Shell scratches her head. "It's weird. You sure it's not in here?" She scans the station wagon's contents now carefully stacked by the door. "That a-hole border guard, he take it?"

"God. How the hell did I forget my suitcase?" Mum takes off her glasses, without which she's suddenly shrivelled and hollow like one of those harvest dolls with the dried-apple faces. "You said you got it from my room."

"I did?" Shell just remembers her arms being full with

her own stuff and the way her groggy headache thumped in her temples.

"You remember it being in there, Shell? I mean, it's not sitting in the bloody driveway?"

Shell unzips her bag. She shakes out her biggest T-shirt, soft faded cotton announcing *Black Market Clash*. "You could wear this, Mum. Like for pyjamas."

"Or maybe it *was* that border guard," Mum says, opening the motel door. The parking lot and the Waffle House sign are right there, smack-dab outside their bedroom.

Through the curtains, Shell watches Mum search the station wagon, beginning at the back and working frontwards. The car's interior light suspends her movements within the surrounding dark and holds them, gold-lit squares of activity, like nights in Algonquin with Dad when the lantern turned their tent into a translucent red pearl, just hanging there in the black swath of fresh air, yellow moon, and brightest stars.

Mum dumps the Goodwill bag on her bed. Their old cutlery set—bundled with elastics—tumbles out, as does a washed-out tablecloth of indigo batik, a set of stained plastic cups, a pair of oversized T-shirts, one fluorescent pink, the other fluorescent green. Some of Dad's old books end up on Mum's mushroom bedspread too; Shell picks up Noam Chomsky's *Towards a New Cold War* as well as a bundle of spoons.

"What? You're giving away our silverware?"

The flat handles are embossed with a rose pattern, *Made in Korea* stamped on the back. Shell loads the bundled forks, knives, spoons into her bag.

"Can't give all my stuff away."

"Not stuff, Shell. Crappy old junk we don't use anymore."

The avocado-coloured Tupperware cups are grubby with Shell's childhood fingers and the bottoms buckled with melts and burns. These, along with a pungent smell of plastic and old milk, go in Shell's bag too.

Mum sighs. "I just have to go to sleep."

She comes out of the bathroom in the fluorescent pink shirt, a grey motel towel for a skirt. After a cup of milk and a stick of Shell's Trident to clean her teeth, Mum curls up under the covers. She turns her bright pink back to Shell, who reads Noam Chomsky by the light of the TV. When Mum starts to snore, Shell gets out her Player's Lights and Jameson and, silently opening the motel door, crouches by the Datsun. Sipping, smoking—the night passes, shaved away by the steady buzz of traffic.

THERE'S BREAKFAST IN the lobby until ten.

Like Shell, Mum wears the same clothes as yesterday—black jeans and lilac turtleneck—and combs her hair with her fingers.

The triangle-shaped Christmas tree in the lobby has fake presents underneath.

"Merry Christmas," smiles the wrinkled silver-blond lady at the reception counter, barely glancing away from the TV hanging from the ceiling.

"Isn't she way too old to be working?" Shell asks.

"It's the sun, Shell. I bet she's younger than me."

Along with thin coffee, Shell has two Styrofoam bowls of Raisin Bran; Mum fills up on hot goopy stuff called grits. They share a green banana, and Mum sneaks apples and oranges into her purse.

Mum pumps gas at the Texaco across the road while Shell finds the restroom at the back. She smokes half a Player's Light, squatting above the toilet, denuded of its seat.

A mum and kids are waiting outside the restroom door. With lowered gaze, Shell hands the mum the long stick with the key.

"Eww!" a little-boy voice cries as she walks quickly away. "Cigarettes!"

THE I-8 IS thick with holiday traffic and the radio is all about Christmas, so Shell keeps the tape player going. So long as it's nothing too crazy, Mum says, which means no Talking Heads. Instead, Joan Baez sees them through the bottom end of Georgia, and crossing into Florida it's "Folsom Prison Blues."

Shell looks up at the flatlands flashing by then goes back to her *Essential William Blake*. The air coming through the ventilators gets thick, then full-on humid. Only RVs and cars hauling boats are slower than their brown Datsun. Pickups with stickers for the Florida Gators, beefy motorcycles, low-riding Corvettes whizz past Mum and Shell, all high on sunshine and soda and something else. Cocaine? Shell's seen *Miami Vice*.

"Jesus Christ." With a wailing horn, a rusty Town Car cuts in front of Mum.

"Keep up your speed, Mum. Limit's up to seventy now."

"Next time you'll be driving too, Shell," Mum says, wringing the steering wheel between her hands, afraid to move her head. "It's a skill every woman needs to learn."

In her side mirror, Shell's gold sunglasses shine like Joe Strummer's on the cover of that rare Clash single Shell traded for with a skater at school. In exchange, he got a bottle of Drakkar Noir cologne Shell had shoplifted from The Bay.

The Kmart on the outskirts of Jacksonville is so big it has groceries. Ham and cheese and bread, mustard and relish fill Mum's basket, as well as toothpaste and a brush, a set of pocket combs, a bottle of Keri lotion, and sunscreen. Large one-hundred-percent-cotton underwear comes in a three-pack: pink, mint, robin's egg blue.

"God," Mum keeps saying. "It's so stupid to buy this stuff when it's just sitting in my suitcase at home."

Shell offers to buy the underwear for Mum for Christmas. Then she remembers she has no money, so she goes to smoke by the Datsun.

Despite the clear sun, the air is brisk and the wind comes hard. Somewhere off, it smells of rain. Shell pulls up the collar of her jean jacket.

"I thought it was supposed to be hot here," she says when Mum comes back.

They load the bags into the car. Mum takes off her coat then puts it back on. At the far end of the parking lot there's a stretch of grass where Mum spreads out the tablecloth from the Goodwill bag. She digs into the cooler. Instead of Mum's plastic cutlery, Shell finds the bundles salvaged from the Goodwill bag. With the old rose-handled knives and spoons, Mum makes sandwiches. Shell uses Chomsky for a plate; Mum gets William Blake.

"You buy any clothes in there?"

Mum shakes her head; she'll just wash what she has on. She opens the map. "Some hours to go yet." Plus, they have to stop somewhere and get a turkey.

"It's Christmas tomorrow, Shell. Remember?"

TINSELLED DOORS AND palm trees hung with Christmas lights line the streets of suburban Fort Myers, but there's no snow and the tiny bungalows seem to be painted for Easter instead: pink, mint, baby blue, sort of like Mum's new underwear. At Publix, Mum asks about the Conch Lane address.

"Yeah, it's a little far," says the cashier who rings in their lamb—they're fresh out of turkeys. "Kind of a bed-room community, you might call it. Just take a left at the lights and go straight down to the end."

They take Conch Lane—inland for an entire hour—as far as it goes. Then Mum turns into an asphalt drive; at the end is a white split-level divided into units.

"Where's the beach?" Shell thought Mum said it was close.

"'Steps from the water,'" Mum says, slamming her car door and comparing the number on the building to the one written on the slip of paper tucked in her wallet: one thousand and fifty. "That's what she told me."

"Well, she lied."

The key is in the main-floor mailbox. Mum and Shell

drag their luggage and Publix bags up a narrow spiral staircase to the second floor and into an apartment full of white wicker furniture and tropical plants made out of papier mâché. There are two doubles in the bedroom and the living room has about ten lamps and everything is accented with seashells, all kinds of them, encrusting picture frames and coasters and lampshades and the stately mirror hung above the couch. A set of sliding doors gives way to a balcony no bigger than a shower stall, the view from which is of a narrow irrigation creek with a concrete walking path snaking alongside.

"There's the water we're steps from," Mum says.

Shell turns on the TV. "At least she didn't lie about the cable," she says, clicking to *Murder, She Wrote*.

Mum steps onto the balcony, sliding the door closed behind her. She unfolds a patio chair and sits, hugging her winter coat around her. Mum holds her back straight and stiff. Her neck is thin and delicate compared with the size of her head, enlarged by a mass of coarse steel-wool hair, extra puffy with the humidity and needing a trim. Unlike Shell, Mum never cries or yells or drinks whiskey to get to sleep. Even when Dad said he was leaving, all Mum did was go for a long walk by herself, returning with the employment section of the *Somerset Free Press*. "We just have to go on," she had said. Well, Mum's mum had been a real-life pioneer, homesteading in a sod house on the Prairies where it's minus forty in the winter. She'd come through the Great Depression. "You don't know from hardship," Mum will always say when Shell refuses to mow the lawn.

It's dark when Shell knocks on the patio glass. "What's for dinner?" she shouts. Mum finally turns around, her eyes pink with tired.

Mum changes into the fluorescent green T-shirt and leaves her turtleneck to soak in the bathtub. Rain spatters against the windows, so they eat their spaghetti and toast in front of the TV instead of on the balcony like Mum said they ought to. The bottle of California wine is for tomorrow, Mum says, but they can have a slice of Publix apple pie, which they heat in the microwave just as the rain turns into a downpour: runoff gushes from the eaves, wind rips and whips, loose palm fronds batter the doors to the patio, which Mum is sure in Florida is called a *linah*.

"Should we leave milk and cookies for Santa?" Shell asks when Mum says good night.

Mum frowns at Shell, who, stretched out on the flowered couch, boots on the cushions, barely looks up from *The Handmaid's Tale* and, beyond that, a *Family Ties* Christmas episode muted on the TV.

"Well," Mum says, closing the bedroom door, "at least be glad you're dry and warm."

BRIGHT SUN SLICES through the bedroom blinds.

"Looks like Santa came after all," Mum says when Shell comes out in her nightgown. Mum is reading Shell's Simone de Beauvoir, dripping coffee down the front of the green shirt. There is porridge on the stove and coffee in the pot. A bag of Hershey's Kisses and a tube of Kmart brand key lime pie lip balm rest next to the place

Mum set for Shell at the round table with the glass top.

"Thanks." Shell pushes the chocolate and lip balm away.

"It's nice here." Mum went for a walk along the irrigation creek. She saw a pelican and signs warning of alligators. The storm cracked a palm in half and Shell should see the hibiscus and lemon trees just there out back.

"Cool." Shell opens her novel, spooning porridge.

Mum's turtleneck is hanging on the balcony. It's dry by the time Shell gets on her jeans and washes her face with coconut-scented hand soap. Mum makes the sandwiches and— "Shell, you'll navigate"—writes out their route to Sanibel Island. But they'll have to be home in time to cook the lamb. Say about four.

The air is clear and fresh, but despite the wreaths and plastic Nativity scenes up and down Conch Lane, it could be any day of any year and just about anywhere in the Christian world. It's just stillness—even the breeze is sparse—no people in sight. Few drives even have cars.

"We the only suckers here?" Shell asks.

"Just you wait," Mum says, starting the Datsun. "Dollars to doughnuts they're already at the beach."

TRAFFIC IS THICK all the way across town and west up the coast. The Datsun—the only rusty brown car in Florida, Shell is sure—gets swept up in the shiny, top-down island flow. The causeway connecting Sanibel to the mainland is three separate bridges, one for each mile, and seems to go on forever. Crystal ocean stretches out on either side, as far as Shell can see.

Somerset is gone. Back there, way behind.

Mum breathes that "it's all so beautiful" and keeps swerving to look at the wide blue water. White triangles of boat sail every which way, and birds — also white — sweep across the azure sky. Then, at the end of the last bridge, they follow the main road to Sanibel's first available beach parking lot.

"Ten dollars an hour, ma'am."

Mum's eyes harden on the attendant. "What?" The Datsun idles as she does the conversion to Canadian in her head.

Behind, horns toot; someone's stereo's got Johnny Mathis singing about chestnuts.

Shell slouches, her head sinking well below window level. "Heck, Mum, it's Christmas."

There's only a few spots left at the back of the lot. Families, couples, cars of teens — from the Carolinas, Georgia, Quebec, and Ontario — gather up umbrellas and picnic baskets, water wings and surfboards. More than a few wear Santa hats with their bathing suits. Mum and Shell grab the cooler and join the queue flip-flopping down to the water. And whether it is dimpled or taut, pimpled or sleek, black or tanned or white as baby teeth, there's as much naked skin on Sanibel as there is beach. Mum and Shell shuffle along, sweating in their denim and long sleeves and heavy lace-up shoes.

"God, I wish I had my sandals," Mum mutters.

"Ah, it's not that hot," says Shell through her teeth.

While the lilac of Mum's turtleneck sort of fits into the colour scheme of the beach, Shell's faded black T-shirt, jean jacket, and thick plaid button-down absorb the bright white sun, which is starting to beat. At least Shell's collar is open, unlike the tight folded cuff encircling Mum's neck.

"It must be over seventy," Mum says, her voice tight. That means the low twenties in Celsius. "We'll have to get on some sunscreen."

The salt air smells of fries — the earthy hand-cut kind with skins still on — and the ocean surf peels, steady and strong. Children squeal right along with the seagulls. The beach sand is pink as cotton candy . . . or, no, not sand. The Sanibel shore is made of millions and billions of tiny seashells, all crushed up and ground up and powdered. Those shells still intact glow the same pastel colours as all the bungalows in Fort Myers. Mum calls the limber white birds scurrying along the water's edge sandpipers; for every ten of those, there's a yellow-beaked heron.

Mum and Shell trudge past beach towels and bare bodies, sandcastles and transistor radios, coconut lotion sweetening the breeze, until Shell deems them far enough removed from fellow humans that they can set up their own picnic.

"Well, this old thing sure's coming in handy," Mum says, spreading out the Goodwill tablecloth.

A girl in a bikini wanders by, drum-tight skin the colour of caramel, sharp diamonds of hip bones catching sun. Shell shrinks up inside her thick clothes and, next to Mum on the tablecloth, tries to sit cross-legged, but her jeans are too tight. They eat sandwiches and cookies from the cooler. Thick, salty waves crash in, brave and vigorous, and then, tired out and mollified, pull gently back again.

Even though her face and neck are white with Banana

Boat, Mum drapes the fluorescent green shirt over her head before she heads up the beach, plastic bag in hand, to do some shelling.

"Back in a bit."

Shell stretches out with *The Handmaid's Tale*—Offred's affair with Nick is pretty hot. Behind her eyes, Shell sees herself as Offred and Nick comes up as Maček, which makes her wish to get back to Somerset soon. Even in winter, Maček wears a leather jacket and high-tops, and his hands are so dry and calloused he doesn't need gloves.

Mum comes back with her pants rolled to the knee. The splotch of purple veins on the back of her right calf is new. She's carrying her sturdy lace-ups and her plastic bag is heavy with shells.

"People all the way down have these special rakes for digging." Mum brushes sand from starfish, sand dollars, lavender mussel shells, and—her prize—a delicate jujube shell the same colour as cranberry juice. And when she'd stooped down for the starfish, all these people came over wanting to see what it was.

"Shelling is serious business here," she says. "You should go see."

Shell puts on some more sunscreen and walks down the beach.

"Don't be too long," Mum calls out. "We need to get that lamb in."

She takes off her Docs, ties them together by the laces, and, slinging them over her shoulder, walks the tide line—jeans rolled up like Mum, ball of socks in her pocket. Her bare feet crush into seashell: teeny tiny ones small as her pinky nail, rosy chunks of conch, limbs of starfish. She passes a dozen or so separate shellers wading through the surf, trawling with long-handled nets. One or two, then a third, stoop over and call out—"Sea urchin!" "Blind-eye drill!" "Banded tulip!"—holding up their treasure for all to see.

When her feet are prunes and jean jacket pockets full of the tiniest shells she can find, she sits on a hunk of drift-wood and smokes. The sun begins to fall and her tummy rumbles for lamb. Ahead, the shellers have gathered—some twelve or fifteen scattered across the shore, nets and rakes slung over their shoulders. They're heading home for turkey or goose or whatever, unless they're Jewish, and Mum said a lot of people in this part of Florida are.

Some yards back, Shell follows them up the beach, eyeing the tidal plain for any dregs they might have over-looked. The tide rolls in and out. There in the wake is a bright red ribbon of seaweed. Shell stoops, catches hold. She pulls, and within the disturbed sand a smooth arc of something pink and nutty bubbles up, just inside the tide mark. It's only from the *Budget Guide* that Shell recognizes the long spindled shape of the mighty Junonia.

Flash—she dips down, scooping the shell from the wet sand before the ocean sweeps in to reclaim it. Sleek as a new-born baby, tapered as an acorn, the Juno's volute's creamy background is patterned with rows of rusty square dots; the whorl that caps the top begins tight but widens out, meeting, eventually, the smooth cuff of the shell's outer lip.

Down the beach, Mum is waving the fluorescent green shirt: time to go. But Shell remains grounded, glued to that Sanibel spot. Look—it's pure luck she holds in her hands: some kind of message, surely. Then, the treasure cradled in her arms, Shell runs up the beach towards Mum, crazy with the sudden feeling that everything is going to be all right.

"Juno! Juno!" Shell calls out like *bingo*, like *jackpot*. "Juno's volute!"

"Shell!" Mum cries back, waving the shirt. The cooler is all packed up, tablecloth folded away. "The lamb!" she cries. "Let's go!"

The crowd of shellers between Shell and Mum turns to look. Three women break away and walk back towards her. Shell stops. She hugs the shell to her chest, tucking it within the layers of her plaid.

The approaching shellers slip in the wet sand, trailing footprints that the sweeping tide washes away. Because one is really tall and they are all pretty old, she thinks of Dorothy, Blanche, and Rose from that show Mum likes, *Golden Girls*. As they get close enough, the texture of their orange skin becomes leathery; their tight, pearly lips hold stretched smiles.

"What'd you find?"

Shell, her Docs still slung over her shoulder, steps back as the women surround her.

"We just want a look," says the tall one—Dorothy. A giant black camera hangs from her neck.

These Golden Girls are in shorts and tank tops, their fallen, wrinkled flesh loosely jiggling. White and silver hair is stark against their tans, as is the twinkle of their jewellery.

Shell shows them the Juno. The women gasp.

"All my life I've been searching for one!" says one with lots of makeup — Shell thinks of her as Blanche. She, Blanche, lowers her sunglasses. Her lids are powdered with green and red for Christmas.

"And look, it's so big!" says the third, who must be Rose.

"You want to hold it?" asks Shell.

Rose takes it first. The rings on her fingers clink as she caresses the smooth surface.

Mum comes up without word or sound. The women stand back, opening the circle to let her in.

"Look what your daughter found," says Dorothy. She tells Mum all about the Juno. "And it's so unusual to find one this late in the day." Can she take a picture?

Mum shrugs. Shell shrugs. Shell holds the Juno away from her, offering it to the camera. But no, Dorothy wants Shell in there. She's to say cheese.

Snap.

Dorothy winds the film. Now Mum's to get in. Blanche takes the cooler from Mum and nudges her towards Shell. "Oh, go on," she coos. She says they are a lovely mother and daughter. And aren't they smart to leave Dad at home with the turkey. That's what they all did this fine Christmas Day.

Mum is stiff beside Shell. Shell tries her best not to smile, but the three women tease her — "Oh, come on, honey" — until her face breaks open. Then she feels Mum's arm around her shoulders and Mum takes a deep breath like she always does before someone takes her picture.

"Cheese!" they say.

Dorothy gets some close-ups of the shell, marvelling again at the size and the sheer luck of finding such a specimen. She says she'll mail them copies of the pictures, so Mum writes down their home address on the back of a Publix receipt.

"Canada!" Dorothy shows her friends the receipt. Well, then, welcome to Florida. So far from home, and isn't that quite the souvenir your daughter's got to take back? And Merry Christmas, Merry Christmas, Merry Christmas, they wave, walking up the beach.

Mum and Shell wait as the three get some distance ahead. Mum rolls the shell between her hands, eyeing the markings. "Gorgeous." She lifts it to her ear, listening for waves.

Then Shell tucks the smooth, nutty cone back into her jacket.

"Ready?" says Mum.

Shell says yup. Then, wait, no. Though she won't say it, Mum looks so hot in her turtleneck and jeans and no sun hat thanks to Shell and the left luggage back in Somerset. Shell pulls the Juno from where it comfortably rests against her ribs. With two open hands, she gives the shell to Mum.

"Happy Christmas, Mum," Shell says, taking the cooler.

SHELL CALLS DAD while the lamb is roasting. She can smell the meat out on the patio where she leans with the portable phone.

Valery is making *mole* chicken for Dad and some friends. He says she is homesick today especially, so the *mole* helps.

Shell doesn't ask what place Valery is homesick for. She pretends she knows what *mole* means and that she isn't homesick for Christmas morning with Dad—homemade toys and pioneer waffles, down to the pond for a bumpy skate. And Shell pretends Florida is a drag—you should see all the fat people, Dad, and shooting ranges—just like she pretends for Mum that Toronto is too busy and clangy, full of bankers and art snobs, she'd never want to live there.

Valery is mispronouncing Dad's name in the background. Shell says a final Merry Christmas and clicks off the portable phone.

MUM AND SHELL watch cable news, pink dinner plates on their laps filled with lamb and potatoes, apple pie on the side. Mum reaches for more wine before Shell polishes it off.

The Juno is on the wicker coffee table, TV reflected in the bony shine.

"Somehow shells always look better in the water," Shell says. "Rocks too. They're so bright purple or orange, but as soon as they dry off, it's just a regular rock."

Mum picks up the Juno. "This one is different. It's beautiful wherever it goes." Mum says it all depends on how you look at it.

"Like how?" says Shell. "It's just big is all. It was better hidden in the sand."

270

"It's not the shell itself," Mum says. "It's a memory now. A whole new thing."

Mum finishes her wine and goes to bed. Shell turns off a *Simon & Simon* rerun and gets into the bed beside Mum's. Somewhere she hears the push and pull of water. Or maybe it is just the dishwasher, rinsing away Christmas.

New Roof

Barb Nutt has a realtor friend, Priscilla. Her candy-apple Mercedes is parked in the driveway behind the brown Datsun, its rear end hanging out across the sidewalk. If Dad were here, he'd make her park on the road. And he'd stand on the porch with his arms crossed while she did it.

Shell hunches over her desk. While Shell was living in the basement, Dad's mountain ash filled in the view from the window of her old bedroom. It's her new bedroom now, the smell of fresh Eggshell still in the air. Shell's fingers are poised on the keys of Mum's Smith-Corona, salvaged from the garage sale she had with Barb a few weeks ago over at the Nutt place. Shell also saved her life's favourite books—*Alligator Pie, Jacob Two-Two*, and all her Judy Blumes—as well as the paper Swiss Chalet hat Kremski gave her when he worked there as a dishwasher.

It fits now, though when she'd gone as Kremski for Halloween, it kept falling down over her eyes. For Kremski's Drum rollie, Dad had painted a pencil stub white and taught her to clench it between her molars, while Mum had rubbed brown oil pastel into Shell's chin for the shadowy beard. Kremski rode over on his bicycle and Dad had them pose for a picture on the steps. But at school all the princesses and ballerinas asked her what she was supposed to be and "Kremski" came out clunky and ugly.

Priscilla locks the Mercedes and smooths her beige linen pants. Her hair is white gold; a shiny hard-shelled purse is hooked on her arm. She peers up the driveway into the back, a hand on a round hip. Then she steps around to the front, scanning the brickwork and state of the porch. She cranes her neck to take in Shell's window. Catching her sunglasses as they slide from the perch on her head, the diamonds on her left hand flash.

Shell's weekly letter to Carla in France is overdue and there's a lot to type about this time. Like how she can't believe she's in grade twelve and neither can she stop thinking about Maček. She hasn't seen him for a long while. "You know that kid Gil?" Shell types, the Smith-Corona's stiff *o* and *l* sticking. "Well, he said Dan got busted, so Maček is lying low until things settle. Downtown is pretty dry now. Not much for smokables. You would hate it! Sometimes I think maybe you were right, Maček does 'like' me, but other times I'm just his buddy, you know? Like maybe if I had a nice long ponytail, then he'd see me as a real girl and not some—"

The doorbell chimes downstairs. Shell freezes at the

keys. Then the screen door slams. "So," Priscilla says when Mum welcomes her in, "Barb tells me you're an artist."

Mum clears her throat. "No. Not quite."

"But you are thinking of listing. Yes?"

Mum goes, "Hmmm," then laughs a bit. "Well, yes."

"It's a big decision." Priscilla understands that. "But the house does have good bones. And with that garage building out back, it could have a lot of appeal for just the right people."

Mum explains how they'd made pottery back there. It's fully wired and there's a gas line, a feature Priscilla says is "fabulous." A real selling point.

Mum leads Priscilla through the house—living room, dining room, kitchen, down to the basement, and up again. At the first creak of footsteps on the stairs, Shell releases the letter from the typewriter, smearing the ink, and ducks into her closet. Crouching in the back, among boots and jigsaw puzzles, she pulls a pile of winter coats over her head.

"Ignore the mess," Mum says as she opens Shell's door, pushing against the heap of laundry blocking it from within.

"Oh!" Priscilla laughs. "Wow. Someone doesn't like to clean."

Mum laughs too. "My daughter assures me there's some kind of order going on in here."

Beneath Mum's wool duffle coat, Shell sweats, rolls her eyes. She rubs one of the coat's bone toggles, which she'd always thought of as being made from reindeer antler. Dad had said yeah, it's Rudolph. But what about his shiny nose? "Oh, stop," Mum would say. "Let her have her fantasies."

Priscilla's beige outfit flashes past the crack in the door, then the red and white check of Mum's blouse. The floorboards creak. Mum and Priscilla are leaning over Shell's desk, looking out the window.

"South-facing?" asks Priscilla.

"That's right."

The closet door opens next—"Plenty of storage room in there"—then closes quickly again. Mum leaves Shell's bedroom door open when she finally leads Priscilla to the lemon-scented bathroom, counters buffed and toilet lid down. Mum's back bedroom is last, the good lacy spread on the pioneer bed.

"Anywhere I don't have to pick weeds or shovel snow," Mum sighs when Priscilla asks where Mum is thinking of moving.

Well, in that case, she'll have to let Priscilla show her some condos. "There's a new development out by the Indian Museum. Close to an excellent high school for your daughter...um...I didn't catch her name."

"Shell," Mum says, leading Priscilla back down the stairs.

When the back door shuts and the house is quiet, Shell sneaks down to the kitchen. Priscilla's polished purse is just sitting there on the counter. A stack of crisp bills thickens the wallet inside. Shell takes a ten-dollar bill and also helps herself to two king-size Rothmans—tucks one behind each ear—and three Werther's Original candies.

She eats bread and honey while Mum's and Priscilla's heads bob in the windows of the studio. They keep pointing up at the ceiling.

Mum leads Priscilla back through the yard, so Shell finishes her sandwich at the top of the stairs. "I like what I see here," Priscilla coughs from the front hall. "Someone did a good job fixing up the place." But the ceiling in the studio is full of mould and because of that she doesn't even need to climb onto the roof to know the shingles need replacing. "I won't show this house until someone does that work," she says, rattling her car keys. Oh, and Mum simply must cut down the brush in the back. "Fill in that old pond. Plant a few petunias. It could be pretty."

Shell is sucking on a Werther's as the Mercedes pulls out of the drive and disappears up Cashel Street. "Screw you, lady," she calls out loud enough so Mum can hear.

"P.S.," Shell types to Carla, "send more of those Gauloises if you can and don't forget to *be honest* about me and Maček. I mean, to think about him, *so much*, it's not just nothing, right?"

MUM CALLS THE roofer Priscilla recommended. He comes early, before school, knocks on the back door. Mum is downstairs ironing her skirt, so Shell answers. But only because he saw her through the window, her arm stuck in the Cheerios box, before she could scurry away. *Murray* is stitched on the breast of his blue work shirt, a clipboard under his hairy arm and a faded anchor tattooed on the back of his wrist.

"Roofer," he says as Shell opens the door. His eyes dart from Shell's army boots to red velvet stretchy pants to cowboy shirt to raccoon eyes and pile of crimped hair.

"Hey Mum," Shell hisses, creeping down the basement stairs towards the smell of steaming cotton. "Roofing guy's here."

Murray climbs the extension ladder Shell and Mum had propped against the side of the studio. Mum waits at the bottom, her arms crossed, while Murray paces up one slope and down another, making notes on his clipboard. Shell's leaning over the sink drinking the milk from her cereal bowl when Mum comes back in. She attaches Murray's quote to the fridge with a magnet. The shiny ceramic orange says *Edison Estate, Fort Myers, FL* on the dimpled bottom.

"How much, Mum?"

"Three thousand dollars." Mum sighs.

"God," Shell says, rinsing her bowl in the sink. "Guess you can't sell the house, then. Right?"

Mum frowns and grabs her car keys: Shell is to get a move on. And don't forget to pack a lunch of some kind. There's still muffins in the fridge.

The morning is warm, hot even, for it is already June. Mum, then Shell, climbs into the car. "Maybe you can hire some handyman guy to do it cheaper?"

"I was thinking Soren Nutt," Mum mumbles as she backs out onto Cashel Street. "He's back from Queen's and looking for summer work."

Shell chokes on her gum. "That guy won't do a good job. Christ, Mum, he's an ass-wipe for sure."

"Shell!" Mum frowns, turning onto Catherine, past the Masonic Temple. "He is no such thing."

Mum speeds up so as to miss the eight-oh-five CNR freight that blocks north-south traffic every morning. On the other side of the tracks, packs of kids start cropping up, heading east to Somerset Tech or, if they are Portuguese or Filipino, to Pope Pius; they run against the traffic lights, break into air guitar, lean against mailboxes to copy homework.

"If not Soren, who?" Mum pulls into the Dutchie's Donuts parking lot on Joyce Street behind Somerset Tech. She glances up into her rear-view mirror as Tony and Gilberto Silva whip around the corner on their skateboards, Big Gulps in hand, hips sashaying. "One of those lumps?"

Shell grabs her backpack from between her feet. "Those're my friends, Mum," she says, slamming the door.

Mum almost hits Gilberto pulling back onto Joyce Street. She toots the horn. As the Datsun trundles away, Tony waves at Shell with his Big Gulp and gives Mum the finger.

SHELL STANDS ON the studio roof. She can see into backyards all the way up and down Cashel Street. This being Saturday, most people have patio furniture out; one guy three doors down is in shorts and has hot dogs on the barbecue and a fourth Canadian open. The high three o'clock sun beats down on Shell's bare arms. Her jeans are tight and moist with sweat, and Mum's black Amnesty

T-shirt is the wrong colour to be roofing in. The worst part is how her hair keeps slipping out from Dad's old Expos ball cap that Mum said she ought to wear with such strong sun.

Shell swigs the last inch of water from a plastic bottle and crouches, not quite taking a break. Mum should be back from Hobbs Build-All soon, with enough new shingles for Soren Nutt to start laying them first thing tomorrow morning. Mum's paying Soren six hundred dollars, flat rate, for what should be three days' work. But Shell has to scrape the old ones off first; Soren's not doing that grunt work. Shell stands, her spine knotted. And because the leather work gloves Mum found in the shed are hot and way too big to wear, her hands are calloused, swollen, the nails black with tar resin. There's just one last patch of old shingles now, along the peak of the western slope. Shell grabs the pitchfork. She started at the bottom edge of the eastern slope around ten this morning. As morning turned to afternoon, Mum coached her and fetched water and snacks and then lunch, and did not say anything when Shell swore or said how much roofing sucks. And it truly does suck, even with Mum paying her six dollars an hour, because the rafters are rotting, especially along the eastern peak.

"Christ," Mum had said as Shell pried the ruined shingles with the pitchfork, exposing wet black wood underneath. "I just want to get rid of this goddamn house, Shell. Even if we rent something."

Shell crouches into the roof's steep slant, slides the pitchfork prongs under the remaining gritty green shingles before wrenching them up, tarpaper tearing. While some shingles pop off as easy as a bottle cap, other areas are stubborn. Once this last swath of shingles is loosened, Shell switches to the coal shovel and pushes them—with great echoing scrapes—off the front of the roof. They scatter in the air before slapping down upon the wide heap of ripped-up shingles below. This morning that spot down there was a weed patch, and before that rows of squash and beans used to grow.

It's nearly four when Mum comes back. The dump closes at five, so they leave the shingles where they are, though Mum would prefer to just load them into the back of the Datsun and get them the hell out of her sight.

"God, even just one load," she says, frowning at her watch.

"Can't Soren do it?" Shell winces, pulling off the Expos cap. Hot, thick hair, dry enough it might as well be barnyard straw, tumbles out and sticks to her neck, back, and sides. "Isn't that what you're paying him for?"

"Okay," Mum says. Shell is right. "And some buddy of his is supposed to have access to a truck or something."

But together they do unload the back of the Datsun. There are twenty packs of new shingles, wrapped in brown paper, three feet long by two feet wide and four inches high or so, thirty pounds each. Mum also bought a dozen boxes of galvanized nails, a thirty-pound roll of felt underlay, a tin reel Mum calls a chalk line, and strips of flat four-inch flashing for making a drip edge.

"That's it?" Shell says, wiping her face with her hot red hands.

Mum pushes up her sunglasses and, with Shell, looks

around. The yard is littered with chunks of tarpaper and scraps of shingle that didn't make it onto the pile, and the air is hung with the sick residue of old asphalt, as well as the char of the neighbour's meaty barbecue. Shell smiles, woozy with nausea.

SHELL IS TECHNICALLY allowed to sleep in the next morning, Sunday. But the phone rings at about seven o'clock and she can't get back to sleep after that. She had fallen asleep reading so early the night before. Mum had come in, switched off her light, and removed the glasses from her face. Mum shuffles around downstairs getting herself an early breakfast; Soren is due at seven-thirty. Shell stays in bed. She reads *The Rime of the Ancient Mariner* for about the tenth time since Mrs. Poole assigned it to the class last week, and then, eyes closed, she tries to not forget about Maček: voice like a rake pulled through gravel; the feathers of his shaggy hair falling back from cheeks dull with acne scars; rare smile showing off his Dracula teeth. Has it already been a month since they played pool at Wizard's? Leaning against her pool cue, Shell told Maček that when Wizard's was a movie theatre she saw *Star Wars* there, her first real movie. Now a dozen pool tables dominate the floor, the green felt tops catching in the light of low-hanging lamps suspended on wires from the high cathedral ceiling. Maček took his shot—his number three banking. Would she believe him if he said he'd still never seen *Star Wars*?

"You're not missing much," Shell had promised, calling

nine in the corner and then sinking it. Shell wouldn't or couldn't let Maček beat her.

How'd she get so good?

"My dad." Shell shrugged. "I can skate and throw a football too."

Maček bought them Cokes between games, and they smoked Shell's Gauloise. The Who was playing too loud; some off-duty stripper from across the street kept putting "I Can See for Miles" on the jukebox—not once or twice, but three times. Later, a bunch of Somerset Tech kids walked over to the train bridge to drink the forty of tequila that Jason, a bug-eyed kid with an acne disorder, had got from the Mohawk reserve. Maček and Shell dawdled behind the others, then deked back to St. Paul's, where there's a parkette and benches. Maček rolled them a joint, warning her that this batch of hash was crazy potent. They sat near the maple tree where Shell goes to fall asleep in the long, lush grass, reading poetry instead of sitting in boring old Creative Writing class. "What a drag, man," she had said of that class. "Too much cornball writing."

Yup, Maček's was strong hash, but beautifully so, glowing. When they got to the train bridge, they shot a tequila each then shimmied down the ravine away from the others, close to the eggy water of the Somerset River. In not too many words, Maček told Shell about the Slovak part of Czechoslovakia where his father still works in a munitions plant and his mother stays home to raise the goats. He grew up on that milk, warm and thick and smelling of grass, plus soft fresh cheese. After his military service, Maček went to East Germany, then hid in an arms truck to get into West Germany, where he got a visa because his mother's cousin Jakub was in Somerset with his own roofing business. He laid roofs seven days a week that first summer in Canada. Then Jakub fell off a three-storey century mansion in north Somerset, some rich lawyer's place, and broke his neck. He's alive, "kind of," Maček said. Maček's visa ran out and instead of going back he picked tobacco and then, at a party, hooked up with Dan. Maček had touched the bulge in the breast of his jacket, zipped up despite the night's warmth. It could have been a baseball in there, but instead it was about four hundred dollars' worth of Moroccan hashish.

And where was Dan? Shell had asked.

Maček shrugged. "Maybe with that girl ... um ..."

"Kate?" The really pretty one—Irish or Scottish— with jade-green eyes and heaps of curly auburn hair.

"Yeah. Her." Maček said he'd better go back to Wizard's to wait for him. They had to meet someone later.

"At midnight?"

Maček helped her up, a firm grip on her elbow. Then he walked Shell to the bus stop and waited until the number twenty came. And he stayed and watched as it pulled away—hands shoved deep into the pockets of his tight black jeans, the thinness of his bandy legs accentuated by his high-top Adidas, delicate gold chain around his ropy neck glinting. She had dreamed about Maček all the next day, felt him as though he was an apparition, a shadow of her psyche, always with her, watching. Then Monday at school, Gilberto Silva bummed a smoke and said Dan had been busted on Saturday. "Right out front of Wizard's."

Shell's heart had turned to ice. "And Maček?"

Gilberto said no, he hadn't been there. But if Maček knows what's good for him, he'll be lying real low. "Heard he's here illegal, eh."

Shell had nodded. "I know."

BY EIGHT-THIRTY, SHELL'S bedroom is hot and stuffy. When she goes downstairs, the house is quiet. Mum must be out with Soren, but the backyard is empty, the pile of shingles unmoved.

"He's not coming," Mum says, coming up from the basement as Shell fills the coffee carafe with water.

"Soren?"

Mum folds her arms. "Little bugger got a job house painting."

"Jerk," Shell mutters. "I knew he'd bail."

Mum's lips are thin and her face so pale Shell can make out a faint pattern of freckles she never had before. "Make me a cup too," Mum says as Shell's measuring out coffee. Mum turns to the back door. Through the window, the naked plywood of the studio roof is orange in the sun, but with spots of brown age and black rot. "God, what if it rains before I find someone?"

"He should have to do the work anyway, Mum." Shell turns on the coffee and bangs around in the cupboard for a plate. "We got it all ready—I mean, you bought new shingles and everything!"

"I know, I know."

"Did the shithead at least call you himself?"

Mum shakes her head and turns back from the door. "Barb."

"So now what?" Shell drops a heel of rye bread into the toaster. Then another for Mum, when she asks.

"Look around for someone else, I guess. Someone cheap."

MRS. POOLE PUTS on a crackly LP of a British guy reciting *The Rime of the Ancient Mariner*, complete with crashing waves and bird cry. Two girls with ponytails and jean skirts keep whispering, so Shell tells them to be quiet, and then Mrs. Poole snaps her fingers and shushes all three of them and that makes Shell really mad. She was going to tell Mrs. Poole about how she stayed up all night reading poetry—and why does Blake spell *tiger* with a *y*, anyway?

Shell smokes half a Gauloise in the pit, the smell of toasted French tobacco enriching the chemical haze of everyone else's Player's Lights and Exports, Canadian brands Shell hopes to never have to smoke again. And while other kids are talking hangovers and Driver's Ed, Shell squints up into the gold of the sun. "Tyger, tyger," she whispers. The beauty is in the repetition, right? Or is it the word itself? "Horse, horse," Shell whispers next. "Bear, bear. Giraffe, giraffe." None are even close to "tyger." The second-period bell rings, clearing the smoking pit. But it's way too nice to go do free-fall prompts in Creative Writing, so Shell takes her books and lunch to the parkette behind St. Paul's. She could really use a sunny nap.

The grass is still a bit damp. Shell sits on her jean jacket and leans up against the thick maple that is her favourite, grooved perfectly to support her back. It's only ten-thirty, too early for her sandwich. Shell opens Blake and polishes her apple. There's lots of squirrels around, plus homeless guys milling around garbage cans, grandmas in thick coats and broken shoes pulling fold-up carts, and young mums hunched over collapsible strollers. They're all heading towards the back of the church, where they disappear into an unmarked door and then come out again with full shopping bags; a few old white men and some young brown guys in baseball hats carry out cardboard boxes perched on their shoulders.

"When my mother died, I was very young," Shell reads out loud between bites of McIntosh, "and my father sold me while yet my tongue / could scarcely cry 'weep' 'weep' 'weep' 'weep'/ so your chimneys I sweep and in soot I sleep." She thinks about that, savouring the repeated "weep" and how Blake makes rhyming poems seem okay when Leonard Cohen or Ginsberg do otherwise. When Shell looks up again, she sees someone who could be Maček.

It is Maček. His gold chain catches the light and his head is down, watching his Adidas taking their quick steps. He's coming right towards her. Shell sticks Blake in front of her face. Before she can think of the right words to say, Maček turns sharp, picking up the path with the poor mums and grandmas and brown people, leading to the back of St. Paul's. Then he disappears into that same unmarked door, just behind a pair of women in bright orange head scarves.

Shell is fast packing up her bag. She stands, shakes cramps and ants from her legs, and wanders over to an outlying bench right where the parkette meets the sidewalk on Clayton Street. When Maček comes out of the church, he clutches a yellow No Frills bag in each hand. His face is barely visible the way his shaggy hair falls forward. The clothes he wears are the same as always—leather jacket, jeans—but look too big for him now. Shell swings her backpack onto her shoulder and takes the path back into the park, striding towards him oh so natural. She smiles. Inside, her heart is going *bam-bam-bam*.

"Hey! Maček," she says, a bit too loud. There's about three yards between them. "What's up?"

Maček looks up, eyes big as golf balls. He stops. "Hey," he says, swallowing. He looks around.

"How are you?" Shell smiles huge to make up for Maček's grimace.

"Fine." Maček's voice is flat. He tucks his arms behind him so the bags bang the backs of his knees.

"Haven't seen you around for a while."

"No," Maček says.

Maček and Shell move over to let the women in the orange scarves pass. They are young-looking from this close; the No Frills bags that weigh them down accent the colour scheme of their drapy outfits.

"So," Shell says. "What are you up to?"

Maček's face goes red. "Tough to say."

"Oh." Shell steps back, swings her pack onto her other shoulder. "You want a Gauloise?"

Maček's eyes narrow and his brow creases. "Really?"

Shell shrugs. "Yeah. I mean, they were your favourite before."

Maček's hard mouth allows a brief smile. "Okay."

They sit on a bench near Shell's maple. The grocery bags slump over at Maček's feet. Shell tries not to look too puzzled over the contents: Kraft Dinner, Skippy peanut butter, loaf of white Dempster's, tins of baked beans, and mandarin segments in light syrup. Maček inhales the tobacco so deeply Shell is surprised any smoke comes out again. His body relaxes. They both watch his hands: stocky nicotine fingers and knuckles rough with dry skin.

"Been lying low," he says.

"I heard."

"Been broke. Sleeping on Dan's sister's couch."

"How's she?"

Maček shrugs, winces into the sun. "Monica's got a bad back and two kids." He glances at Shell. "They'll be wanting lunch soon." He nods at the back of the church. "St. Paul's gives the best food, but it's only once a week."

Shell swallows. Her stomach knots. She wants to puke up her apple and her Blake poems and her dreaming about Maček when he's been hungry and without a bed and supporting a family not even his own. "Okay, yeah," Shell stutters. "I was going to eat my sandwich soon and—"

"You should be in school, right?" Maček drags on the last of the Gauloise.

"Yeah, well. It's just so nice out today and I was reading anyway, so it's like self-schooling or something."

Maček stands up, a bag in each hand. "See you around, Shell," he says, turning, going.

His shoulders round against the strain of the groceries and, it's true, his tight black jeans have loosened. But he still walks tall, his body sort of muscles along. He's at the edge of the park, turning south, when Shell calls, "Wait," and goes running up after him, ducking around an old man with a full grocery bag hooked on the handle of his walker. Shell catches Maček's arm. His eyes narrow at her.

"You want a job?" she breathes, bursting.

"Huh?" Maček's brow gets all ridged.

"Because I got one for you," Shell says. "Or my mum does, I mean."

"What?"

"Roofing."

Maček leans back, the handles of the grocery bags cutting into his palms. "Okay," he says. "I'll consider it."

"HE'S TAKING AUTOBODY at school," Shell lies to Mum. "And he has at least a year of roofing experience." Which is true.

"How much does he charge?"

"Don't know. Whatever you were set to pay Soren."

Mum says she wants to meet him first, this "friend of a friend" from school who Shell says is a bit older but she doesn't know by how much. "He was in the Czech army, so as old as that. Okay?"

Dan's sister doesn't have a phone, so Maček calls Shell from a pay phone, right at seven like they had agreed in the parkette. It's weird to hear his gravelly voice on the other end, and the way he says "Shell?" truly makes her feel weak. Now they know each other. Now they are something more than whatever they were before.

MAČEK KNOCKS AT seven forty-five the next morning, right on time. Shell has been up and dressed since six, typing to Carla in her room: "Buddy, guess who's on his way over???"

"Hey," Maček growls when Shell opens the back door, his accent flat and voice fatigued. And his face is pale, chin and Adam's apple cut from shaving. Maček takes his coffee black. Nothing to eat because, he says, it's still too early.

"You sleep any?" Shell asks.

"A few hours, yeah."

"Me too."

They sit at the harvest table, talking about nothing at all really, until Mum comes down. "Shell? When's your friend due —"

Shell stands up, then Maček. Mum is in a skirt and blouse, nylons, her hair combed and wet, glasses steamed. Her eyes fall on Maček. The muscles in her neck rope up.

"Hello," she says.

Maček says good morning and offers his hand. They shake. They look each other in the eye for what seems like forever.

"Thanks for coming," Mum says.

"You're welcome, ma'am," Maček says, coughing nicotine.

Shell follows Mum and Maček out to the back. Maček scans the yard, then the pile of new shingles. He ascends

290

the extension ladder quickly, his sneakers barely touching the rungs. He walks the roof. Mum and Shell look up, wincing into the new-day sun.

"Two days' work," Maček says, coming down.

"But can you get the shingles up there? They're real heavy."

No problem.

Mum crosses her arms. "How much?"

"Five hundred. Flat. Work guaranteed."

Mum shades her eyes with her hand and tries not to smile. "Okay. Come on Saturday. Early."

Mum drives Maček and Shell to school, and Shell talks the whole way about what a jerk Soren Nutt is. "You know that guy?" she asks, turning to Maček, sitting in the back, looking out the window. Shell shivers to see Maček wearing a seat belt in Mum's Datsun like it's an everyday thing.

"No," he says.

"Well, you're lucky, because he's always been a bully, though my mum doesn't seem to think so."

Then Maček nods off, chin to his chest, waking when they bump over the tracks. Mum lets them out at Dutchie's Donuts. When the Datsun is gone, Maček pulls up his collar. He's got to go. And Shell needs to get to class. "But see you Saturday. And thanks."

Shell says, "It's cool." Her knees turn to fondue. She's so slow getting to English class Mrs. Poole has already shut the door. But Shell is smiling so big she doesn't get sent down for a late slip. The room is quiet; pens and pencils scratch. Instead of working on her analysis of leitmotifs in *Hamlet*, "Dear Carla, Guess what?!!!" is what Shell writes at the top of a fresh binder page. "Maček was at my house this, the most glorious of mornings!" She tells Carla about the black coffee and no breakfast and how polite Maček was, skipping over the reason why Maček is working for Mum, because what if there really are mail censors like Chomsky says and Maček gets traced and then deported? The important thing is that he's going to fix the roof, right? "Isn't that amazing?"

MAČEK DOESN'T NEED much, just Dad's tool belt, a hammer, and some water. Plenty of nails. Sunscreen? No. But he'll wear the Expos cap. He takes off his jacket, one careful arm at a time, folds it in half, and lays it across a lawn chair. He is thin without it, a turtle denuded of its shell. But a turtle with shaggy hair and Dracula teeth. Maček wears his blue button-down undone; underneath, Dan's faded Slayer T-shirt is tucked into beltless jeans. He nods at Mum and Shell then shimmies up the ladder with the roll of underlay on his shoulder, which he applies quickly, but only after patching all the rot with fresh plywood. Maček's hammer echoes for hours.

When Mum and Shell come back from the co-op, Maček already has two packs of shingles nailed down.

"You used the chalk line?" Mum asks. "By yourself?"

Maček shrugs. "There's a trick to it."

Before lunch, Maček washes in the bathroom upstairs—Mum already cleaned the counter and closed the bedroom doors—and then he sits at the table only when and where he is told: in Dad's old place. He has three bowls of Mum's homemade minestrone soup and two sandwiches of cheddar on dark rye. Mum keeps jumping up whenever his bowl or plate needs filling. She bought Polish pickles at the co-op, without Shell even asking her, and a Cellophane bag of German gingerbread. Maček eats like Kremski, with no knife, napkin tucked into his shirt, and though he goes fast, he does so without slurping. His eyes water when he bites into the ginger-bread. His mother made the same kind at Christmas. "For after midnight Mass."

"You're Catholic?"

Maček pulls the gold chain out from his shirt and shows Mum the charm: a crucifix delicately engraved with flowers and a word in Czech. His mother gave it to him when he left. "Three years ago now."

Mum says he is brave. Is he here alone?

"There's my cousin, Jakub." Maček takes another cookie. "But he's a vegetable with a broken neck."

Maček works until three o'clock. When he unclips Dad's tool belt, the whole eastern slope is covered. Mum and Shell climb up the ladder while Maček's washing tar from his nails and brown sweat from his face and neck. "It's great work, eh, Mum?"

Mum nods. "Just terrific," she says of the new green shingles laid in perfectly straight rows, not a single gap or nail head showing. After strong tea and more ginger-bread, Mum and Shell drive Maček downtown.

"See you tomorrow, ma'am," Maček says, getting out in front of Mister Sound. He tucks his fifty-dollar advance into the back pocket of his jeans, slings his jacket over his shoulder.

"Now he better not go spend that on cigarettes," Mum says into the rear-view mirror as Maček disappears up the block.

"Oh, come on, Mum!" Shell says. "He's not like that." But as she too watches him go, she hopes Maček does stop on the way back to Dan's sister's and get himself an extra-large king-size pack and, thinking about Shell, smoke one after another.

IT SMELLS SWEET and smoky downstairs, like steamed pudding and strong coffee; like Sunday mornings used to be, with Dad around. Maček, flushed with yesterday's sun, is at his new spot at the harvest table when Shell comes down. She's showered and dressed in her least dirty jeans, crimped hair sticky with Alberto mousse. Shell smiles at Maček, not too big.

He stands up, napkin tucked into the neck of the same Slayer T-shirt. He nods, blushing through his sunburn. "Good morning, Shell."

Mum's got the waffle iron going: the first time since Dad left.

"Mum, hey, I thought you sold that thing at Barb's."

"Nope." Mum lifts the iron's heavy black lid. "And it's a good thing, because we've got a real waffle fan here."

Mum bustles around brewing coffee and chopping banana. Has Maček had real maple syrup? How about farm-fresh apple butter? Too bad there's no bacon. "Next time," she promises.

"Shouldn't you be working?" Shell whispers, sitting

down across from Maček. She eyes Mum, who is actually whistling as she takes a tray of warm waffles from the oven. Rushing over to the table, Mum forks a pair of steaming, perfectly brown waffles onto Maček's plate.

"Shell? Honey, how about you?"

"Huh?" Shell hasn't been a honey to Mum in ten years at least.

"One waffle or two?"

Shell glances at Maček, who has syrup on his whiskered chin. "One for now. They're awfully big, eh?"

"Big and so good," Maček says, steam rising as he cuts into a puffy waffle with the side of his fork.

It's nine o'clock and two pots of coffee later when Maček clips on Dad's tool belt. He has to set it to a bigger hole now, he jokes. Mum squeezes suntan lotion into his open palm.

"Really rub that in," she says. "Especially on your face."

While Mum and Shell clean up, Mum shakes her head and says, "He's a smart guy, that one."

Shell rinses what little remains on Maček's plate into the sink. "That's why he's here, Mum. You know?"

Mum catches Shell's eyes. They stand in the silent, sweet kitchen, separated by the open dishwasher, Shell holding Maček's plate and Mum his coffee mug; Dad made them both out in the backyard studio. "I do know, Shell."

IT'S COOL IN Mum's room. Shell lies in the pioneer bed, on top of the wrinkled sheets, oily with body lotion. The light is out and the box fan on low. Maček's crouched figure is visible through the window if she props up against the pillows. It's probably wrong to be watching without him knowing, and it's probably wrong to likewise imagine he is her husband and they have children, and while Maček stays home to raise them and build airy wooden houses, Shell becomes a famous poet and travels the whole world. *Click-clock* goes the echo of Maček's hammer. *Click-clock.* His blue button-down lies abandoned by the eastern eave and when he stands to reach into his tool belt, the gold cross around his neck glints in the sun. Shell's face gets warm just seeing that. He lays a shingle then fixes it in place — one, two, three nails across; and when the angle of the roof cuts him off from view, she picks up *A Sadder and a Wiser Man* and reads about Coleridge's life — his addiction, depression, constipation, hatred for his wife. She pencils down some notes for her final essay, comparing "Kubla Khan" and that movie *Citizen Kane*, which Shell has never seen, just read about, but they have the film strips at the public library. On Monday, tomorrow, she'll call ahead to book a viewing room.

Click-clock, click-clock.

And when she's bored with Coleridge and all the inset pictures of ladies in lace collars and men with mutton-chops, she memorizes Blake. She has "The Tyger" and "The Sick Rose" down pat, but keeps messing up the one about the chimney sweep: "When my mother died I was very young...crap...and my father sold me while... um...yet my tongue / could scarcely cry 'weep' 'weep' 'weep' 'weep'/ so your chimneys I sweep and in soot I sleep."

"Weep, weep, weep, weep," Shell whispers.

Click-clock, click-clock, goes Maček's hammer.

Breeze cuts through the window screen, kissing Shell's toes, the contours of her face. "Weep, weep, weep, weep." Suddenly Shell's eyes surge with tears. Because she loves Mum so much and Dad and even Valery, with her chocolate chicken and caramel eyes, and she loves Maček too—of course she does!—but with those words she knows she'll have to leave here—the cool bed sheets that smell like Nivea and the rap of Maček's sturdy, steady hammer. She'll have to go someplace where the library has more books and the essays she writes can be longer and harder and so beautiful and in a way Somerset can't ever understand. And she'll have to go soon. A world lives out there. She's already seventeen.

TO CELEBRATE THE brand new roof, Mum's going to treat them all to a takeout supper. Maček gets to pick the place. Swiss Chalet is his favourite. While Mum goes for the food, Maček showers and Shell sets the table, including wineglasses for the Chardonnay Mum tells her to bring up from the cold room. Maček comes down in the Neil Young T-shirt Dad gave her and because it fits him so well, she says he can have it. They have lemonade and cigarettes on the back porch. Maček smells of Pert Plus, his face rosy from scrubbing.

"I like your mother," Maček says.

"Yeah, she's okay."

"She misses having a man around."

Shell blushes. "You think?"

"Sure. But you guys are doing okay."

"Yeah?"

"Sure. I mean, I wish my mother could be like yours. Tough but really nice and happy with that."

They eat at the table and use real plates. While Mum and Shell have the quarter chicken dinners, Mum got Maček a half chicken. "I bet you're hungry," she says, "after all that hard work." Then they eat, silently dipping succulent chunks of falling-apart chicken into the special sauce that comes on the side, spicy and a hint of sweet. The hand-cut fries get dipped too, along with the toasted buns.

"My cousin used to drink this sauce straight," Maček says in his slow, flat accent. "He'd order extra, glug it back."

Shell laughs, the wine flushing her with love and lightness. "Yeah. We have Swiss Chalet stories too, right Mum?"

"We do?" Mum says, sipping from her greasy wineglass.

"Yeah," Shell scoffs. "From Kremski."

Mum's face clouds and she sets down her glass. She continues to eat, fry by fry, as Shell tells Maček about the Soviet artist and Swiss Chalet dishwasher who was Dad's best bud all the time Shell was growing up. He can still be seen riding around on his old bike, picking garbage and cigarette butts. "Wait!" Shell cries, jumping up from the table. The paper Swiss Chalet hat is under her bed, tucked in the horsehair button box. She pulls it on her head and runs back downstairs. "Ta-da!" She digs into her cooling meal while, mouth full of food, telling Maček all about how she went as Kremski for Halloween and how he was such an inept camper when they went canoeing in Algonquin, he actually brought a suitcase. "Well, after all, the guy was Soviet."

Maček wipes his mouth without untucking his greasy napkin; sauce smears across his cheek. "So?" His face is stone, like Mum's, and his jaw is clenched. "How's that funny?"

"It's not funny," Mum says. "It's too bad."

Shell feels her grin dissolve. She looks from Mum to Maček to her dirty plate and pulls Kremski's hat gently from her head. Folding the yellowed paper neatly, she holds it in her lap.

Mum refills Shell's wineglass, then Maček's, emptying the bottle. She takes their empty plates into the kitchen, returning with a breadknife and a Sara Lee chocolate cake, the box sweating with thaw.

THEY STAY UP late drinking tea and looking at old photos — Sanibel Beach, the house right when they moved in, Mum's mum out on the Prairies. Maček eats the last piece of cake while Shell puts on Bob Dylan. Then Mum says she's going to bed early. Does Maček need a ride home?

"Don't trouble yourself at all, please." After all that food, Maček says he'll walk.

"Well, don't forget it's Sunday. You both have school in the morning."

Now they are alone. Now they can smoke. Stars are out, so are the bugs, and the night air is damp.

"How's Dan's sister?" Shell asks, taking one of Maček's cigarettes and leaning up against the rail of the back porch. Carla's care package from France will be here any day now. Along with Gauloises and Hariboo, there's probably going to be something for Shell's birthday too.

Maček touches the pocket of his jacket; the envelope with four hundred and fifty dollars is tucked safely away. "Things'll be better now." He says Dan's going to be out in two months. As part of his probation, he'll go back to Somerset Tech. "Autobody."

And what will Maček do?

"Was thinking roofing, house repairs." Maybe Shell's mum can spread the word. "She's got lots of single friends, eh?"

"You mean *shingle* friends?" Shell laughs. Sure, Maček could get a business going. "Like when we move, we'll need help for sure, if you're into that too."

Maček says right on. Where they moving to?

Shell shrugs. "Maybe some condo. Got to get rid of this place first, though."

Their teacups cool. Words dry up. Hey, the stars will be even better up on the roof. Shell gets her jean jacket from inside and climbs up the ladder first, Maček right behind. She can barely see her hand in front of her face, but she can see the Milky Way and, below, the next-door neighbour's eating popcorn from a huge steel bowl, the TV flashing blue.

Shell and Maček sit on the peak, the soles of their

sneakers braced against the rough texture of the new shingles, which smell like a gas station or the inside of Canadian Tire. Maček flexes his hands, hammer-stiff, and pulls out his cigarette pack. There's a joint inside, which he invites Shell to light. She does—checking that Mum's window is dark. The rich spice of hash infuses her lungs, warms her tongue. "Oh, how I missed that."

Maček thought it would be so.

"And I missed you too," Shell whispers, so quiet she might have been the only one to hear it.

They only need a few tokes, Maček's hash is always that good. They laugh, remembering things about Carla that were so great, like how she'd always show up at parties with Harvey's leftovers. Or the time they got high on the dock and Carla fell into the Somerset River. *Splash.* Her hair smelled like egg for weeks and she even had to throw out her coat. Then Shell gets worried because can't the whole neighbourhood hear their voices? "Someone'll call the cops."

So Maček takes her hand—his palms warm and rough as an emery board—and they shimmy down to where the grade is less steep and stretch out on their backs. Eyes to the wide starry sky, Shell's right hand in Maček's left, night washes them, watches them. "We're safe here, Shell." And they are.

When Shell wakes up, the sky is violet. Maček's jacket is tucked around her, keeping in her warmth. Maček is sitting up on his elbows, watching the coming of sun. Shell blinks rapidly, wetting her contact lenses.

"Hey." She sits up. "Who knew a roof could be so cozy?"

"Only because I made it so." Maček coughs. "Just for you."

"Yeah?"

"And for your mother too."

The sunrise is rose, is burgundy, is gold. Shell climbs down the ladder first, then Maček. At the back steps, he takes back his jacket. "Your mother won't be happy to see me here."

Shell yawns. "You'll be okay?"

"Yup. Buses are probably running."

"Got your cash?"

"I do."

"And your hash?"

Maček laughs.

They stare at each other's feet, noses running.

"Okay, so I'm going to call you," Maček finally says.

Shell nods. "Any time." Then she swallows, takes a breath, and, like diving into deep water—a lake, an ocean, the far end at Earl's Park pool—she reaches out for Maček, pulling him into her, her into him. It's kind of a hug at first, but then she kisses Maček, fast and messy and on the lips, then runs up the steps before Mum's alarm goes off, because, look, the sky is nearly blue.

When she shuts the back door, Maček is still there, waiting, at the bottom step. He lifts his hand. Shell waves too.

THE NEW PEOPLE moving into the house are musicians: cello for her, violin for him.

Priscilla says the studio out back was the selling point—a perfect space for practising and teaching

302

too. "And the new roof is really tremendous," she says, smoothing the Sold sticker over the wooden sign with her giant name and smiling face.

Shell pretends to read *The Second Sex* on the front steps.

The spikes of Priscilla's high heels sink into the front lawn. A robin, going for the shiny orange fruit of the mountain ash behind her, dive-bombs her head. Priscilla lets out a small cry and dashes like a deer to the sidewalk, where she shakes hands with Mum. Then her candy-apple car glides away.

"The change will be good for us, Shell," Mum says, sitting down next to Shell, who can't look up from the black words on the white page. Simone de Beauvoir swims behind eyes full of tears. "And anyway, you only have until September, when you go to university. You can't live here forever."

"Yup," says Shell.

"You *are* going to university, Shell," Mum says.

"Yup," says Shell.

"You won't make the mistake I did."

"Nope," says Shell.

THE PILE OF books on the floor by the window is more like a wall and is as high as Shell's waist. Her room in the condo Mum bought is barely big enough for a twin bed; she will have to sell at least two boxes of paperbacks at Rambler Books on Clayton, where Sorensen Sports used to be. All the studios above have been renovated into apartments. Bright pink petunias drip from the planter on the ledge of Dad and Kremski's studio window.

Shell takes down the *Bad Moon Rising* poster she special-ordered from Mister Sound, and sneezes when she opens the horsehair button box under her bed. The dust is fine-ground, pink and grey: a baby and an old lady mixed into one soft silt. She hasn't touched the box since moving up from the basement. The treasures inside are distant and familiar: a jagged slice of green glass, a necklace of pasta, a rusty roller skate key, the Polaroid of her naked self that no one else in the world will ever see. It is the whole of Shell's heart, dissected: Dad, the pond, the cardinal bush, the smell of Mum's warm jam, the taste of Dad's beer, the scratch of his beard. She shuts the box.

Shell is still. She might stay this way forever, buried in the heavy soil of not wanting to grow anymore. In time she will calcify, fossilize, become another midden hunk for the cellist and violinist to unearth, polish up, set in the windowsill above the sink where Mum's glass medicine bottles will never be again.

In the hallway, the telephone rings.

She wants it to be Maček calling—to say hi, how's it going, to see if maybe Shell wants to meet up to shoot pool again. But what if it's not Maček?

Somewhere, a bird's wings are beating. A robin is feeding from the mountain ash Dad planted outside Shell's window so long ago. And also the beating is blood in her ears, blood in her heart, pumping forth because that's just what it does.

Shell counts the phone's tenth ring.

Mum shouts from the bottom of the stairs. "Shell! That'll be for you if anyone."

Shell pushes away the button box. She rushes to the ringing before Maček—it has to be him—hangs up.

"Hello?" Shell says into the receiver, twisting the cord around her wrist.

Acknowledgements

Thank you:

The Canada Council, Ontario Arts Council, Kim Harrison, Maurice Carroll and the magical house in Sixmilebridge, County Clare, Ireland, where much of this book was written; Joanna Reid for excellent editorial feedback and ongoing interest in what I write; Sarah MacLachlan, Laura Meyer, Barbara Howson, Jenna Simpson, Alysia Shewchuk, and especially Janie Yoon, a true friend and most insightful, patient, and supportive editor; my agent, Martha Magor-Webb; my mom and brother; my dad and Sara; Linda and Michael Hutcheon for your kindness; my friends; my Carleton colleagues; my dearest darling Chedo; our daughter who teaches me how much my parents love me, the lesson of this book.

Permissions

© Dawn Johnson

NADIA BOZAK is the critically acclaimed author of the novels *El Niño* and *Orphan Love*. She is also the author of *The Cinematic Footprint: Lights, Cameras, Natural Resources*, a work of film theory. She is currently Assistant Professor of English at Carleton University in Ottawa.